NEW YORK ECHOES 2

ALSO BY WARREN ADLER

Short Story Collections
New York Echoes
Never Too Late for Love
Jackson Hole, Uneasy Eden
The Washington Dossier Stories

Novels
Funny Boys
The War of the Roses
Random Hearts
Trans-Siberian Express
The Children of the Roses
Banquet Before Dawn
The Henderson Equation
The Casanova Embrace
Blood Ties
Natural Enemies
Twilight Child
We Are Holding the President Hostage
Madeline's Miracles
Private Lies
The Housewife Blues
Cult
Mourning Glory
Undertow

Mysteries
American Quartet
American Sextet
The Witch of Watergate
Senator Love
Immaculate Deception
The Ties That Bind
Death of a Washington Madame

More information at WarrenAdler.com

NEW YORK ECHOES 2

SHORT STORIES

Warren Adler

PUBLISHED BY:

STONEHOUSE PRESS

300 East 56th Street
New York, NY 10022

New York Echoes 2
Copyright © 2011 by Warren Adler
All rights reserved

ISBN-13: 978-1-59006-011-7 (print)
ISBN-13: 978-1-59006-027-8 (ePUB)
ISBN-13: 978-1-59006-028-5 (Kindle)

Copyeditor: M. Elizabeth Palmer
Cover Design by Jowdy Design
Cover Modification by Adam Figueira
Interior Design and digitization by Elizabeth Beeton

Manufactured in the United States of America

Publisher's Cataloging-In-Publication Data
(Prepared by The Donohue Group, Inc.)

Adler, Warren.
 New York echoes 2 : short stories / Warren Adler.

 p. ; cm.

 Available also as an e-book.
 ISBN: 978-1-59006-011-7

 1. New York (N.Y.)–Fiction. 2. Interpersonal relations–Fiction. 3. Short stories. I. Title.

PS3551.D64 N49 2011
813/.54   2011905680

CONTENTS

INTRODUCTION

My mother used to say that there are two places in the world: New York City and out-of-town.

In my callow youth, I did not take her seriously and hungered to see and experience out-of-town. I did. I lived in Washington, D.C., Los Angeles, Jackson Hole, Wyoming, and traveled extensively. I've concluded after many decades of observation that out-of-town is fine and offers many singular interests, intimate pleasures and varied personalities, environments and landscapes.

Many places out-of-town have served me well, providing backgrounds for many of my books and stories. Indeed, I am grateful for the nourishment that out-of-town provided my imagination.

Still, at the risk of being dubbed a jingoistic ingrate and mindless booster, I have finally concluded that mother was right. What she meant, of course, was that New York City was unique, a world apart, a place like no other spot on the planet, a diverse, complicated mosaic of the human condition in all its splendor and richness. It is a city of both reality and imagination where hopes and dreams permeate every atom of its human and material structure.

In this dreamscape, millions of humans brush against one another like ants in their busy underground corridors, each bent on pursuing tasks that give meaning to their lives. The city functions by the grace of a thousand little miracles. One can feel the pulse of life here, the heartbeat of creative energy. It is a glorious paradise where everyone worships at a million shrines, privately and secretly bowing to the Gods of fame and fortune.

Aspiration and self-fulfillment rule in this arena of hot energy. It is a fabulous potpourri for all ages and inclinations. In this city, one can be oneself, and all differences are respected and celebrated. Every day is a feast for the senses. One sees and feels it on the city streets, on the subways and buses, in the theaters and concert halls, in the restaurants, in the tunnels and on the bridges, in the houses of worship, in the stores and the parks, in the faces of its citizens who pretend not to look but observe everyone else with laser intensity. It is ever changing, always in flux, never resting, a city that never sleeps, always conscious, always alive.

There is an underside as well, a pervasive and always-present sense of human struggle, sometimes tragic, often confusing, even heartbreaking. That part cannot be ignored if the author is on the trail of truth.

What a fantastic environment for a writer of the imagination, a storyteller seeking truth, intensity, excitement and suspense. It is a gift to live here.

That is why, after roaming the world for decades, stories set in New York are pouring out of me like an endless river. My first *New York Echoes* collection was published in 2008. Famed actress Cynthia Nixon read six of the stories, now available on Audible. Her passion and understanding of these stories is a rare treat.

This is the second collection. My hope is that there will be others. I've included two stories, "The Other People" and "The Girl in the Polka Dot Dress," published in anthologies more than sixty years ago before I began my serious wanderings out-of-town. Even then, I was in love with it, although I had not realized it in my youthful ignorance.

I hope you enjoy reading them as much as I enjoyed writing them.

Warren Adler
Spring 2011

TRUST ME

I was visiting my father in a nursing home in West Palm Beach, Florida. Visiting might not be the correct description. Viewing him would be more accurate. He had Alzheimer's and didn't have the foggiest notion who I was. All he did was sit in his wheelchair, staring out in front of him, his eyes glazed and indifferent. Occasionally he made strange sounds. It tore me up to see him like this.

I was there more out of guilt or duty or obligation. I doubt if it had anything to do with love. The man I loved, who was my father, had slowly disintegrated. He had simply disappeared. What I saw before me was merely a vague shadow of a man, barely recognizable as such. It has been said that a man's soul leaves him on death, what they call "giving up the ghost." My father's ghost had left him years ago.

Most of the nursing home workers on the floor were surly and couldn't care less. I guess they thought it was pointless to show any real caring since the patients didn't give a damn. It really hurt to observe that, although I understood why it was so. After all, who would take such jobs? It was depressing and thankless and low-paying.

That's why, I suppose, my attention was directed to a small lady with blue-gray hair, who walked among the living dead slumped in their wheelchairs. She stopped to talk to each of them, bending low to catch their eyes, smiling and offering pleasant inquiries as to their health and outlook as if they were normal human beings. Of course, they didn't answer, but that did not daunt this lady, and when she left them she would squeeze an arm or a shoulder and offer a farewell that surely fell on deaf ears.

"Remember, you take care now," I heard her say.

She came to my father and performed her routine. I thought I saw a brief spark of recognition, but I wasn't sure. She bent over him and gave him a bear hug. Miraculously, he smiled and hugged her back. He had never done that for me.

"He's a cute guy," she said with a perky laugh, blue eyes twinkling behind silver-rimmed glasses. She had the clear, contented look of a person who took joy in helping other people.

"My dad," I said when she turned her glance at me.

"I mean it. He is cute," she said.

He didn't seem cute to me.

"You come here often?" I asked.

"Make my rounds every day. Just a volunteer, though," she said. "Visiting my kids." She turned to my father. "Right, Paul?" Once again I saw a vague response of recognition in his eyes.

Somehow her presence took the edge off my gloom. I had dreaded this visit, just as I had dreaded all those that came before. I could not remember ever meeting this woman at the home, and yet she had the look of someone I had known.

It puzzled me and since she was so open and friendly, I knew it would not be an intrusion to make some inquiries.

"Where are you from?"

"I live a mile from here."

"I mean where you grew up."

I studied her face, inspected the blue eyes, the lips that smiled broadly, wrinkling her face. I figured her for late sixties.

"Pennsylvania," she said. "My father was a coal miner."

"Never been there. But I do think we've met before."

I told her that I was from Manhattan, a lawyer. I was married with two kids, both grown and on their own. For some reason, I felt compelled to volunteer these details. Often these days I was meeting people that were vaguely familiar, faces out of my past, except that they had not aged. It was, of course, an illusion. Only the image, the snapshot of memory in true time, stays the same. People change.

"I liked Manhattan in the old days," she said, smiling, showing an even set of obviously false teeth.

"You lived there?"

"No." She laughed. "I once worked in Brooklyn for a few months. I hear it's still there." It was then that she winked at some imaginary person over my shoulder.

Of course. I knew instantly. This was Jean Moran. Jean Moran forty-odd years later. A chill rolled up and down my spine. Jean Moran. I wanted to rise up and hold her in my arms. But I didn't, for reasons that you will soon know.

"I lived there when I was a kid," I answered, suddenly stunned by my recall.

She looked at me suddenly as if I had caught her attention. I felt her brief intense inspection and then she smiled again and said goodbye with a cheery wave. I watched her walk spryly down the polished corridors until she turned a corner and was out of sight.

Memories, I thought, looking at my father to whom memory had already died. Memory is history and history is the record of your life, our lives. I felt an overwhelming pity for my father. I know, Dad, I said in my heart. Without memory there is nothing.

Perhaps it was because all memory had vanished in the minds all around me that my memory suddenly became so acute. This was the

Alzheimer's floor. But Jean Moran, the young Jean Moran, emerged in my mind full-blown in present time, the Jean Moran who had touched my life so deeply and profoundly when I was eleven years old.

As I sat there watching my mindless father, time slipped away and I was back in my parents' apartment in Brooklyn. We lived in a one-bedroom apartment in an ornate building in the Crown Heights section.

In the style of the times, the building had a large lobby presided over by a doorman. The lobby was dominated by a huge fireplace with an electric simulated fire and suits of armor on each side of it and, in front of it, a suite of dungeon-like furniture. This passed for elegance in those days. It even had a name, which escapes me, except that it ended in "Arms," which, I assume the owners used to summon up images of old English castles.

It had the aura of "fanciness," although the people who lived there were no more than three decades out of the ghetto and most of them had been hauled across the big pond by their parents escaping the pogroms of Russia. So they were making it in the new world, even though there was a depression on.

Appearances then, like now, had the same shallow façade. My father was a bookkeeper for a clothing firm, but my mother had a keen strategy for making it seem as if he were the owner of the firm. My mother also kept a servant. She called her "the girl," not the maid. A maid was always colored. A girl was a step up in the pecking order of perceived prestige.

I always felt that hiring a "girl" was also the price my father had to pay for Jerry's arrival seven years after me. From my mother's point of view, Jerry put a housekeeping burden on my mother that required the assistance of a full-time sleep-in servant, a "girl."

The girls didn't stay long and with good reason. Neither my mother or father was ever harsh to them, but conditions were rather cramped and, after all, the girls got restless. Periodically, after one of them quit, my father would come home with another, apparently from some agency in Manhattan.

They were always fresh, pink-skinned, shy Irish girls from large families of unemployed miners from the coalfields of Pennsylvania or Ohio. For the most part, they were always pleasant, hardworking, and polite. They had to be. They needed the work.

I am talking, of course, of the deepest darkest days of the depression. Families were starving. To survive, families sent their daughters to New York to find work, any work. Most of these girls had never left home. I think most of them were in their twenties and I'm sure they worked cheap, since we did not have very much money. My father was glad to have a job in those days.

The main problem with working for our family was space. We lived in a one-bedroom apartment. I slept with my brother Jerry on a double bed in the bedroom. A foot away was another bed in which the girl slept. My parents slept on a daybed in the living room. There was one bathroom.

It didn't seem at all cramped to me. I had no other frame of reference. I can place my state of mind at that time in an odd way. I was a bit of a sissy. I still played with dolls, albeit boy dolls as well as girl dolls. When everyone was out of the house, I would stand in front of the mirror with a doll in hand and imagine myself and my doll in various situations. It can best be described as going into a trance, transporting myself through time to another place, imagining myself and my doll, no longer a doll, of course, but a real person, in some exciting situation. It was a lot like seeing a movie in my mind with me and my doll in starring roles. My father hated my playing with dolls.

"He's too old for it," he would say. There was no way to hide his comments in a one-bedroom apartment. Usually my parents would have their confabulations in bed, within easy earshot of us boys and the girl.

"Stanley is still a child," my mother would counter.

"He'll be twelve."

This worry seemed to occupy my father's mind a great deal at the time. Once they raised their voices over the matter, and, of course, I heard every word.

"It's unhealthy, Martha. I think we should throw away Stanley's dolls."

"You'll break his heart."

"He'll grow up to be a damned pansy."

I had no idea what he meant. There was a long silence after that then my mother said:

"One thing I won't do is throw them away. How could we explain it?"

"Tell him dolls are for girls."

"That will only exaggerate the problem."

"I'm not so sure. He's a big sissy, you know. He's not much for sports and such."

"He'll outgrow it."

"I hope so."

All this was very confusing to me, although I thought I knew what a sissy was. I thought it meant coward and I knew I was no more a coward than any of the other boys. I didn't like team sports and probably deprived my father of the joys of rooting for his boy on the playing field. He loved baseball, which was the big neighborhood sport at the time. I could take it or leave it. I was good at track, though, being a pretty fast runner. But who came out to watch track in those days? Besides, it was all over so damned fast.

Of course appearances had a lot to do with my being perceived as a sissy. I was pretty with blond curly hair and big brown eyes. I also had the kind of skin that blushed easily and, at times, I looked as if someone had rouged my cheeks.

Also, my mother made sure I was always neat and well dressed with a perfectly clean white shirt and pressed longies with razor-sharp creases. Looking back, I suppose I might agree with my father. I looked like a sissy. I played with dolls. I didn't like contact sports. By those measures, I was, indeed, a sissy.

Jean Moran, as she was then, is vivid in my mind. She came after Josephine who followed Maggie. I remember those blue eyes, her warm smile and sparkling white teeth. She had a milky way of freckles across her nose and joked with me a lot. But it was the wink, that same wink, that she had given me forty-odd years later in the nursing home that branded her, unmistakably, as the Jean Moran I knew.

Before Jean, I never paid much attention to the girls. They were there to help Mother and take care of Jerry. They were peripheral to me. Yet, especially when Mom and Dad weren't around, they had been put in charge and I was supposed to mind them.

Before Jean came, I think I was a lot more modest about my body, always dressing in the bathroom out of sight of the girls who shared our bedroom. I'm not certain if they were as modest as I was. At least, I never paid much attention until one day I saw Jean Moran naked.

It must have been summer because it became light early. I think it was also Sunday and Jean had gotten up to attend mass. She, like the other girls, was a good Sunday Catholic and crossed herself a lot.

I opened my eyes and there was Jean's beautiful rosy tush no more than a foot from my eyes. Jesus. At first I thought I was doing something wrong by keeping my eyes open, but the best I could do was to narrow the slits and take in the sight. Once she turned sideways and I saw her tits, nice-sized with little red nipples, and, lower, a patch of blonde pubic hair.

She was, I'm sure, totally oblivious to my watching her, but watch her I did as she dressed. I suppose, if I really plumbed my memory, I might mark that moment when I first noticed a hard-on. Naturally, I had had hard-ons before. When my mother noticed them, it was always her contention that they were there because I had to go to the bathroom. Even mothers are ignorant of the sexual progress of their sons.

Once when I was taking a bath, my mother came into the bathroom and I pointed out all the hair that was growing around my dingy.

"Just be sure you don't get it into trouble," she told me. I hadn't the faintest idea what she was talking about.

Handing down sexual knowledge, at least as far as my family was concerned, was not very efficient in those days. Such information was called "the facts of life," and the assumption was that fathers told boys how babies were made and mothers told girls. My father somehow neglected to mention anything in this regard. As a matter of fact, he never ever discussed the subject with me, clinically or otherwise.

I, therefore, had to learn about this mysterious subject from my peers, which was a faulty system at best, especially when you are eleven years old. At that time there was no such thing as formal sex education in the schools. We had no idea about what went where or how, although some of the bigger boys talked among themselves about the thrill you got when you jerked off, whatever that meant.

So here was this ignorant sissy staring agape at a mature naked woman's body and suddenly discovering that the sight of it had something to do with making your dingy hard. I wanted to see more of Jean Moran's body. It sure was exciting and made me feel good. Sometimes she caught me at it.

"Go on with you, peeking at me, you naughty boy."

"I was not," I would protest. A lie, of course. I looked at her every chance I got, through any crack and keyhole.

Naturally she was privy to my parents' conversations about my sissiness, but that probably fell under the heading of information forbidden to servants. I'm sure her folks told her that you only got into trouble by minding your employers' business.

I'm sure, too, that she knew that the sight of her naked or even half-naked body was exciting to me. I have no way of knowing that, but I did have many a quick tantalizing glimpse of her nether parts. Too quick. Because we lived at such close quarters she had developed a way of dressing and undressing under a nightgown, although she did sometimes forget. It was nerve-wracking to sometimes wait up for her to go to sleep, hoping that she would forget to undress under her gown. More often than not, I was disappointed.

She was a good-looking girl and did attract some of the young men in the neighborhood. Occasionally, they showed up to babysit with her when my parents went out at night, although I'm sure my mother had told her that this was forbidden. But that was between her and my mother. I didn't associate it with anything worth thinking about, and I was usually asleep long before my parents came home.

One night I was awakened by a strange sound, repetitious and rhythmical. I listened.

"Trust me?" I heard a male voice say.

"No," Jean Moran replied.

"Trust me?" the male voice said again.

"No," Jean Moran said.

"Trust me?" the male voice repeated.

There was a bit of a hesitation, then Jean said:

"Just a wee bit."

This went on and on. Sometimes Jean said no. Once she said "maybe." Often she said "a wee bit."

Without making a sound, although my heart beat a tattoo in my chest, I crept out of bed and tiptoed to the bedroom door. I knew something odd was happening, but I didn't know what.

Carefully, I opened the door a crack and peeked into the living room. Only the little lamp on the table at the other side of the room was on. I could make out the form of Jean Moran on the daybed where my parents slept. A young man was beside her, leaning on one elbow and moving his hand on her upper body. She lay on her back and I noticed that the upper part of her dress was open.

They were obviously playing some kind of a game. The young man was moving his hand on her body and she was consenting or refusing depending on where his hand was or how she felt. The young man was making a bit of headway, since Jean had trusted him enough to unbutton her dress and unfasten her brassiere. I could tell that had been done, because I could see her breasts were loose.

I watched, mesmerized by the process.

"Trust me," the young man said.

"Maybe."

He got bolder and put his hand under the brassiere. I knew what he was doing, squeezing her tits.

After about fifteen more minutes of "trust me," he had gotten her brassiere off and had even given her nipples a few sucks. Then he started going lower, starting all the way down at her ankles. You can't imagine the effect of this sight on an eleven-year-old boy.

Because the light made it difficult for me to see what was going on down below, I lowered myself to the floor and crept forward through the door's narrow opening as quietly as I could. After all, Jean and her friend were busy as hell. I watched as he challenged her trust all the way up her leg and thigh. Then she had spread her legs and he was challenging this trust all the way up. He had even lifted her dress. I could see her panties very well. They were satiny and seemed to shine in the dark.

At one point, he was getting her to trust him to start rolling down her panties, and when he tried to do it, he had a bit of trouble and needed her to help him. Because of this, she had to lift her body. It was then that she saw me.

"Oh dear mother of God!" she squealed, jumping up.

"What is it?" the young man said, equally frightened.

At her scream, I had dashed back to bed, but there could be no mistake about it. What I had seen I had seen and I can tell you that it was a powerful sight to me at the time.

Of course I couldn't sleep and it wasn't long after my discovery that Jean came into the bedroom. She sat on her bed and watched me as I pretended to sleep. I heard her sigh lightly and, a few moments later I heard her sobbing. When I finally opened my eyes, she had covered her face with her hands. Her shoulders shook and she was sobbing bitterly, stifling it as best she could so as not to wake Jerry.

"Please don't cry, Jean," I begged. "Please."

"You saw that, Stanley," she whispered between sobs. "And I'm so ashamed."

I didn't know what to say.

"If your mommy and daddy find out, I'm going to lose my job. I can't lose my job, Stanley. It would be awful for me."

"Why would you lose your job?" I asked.

"I did a terrible thing. I had no right to have that boy in here. No right to do what I did."

"Aw please, Jean," I said, sitting beside her on the bed, genuinely frightened for her. I also felt a bit guilty, as if I were the source of her pain.

"You don't know what this means," she said.

"I know what it means," I said bravely. The fact that I was attempting to soothe a crying woman somehow gave me the false impression that I was more manly than I was.

"You have no idea. Your mother finds out, that's the end of me."

"How will she find out?"

She continued to cry, but less than before. Finally she dried her eyes.

"You won't tell, Stanley?"

"Of course I won't tell."

"Is that a real promise?"

"I won't tell. I promise."

"It's to be a secret between us?"

"I will never, never tell," I assured her, flattered by her confidence and, I suppose, my power. "Cross my heart."

"Thank you, Stanley," Jean said. "I will never forget that."

The sharing of this secret dramatically changed my relationship with Jean. I was now her confidante and, I believe, her friend. She would say things to my mother, then wink at me in her peculiar way.

She impressed my mother as being more and more conscientious, and my mother was very vocal in her praise of Jean's performance, which pleased Jean a lot. It also validated to her that I had, indeed, kept her deep, dark secret.

We even discussed things together in a more intimate way.

"You really shouldn't play with those dolls, you know. Not in front of your mom and dad," she would warn.

"He thinks I'm a sissy."

"Lots of dads think that about their sons."

That made me feel somewhat better. She had six brothers.

I felt really close to Jean Moran and dreaded the day when she would have to leave.

"I hope you never leave us, Jean," I told her often.

"There comes a time," she sighed.

"I hope it never comes."

To my knowledge, she never invited any other young men in when she had to babysit. If she did, I think I might have been very jealous.

One night—I think she had been with us about seven months—we found ourselves together in the living room. Mom and Dad had gone off to the movies. Jean was sitting in a chair reading and I was on the floor playing with one of my boy dolls. Suddenly I looked up and I noted that Jean's dress had hiked up, showing her bare thighs. I maneuvered myself up to a point where I could see the crotch of her panties.

It wasn't long before she saw me and put her legs together, pulling down her skirt. She gave me a mock look of disapproval, then went back to her book. But after awhile I noted that she was watching me playing with my doll.

"Tell me, Stanley," she said quietly, "that night you saw me playing 'Trust me.' What did you feel?"

I shrugged. I couldn't find a way to describe it. She watched me for a while longer, then moved to the daybed, rolled on her side and leaned on her elbow.

"Did you like watching us play?"

"I suppose."

"Would you like to play?"

I shrugged. Words failed me. She waved me forward and I got on the bed next to her.

"Now start up here," she said.

With some hesitance, but no reluctance, I put my hand on her neck.

"Trust me?" I said hoarsely.

"Yes."

I brought my hand lower.

"Trust me?"

"Maybe."

My hand touched the side of her breast.

"Trust me?"

"No."

But she looked up at me and smiled, showing me that I should press forward. The game, after all, was in the promise.

My hand circled her breast until she finally trusted me to touch it over her brassiere. My God, I felt wonderful. It wasn't long before her beautiful breasts were naked in my hands.

"I'll even trust you to kiss them," she said sweetly. And I did.

Then we got to work on the lower department. By then I had acquired the knack of the game and it wasn't long before her dress was up and her pink satiny panties lay before me. At that point I was somewhat stumped.

"I've trusted you with everything so far, Stanley. Haven't I?"

"Yes," I agreed.

"Now I'm going to trust you with the most important part of all."

"Really?"

"Really."

"But before I do that I want you to show me yours."

"Mine?"

She reached for my hard-on and touched it.

"That," she said.

I really was confused. I had a most confused idea of the geography of sexual conjunction. I was also shy and frightened. A hard-on was a very private thing for a boy. But Jean was so trusting and warm and persuasive that she finally persuaded me to show her my hard-on.

"That is a wonderful, beautiful thing you have there, Stanley. You should be very proud of it."

"Have you seen many things like mine?" I asked.

"I have six brothers and I have occasionally seen other boys. Do you know the use of this?" She caressed it lightly.

"Use?"

She explained it as best she could. In retrospect, I did not think then that she was a woman of great experience, although I know now that she greatly enjoyed this episode in her life.

"Now," she said, "I'm going to show you what I was talking about." She slid down her panties and spread her legs. What I saw sticks with me in vivid detail. I saw it, as they say, in living color. It was, to me then and still in my mind, a marvelous sight, tantalizing. The sheer eye-filling joy of seeing it for the first time can never be replicated. Remember, what I am describing was seen through the eyes of an eleven-year-old boy.

"Now you get on your knees between my legs, Stanley and I want to show you what you must do with this."

She guided me gently and directly into her. My penis even in its present state was still quite small and it slid in very easily.

"This is what the life of a man and woman means, Stanley. It is a beautiful, wonderful thing. It is not a dirty thing, although it can be dangerous, especially to a girl."

She let me pump her for a bit, then gently released me and held me in her arms. I felt wonderful, safe, warm, loving. I did not have an orgasm. I don't think she did either.

I don't know how long we stayed together, probably no more than an hour. But after we had dressed, we sat down on the bed holding hands.

"I'll never tell," I volunteered.

"Of course you won't," she said gently.

"I love you, Jean," I said. "And I promise you with all my heart that I will never tell."

She gave her notice the next day and I never saw her again until a few moments ago, more than forty years later.

But I've often thought about my experience with Jean Moran. How sweet that memory is. Today, I suppose, they might consider our act child abuse, or immoral, or some such euphemism that society has to invent to protect itself from its darkest fears.

I can't even tell you that I truly understood her motives for giving me this lesson in life. Perhaps she was reacting to my father's fears about me being a sissy. Perhaps she just wanted to leave me with this gift of knowledge, to give me the true taste of human nature. Maybe, deep down, she was just lusting, giving in to her own horniness, manifested in a desire to have sex with young boys. To me, whatever her motives, it was a gift more profound and meaningful than any I have received in my life.

I saw her briefly the next day making her rounds, spreading the joy that I know now was her purpose in life. I even stopped her in the hall. She looked up at me and smiled.

"Thank you, Jean Moran," I said.

She looked at me for a long moment. I'm sure she had a flash of memory and saw me as that little boy of eleven.

Then she walked away, but I must have continued to look at her. She turned at the end of the corridor and looked back.

"I never did tell," I whispered.

It was then she did her familiar wink and I was sure she heard me.

SECRET LOVERS

"The hardest part is the guilt," Glen told her. "Being away from you at night and the weekends."

"You could do something about it," Sara replied. This is not the first time she had heard his plaint, for which she had little sympathy. Besides, she had her own ax to grind. She did not like being defined as his mistress, which was the more honest description. She preferred the word "lover" to describe her situation.

And since lovers required—indeed longed for—time together, they had worked out a system that was both practical and geographically convenient. Glen lived with his wife Anne on Park and 68th; Sara lived on Madison and 56th. The law office in which Sara was a paralegal and Glenn was a partner was on Fifth and 59th.

The arrangement worked like this: Glen would arrive at Sara's apartment at six-thirty every morning. The doorman knew him by sight and his arrival was never questioned, especially since both he and Sara were generous tippers and not only at Christmas time. He would crawl beside her in her queen-sized bed and invariably make love to her until eight, when both got dressed and arrived at the office separately.

They congratulated themselves often on their discretion. Except for the doorman and his occasional relief, they assumed that no one, but no one, knew they had been carrying on this red-hot affair unabated for more than a year with little sign of let-up. From her perspective, there was little need for discretion for her own sake, only for his. She was single, twenty-seven years old, tall, willowy, a blonde goddess type, with unlimited opportunities to attract and meet men, but she made a point of turning down all offers. Indeed, she had no desire for other men. Glen, she assured him and herself, was the love of her life and being true to that love was a point of fealty and honor.

Glen's situation was a bit more complicated. He and Anne had been married for twenty-five years. They had one child who now lived on the West Coast and hoped to have a career as an actress. Anne had inherited a tidy sum from her parents, who were both deceased. She was enormously attractive and popular and spent much of her time on philanthropic boards; she and Glen often appeared in the style section of the *New York Times* attending one or another charity event. Both enjoyed their large single-floor apartment, their lifestyle, and each other when they were together. They never fought. Glen was proud of his wife, who was an elegant dresser, an excellent speaker, and, he was certain, an honorable and faithful spouse.

Of course, in a long marriage, the sexual part of their lives had become routine, although Glen made certain that he exercised his sexual duties at least once a week, which appeared to be enough of a requirement for Anne, more like a validation of their long marriage, a kind of periodic stamp of approval.

What had happened was that, quite by accident, since they were thrown together in the workplace, both Glen and Sara had fallen in love. Fallen, of course, was the operative word. It was as if both of them, almost simultaneously, had fallen over a cliff together. It had happened quickly, one of those sudden explosions. At first both thought it was simply lust, that disembodied chemical state where their relationship was measured in the number of climaxes each induced in the other, which were considerable.

They continued to be considerable, but there was a lot more to it, the angst, the despair, the discipline required to maintain the secretive nature of their relationship. Sara felt no guilt, only longing and loneliness when he was not with her at night and weekends. Although she had girlfriends from college and the office, she kept them at a distance regarding her personal life, although she suspected that the more perceptive of them might have suspected that she had a secret lover.

At times, when her friends' curiosity tried to breach her defenses, she parried their thrusts until they gave up their pursuit. On weekends she mostly she stayed home, went to the movies or shows or took long city walks. Glenn's path never crossed hers at night or on the weekends. Glen and Anne's social life occupied a different strata, and Manhattan life was layered strata by strata.

Since they spent a great deal of time together, encouraging conversation ("quality time" they called it), they were quite candid about their situation, deliberately transparent and revealing. Despite the deep intimacy of their relationship, he had made it clear from the beginning that he had no intention of leaving Anne, both for practical and emotional reasons. He admitted that he loved their lifestyle, was comfortable with it, enjoyed the fruits of her inheritance and, although he was head over heels in love with Sara, under no circumstances would he ever marry her.

"I am a cowardly bastard and I know it," he told her often. "Worse, I am in love with a beautiful young woman who, if this goes on much longer, will hurt her chances for marriage and a family."

"It's true," she would reply. "You are a cowardly bastard. And I am a stupid slave to my passion. Yes, this whole affair could ruin my life and I know it, but I am in love. There is nothing I wouldn't do to make you happy. Nothing. I am your willing slave, darling. A damned fool."

"Away from you," he assured her, "there is this awful void. I try my damnedest not to think of you, try to keep you shut up in another compartment. I succeed maybe one quarter of the time. It is a really painful situation."

"Of course, you could always stop the pain," she would say. But she genuinely feared pressing too hard. Since Anne was wealthy and could sustain herself financially without him and had a busy life, she would wonder out loud why he could not sever that relationship.

"Please, darling," he would answer. "I haven't got the guts to hurt her. She has been a wonderful wife. I know it's totally illogical since I am madly in love with you, but I just haven't got the character and courage to untie the knot."

"I'm becoming a nag," she would counter. "I'll stop it now." Then they would make love and that issue would be put aside.

Weighing her options, she could not bear the thought of losing him. As she told herself often, half a loaf is better than none. She forced herself never to fantasize about the future, although she could not help analyzing her situation. She was addicted to him, could not wait for him to wrap his arms around her every weekday morning.

There were, of course, occasional longer absences. Glen and Anne traveled. They visited their daughter on the West Coast, and Sara went home on holidays to visit with her parents who lived in Portland, Maine. Occasionally Glen had to be away for a day or two on business, but they could never take the chance of traveling together. If they were found out and a nasty event ensued, she would never forgive herself and was certain that such a revelation would end their affair forever.

Despite their joyful morning meetings, the angst of separation took its toll on him. Yet he could not stop himself and often would see himself as a victim, caught between a rock and a hard place.

"Leading a double life is not easy," he told her with increasing frequency. "Of course, in many ways, our life together is my real life."

"I don't know how you do it. I couldn't."

It was true. It was a lot easier for her to handle the situation. All she had to do was to be discreet in the office. They never went out together at night and there was little opportunity for them to be found out. Getting in and out of her apartment house was about the only risk he ever took, but even that was not much of a risk.

He did buy her gifts, mostly expensive jewelry for which he paid cash. The fact was that she demanded nothing although she lived far above her means. She rented a well-furnished condominium that was far too expensive, but it was necessary to consider both the geographical implications and the matter of ambiance. She thought it demeaning for her lover to come to her in a dumpy and badly appointed apartment.

While she gallantly refused any financial help, he would, knowing her financial situation, contribute sums to her maintenance, which he literally forced upon her. It worried him that she was having a tough time making ends meet.

"I am your lover, not your mistress," she would contend.

"I fail to see the difference."

"It's one of nuance."

He did not argue the point, fearing that it would open up a path of thinking that he knew she did not wish to confront. There was, of course, a practical consideration. Their affair depended on proximity. It simply would not do to waste time taking a cab or subway to another less expensive place in Manhattan or one of the other boroughs where the rents were considerably cheaper. It was hard enough to get up early and still make it to work on time. Thankfully, Anne never questioned why he left home so early.

"My husband works like a dog," she would often tell friends. "Especially since there is no need."

There was no denying, too, that there was a physical toll on him, a man over fifty, however well preserved. Often, a glance in the mirror in the men's room at the office would show the ashen complexion of a drained man. It was not uncommon for him to offer up his seed, as he characterized his couplings, three times during their nearly two-hour trysts. Hardly more, but never less. He was quite proud of the count and Sara marveled at his stamina.

"I didn't know what love can do," he joked.

"Is there an award for such a performance?" she would giggle.

She had no difficulty in matching his release. Indeed, her previous experience had been tepid in that regard. Occasionally it worried him that he would be inhibited in his marital duty, but he had always suspected that his wife often faked her ardor. At times, he had to merely act the part.

Nevertheless, Glen knew he was a man hanging on a thread between guilt and joy. No matter how hard he tried he could not resolve it. As the guilt grew stronger, so did the joy. He had never experienced such passion, although he had been in love before, but that was before his marriage. He was not a philanderer and was always brutally honest with himself, rational, practical, thoughtful.

He did fairly well as a lawyer, specializing in estate planning and issues that concerned death and inheritance. Through his practice, he had learned a great deal about human behavior. Death, he knew, revealed many secret lives that could no longer be hidden. Up until he met Sara, he had always believed himself a proud and moral man. He had never been unfaithful and he made it a point of honor to insist that most of their living expenses came out of his earnings, although he allowed Anne to buy their exquisite apartment, their expensive art work and furnishings.

Upon his insistence, they did not own a country house, a decision that predated his relationship with Sara, but since then, he had considered this decision wonderfully apt. It would have meant losing time away from Sara. Thankfully, Anne never brought it up anymore.

At times, he wished fervently that he was not in love with Sara, that he could walk away from this relationship, quit cold turkey. His battle with guilt was debilitating and exhausting. It was a condition within him that ebbed and flowed and he confessed to Sara often that it made him feel weak, indecisive, and ashamed.

"You mustn't dwell on that part, darling," she told him.

"It's making me crazy."

"Leave it home. Dispense with such feelings when we are together." She wished she could be more delicate about it, but the idea frightened her and she wanted him to put it aside. She wondered if it was building inside of him and becoming too hard for him to handle.

The conflict was becoming a growing affliction, and, like a virus, ideas to resolve it spread through his mind. Perhaps, he thought, he might find a way to compromise his dilemma, like formalizing the arrangement, confessing all to his wife and attempting to get her to agree to legitimize the relationship with Sara.

Among the French, he had been told, a mistress was quite tolerable. In fact, the former President François Mitterrand's wife and mistress had publicly attended the man's funeral, proof positive that such an arrangement was workable.

Knowing Anne, he was certain she could never agree to such a humiliating arrangement. Besides, legitimizing the idea could prompt Anne to take a lover. Certainly she would attract many takers, especially fortune hunters who would take full advantage of the situation. He could imagine a situation where everybody involved would have additional partners, a giant free-for-all of copulation and a dangerous exchange of bacteria and viruses.

Sara ridiculed the idea.

"As a lawyer, think of the complications," Sara pointed out. "Upon death, who inherits what?"

"Maybe we can put it all on paper. Hell, because I'm a lawyer I could make it contractual."

"The human heart cannot be contracted," Sara had responded, believing it implicitly. "It goes its own way."

"Besides, I would be profoundly jealous if you had another man in your life."

"How am I supposed to feel?" she responded cautiously. "You have another woman with whom you have sex."

"That's different. I am married to that other woman."

She feared going beyond that argument. Another Pandora's box would open. She had often wondered if their numerous couplings were psychologically designed to drain him of any desire for sex with Anne. It was a subject he refused to broach.

"Render unto Caesar's what is his and unto God what is his," he would joke. His meaning was clear.

There were other ironies that plagued him. Despite the limited time frame of their relationship, their conversations were deep, penetrating, and far more honest and numerous than those he had with Anne. Beyond the sex, there was the absolute, or almost absolute, transparency of their revelations to each other. They were able to transmit their inner thoughts and emotions. Both agreed that in the after-play, the intermissions to their couplings, they could empty their minds and hearts without inhibition, like a free association session with one's therapist.

Neither of them had ever been to a therapist. He feared revealing his secret to anyone, not even a therapist who was legally committed to privacy. She did not feel she needed one. What could a therapist possibly tell her? she wondered. That she was a damned fool, a co-dependent or whatever could be defined in the jargon for someone like her, committed to what was most likely to be a hopeless cause? Who needed a therapist to tell her that? Was there a twelve-step program for a committed lover to break her of her addiction?

One favorite topic of their after-play was why they had fallen in love with each other. Why her? Why him? Did he remind her of her father, whom she adored? Was there something in the chemistry of their bodies that stimulated their attraction? Where did this strange all-encompassing feeling come from? For lovers, these were weighty questions. Unfortunately, there were no answers, only more questions.

"We got hit by Cupid's arrows. Leave it at that," he would tell her after all aspects of the issue were tackled without resolution. The fact was that they finally concluded that this was one of life's mysteries and, whatever the consequences, it was the most profound emotional high that each would ever experience in their lives.

Unfortunately, the agony over his guilt began to weaken his resolve. It was becoming too burdensome to sustain. He was losing sleep, becoming disoriented, fixating more and more on the pain of her loneliness when she was away from him.

"As long as I know you will come to me in the morning, I am very content," she assured him. There was a germ of truth in the assertion but it was not convincing.

"Thinking of you alone is painful, darling," he would respond. "You're just a few blocks away, but it seems like the distance of light years."

"Then don't think too much about me."

"Don't you think of me when you're not with me?"

"All the time."

"Doesn't it hurt?"

"Very much, but then I know you will arrive in my bed every weekday at precisely six-thirty in the morning. How many woman can boast of such a wonderful surprise?"

"For me it's become a risk and reward situation. The greater the risk, the greater the reward."

As time went on and the glow of their relationship did not diminish, the guilt accelerated. He was losing sleep. At times he became disoriented and his work suffered. The burden of his guilt became too much to bear.

"I am ruining your life," he would tell her often.

"It's my life," she would counter. "By my lights, you're enhancing it."

"You won't say that after a few more years of this."

"I might say it more so as the years go on."

"I think you've lost your mind. Besides, I'm twice your age."

"So you say."

"My birth certificate says it."

"Your libido is lying."

"It won't lie forever."

"There is always the pill."

She worried about such subjects dominating their conversation. It indicated that his anxiety about her was accelerating. And it was.

Finally, he did realize that he'd have to take charge of the situation, which, he knew, required great sacrifice on his part. He lit upon a rational solution that he knew would be hurtful to both of them, but it was necessary, especially for her. As a trained lawyer, he always opted for rational solutions of benefit to his clients.

In this case, he tried to imagine her as a client. It was difficult to shake the emotional baggage, but he tried valiantly and finally came up with an idea. It took him months to broach the subject.

"This can't go anywhere for you, my darling. I can't live with the guilt. I just can't."

"Is your ardor cooling?" she asked, deliberately flippant, but he knew she was stunned by his assertion, although she had always lived in fear that it would come some day.

"You know that's not true. But someone has to make a move. And that job falls to me."

She had turned ashen and her eyes had misted, but she quickly gained control of herself.

"I've accepted my role, Glen. No need to push the envelope."

"It's a lousy role, Sara. You know it and I know it. And there is no way I can find the courage to fix it. I'm on the horns of a dilemma and if I don't take action you will be the loser over the long haul."

"How lawyerly. What then do you propose?"

She listened carefully as he laid out his plan, refusing to comment, her mind trying to comprehend his so-called rational solution.

"Here's what I propose, darling." He cleared his throat. He had rehearsed the idea over and over again in his mind, had made preparations, had solved the logistics. "I want you to go away from here, to find a new life somewhere else, to forget this episode."

"Can you?"

"Never. But don't interrupt. This is very hard for me."

"I'm listening."

"I want you to accept a million-dollar gift from me."

"Stop this, please."

"Just listen. Anne will never know. I have made arrangements to borrow this money on my own. I want you to take this money and start a new life somewhere else. You have a marketable skill and the money will give you the freedom to explore your options."

Feeling upset and humiliated, she tried to retain her composure.

"I feel like a prostitute. At least leave me my pride."

"I love you, Sara. I love you with all my heart and soul, but I cannot accept the continuing burden of my own guilt. I know what I'm doing. I'm trying to make you an offer that you cannot refuse. In fact, I urge you to accept it, if only for my sake alone. I cannot sustain this life of guilt. I cannot divorce my wife. I am a coward, I know. There is something ugly about this proposal, but I want you to consider it. I cannot continue this relationship, the lies, the dissimulation. Please do it for my sake. I plead with you. For my sake, Sara."

She turned her face away, not wishing him to see her contempt. She could not summon up the strength to reply.

"If you don't take this offer, you will regret it for the rest of your life. I know how you must feel. Sara, I dread the future without you. But if you love me, truly love me, you will understand. Can you imagine how terrible I feel in making such an offer? I hate myself for it, but I know it is the only logical solution. I cannot go on like this. Is it better for us simply to part and leave it at that or for me to make such an offer, if only to give me, selfishly I admit, peace of mind?"

Finally she found her voice.

"So I'm to be bought off, am I? This is what it's all about. Money. You won't leave your comfortable life because of money and you think that money will make me happy. I am insulted, Glen. I reject your offer out of hand. I am appalled that you could sink so low."

"I knew this would be your initial reaction, darling. I'm stuck in a terrible place. Who could possibly understand what I am going through? Think of me as a victim. Think of this money as hush money. Think of it as a payoff for what will certainly be the greatest moments of my life. Think of it, too, as a means of escape for you, a chance to live a normal life without lies and lonely nights. I know. I know. I am trying to buy off my pain. It is my last chance for comfort and peace of mind."

She watched him make his plea and felt herself calming. She knew he was taking an even greater risk. A loan from a bank was certainly something that couldn't be kept hidden for long, especially since it had to be paid back. It would be hard to justify a payback schedule that he could meet, even though he made a handsome salary at the firm. Still, she could not react at that moment.

"Just think about it, darling. This is hard. I know it's the right course for you."

When the offer was made, they were still in bed. He rose, kissed her on the forehead, got dressed, and left for the office. She did not appear that day, which filled him with anxiety and dire thoughts. Nor did she answer her phone. He knew that he had given her a real blow and terrible thoughts went through his mind. He imagined flight, disappearance, even suicide. Especially suicide. Just deserts, he thought, for his selfishness and his cowardice.

As the day wore on he grew more and more panicked. Toward the end of the day he feigned illness, rescheduled all his appointments, and rushed to her apartment.

"Gone," the doorman said.

"Gone?"

He opened a drawer at the reception desk and handed Glen a sealed envelope.

"Left this for you."

He hadn't given the doorman his correct name and when he was handed the envelope he noted gratefully that there was no name on the envelope. There seemed to be an expectation of a tip, as if money was required to keep the matter quiet between them. He handed the doorman a twenty-dollar bill, took the envelope and walked down the street to a Starbucks where he ordered a latté, then found an empty seat at a corner table.

For a long time, he looked at the unopened envelope while he concocted dire scenarios. Was this a suicide note? Had she mailed a letter to Anne informing her of the entire affair? Had she written to his law partners confessing their involvement and threatening a sexual harassment suit, a common occurrence these days? Was she planning some terrible circumstance that would impact negatively on his life?

He let the coffee concoction slide tastelessly down his throat, once again confronting his cowardice and lack of character. Time passed as he looked at the envelope, touched it, slid his thumb along its edges, sniffed at it for any sign of perfume, as if the scent would offer an optimistic preview of what the letter contained. No smell was evident.

He felt devastated and empty, but mostly fearful that the letter contained something ominous. Had she fled, really fled? Of one thing he was certain, this had to be the end of it. Surely a bad ending. When he had revealed his idea he thought he had been more than magnanimous, wildly and extravagantly generous. He was taking a giant risk. Worse, he had forged Anne's name and worked out a repayment plan directing all correspondence to come to his office.

The debt would require the use of his 401(k) from which he would release periodic payments. He had even concocted a fallback plan in case Anne found out about what he had done. He would tell her he had gambled in stocks and lost heavily. He would be contrite, beg her forgiveness, admit his folly, surrender to her mercy. After all, he had become an expert in dissimulation, a master of lies.

If only she hadn't confessed the whole affair to Anne. In that case he would be scot free. She would have left of her own volition, cut the strings, her memories of their affair spoiled by his crass action to buy her off. Thankfully, she had taken strict precautions and had not become pregnant. But suppose she had. A new thought intruded. The old cliché, the tired plot point of a thousand novels, plays, and movies. Would her letter suddenly reveal that new twist and provide yet more fodder for his guilt? A film of sweat broke out on his body. Perspiration soaked his shirt.

In time she would get over the affair, her love for him would fade away, along with his guilt. Never again would he allow himself to get entangled in such a disruptive situation. Never again would he allow himself to "fall" in love. Fall was the operative word.

He toyed with the idea of not opening the letter, assuming it was, after all, merely a letter of farewell, a dear John, which he roundly deserved. But the idea of a hanging loose end seemed worse than the revelation that would be contained there. Then he concluded that it was his ticket to freedom, the key to his unburdening.

With shaking fingers he carefully tore the end off the envelope, blew it open and removed the letter. For some reason, he looked around him furtively as if what he was doing was subject to surveillance.

"Dear Glen," the letter began. "I have decided to accept your offer. I am leaving town as of today. I have sent a letter of resignation to the firm and have packed up and given notice that I will be leaving the apartment. I'm not sure where I am going, probably to the West Coast. As you say, my skills are easily transferable. I will send a note to you at the firm and inform you where you can wire the funds, which I will require to settle up the rent and replace some items that I have left behind. Everything that could be said has been said. Please don't ever try to contact me. Sara."

He read the letter twice. It struck him as a form letter, cold and businesslike. Inexplicably he felt a growing anger. Then he threw the letter in the trash receptacle along with the half-drunk cup of latté. He hoped the guilt was gone, but he wasn't sure.

BAD PATCH

Gordon called them the walking wounded, older people clinging to life, hanging on. He would see them, accompanied by their caretakers, mostly black women who would either push them in wheelchairs or amble beside them as they struggled on their walkers, moving along First Avenue for lunch at the Madison Restaurant where Gordon invariably ate, or other eateries nearby.

Older couples limped along solicitous of each other, or men and women by themselves, intrepid and alone, assisted by canes moved in wary steps along the pavement. He assumed that the reason for so many sightings of these unfortunates was the number of rent-controlled apartments in the area where these people had lived for years and, refusing to be warehoused in nursing homes, had chosen to end their days in quarters that were still affordable.

Some, he speculated, were being subsidized by their children, who were hoping to keep these comparatively inexpensive and prized apartments after their parents had passed on. Perhaps there was a provision in the strange rental practices of New York that made it possible, but he wasn't certain. He discovered that he had grown increasingly observant of this phenomenon as he grew older. He was, after all, in his early eighties, still reasonably healthy, still compos mentis, still viable as an independent self-sustaining mobile human being enjoying all the various emoluments that the big city of New York had to offer.

Many of these unfortunates, Gordon noted, were younger than he, which always brought forth in his thoughts the silent monologue that he should count his blessings and stop complaining about all the minor aches and pains that afflicted his aging carcass. There could be no denying, however, that his generation was passing and mortality was an ever-present reality. Still, the fact was that he was remarkably active and healthy, despite his age. He supposed he should thank his parents for his genes, although his father had died in an automobile accident when he was sixty.

Gordon still played tennis every Saturday at the Roosevelt Island Tennis club, taking the aerial tram over the East River and joining the weekly senior round robin of mixed doubles. His usual strategy of high lobs and short angled shots kept him in the running as a sought-after partner and he often was considered the stronger player on his doubles team, even if his partner was years younger.

After the games, he usually schmoozed with the other players and ladies of uncertain age, some of whom he had bedded with surprising results, thanks to the new drugs that proved remarkably effective in this endeavor. Lately he had reserved his affection for Sylvia Dubrow, a well-preserved widow in her late sixties who lived a few blocks away on Lexington Avenue and still retained an imaginative sexual flair, which was an excellent adjunct to his pharmaceutical assistance.

He dubbed these episodic trysts with her as his manly validation, a term she enjoyed hearing.

"Not very seductive, but it does offer happy expectations."

Athletic and an inveterate exerciser who kept her figure under control, Sylvia did Pilates, attended yoga classes and was a regular on the

Saturday tennis round robin. She had been a schoolteacher and had married an accountant late in life. Consequently, she had no children, which suited Gordon just fine. He had avoided consorting with women who carried the emotional baggage of grandchildren and he detested hearing their ruminations on the exploits of such progeny.

Gordon had a son who lived in Seattle, who called a couple of times a year and was more or less estranged. His ex-wife, who had died a couple of years ago, had had custody of the boy and, as a result, had somehow dislodged from his psyche any paternal feelings, or so it seemed to Gordon, who prided himself on being able to cope with adversity, of which he had seen a great deal in his life.

His own apartment was a rent-controlled one-bedroom on 53rd Street, hardly a fashionable building. It was owned by an indifferent estate, which only made repairs when ordered to by the courts. All the appliances and bathroom fixtures were vintage forties and the mildew was growing increasingly noticeable, but Gordon had lived there for thirty years, ever since his divorce, and he had grown accustomed to its eccentricities. Besides, it had one of those old claw-footed bathtubs, which could hold his six-foot frame quite comfortably and was the envy of Sylvia, who would bubble-bathe excessively after their weekly sexual episodes.

Aside from her sexual adventurism, which was delightfully surprising and effective, Sylvia was one of those women who were persistent and relentless interrogators.

"You are one nosy lady," he would admonish her as they lolled in bed in leisurely after-play.

"Indulge me, Gordon. I am a sponge for knowledge, especially about the men I fornicate with." She had admitted that she had had an extensive history with men before her late marriage, but had renounced such practices in her widowhood, assuring him that he was her last and one and only lover. "Besides, there is a lot less time consumed by the sexual aspect in this time of life, leaving a lot more time for talk."

35

It surprised him how less guarded he had become in what he laughingly referred to as his dotage. He was amazed at his long-term memory as she probed and questioned, and suddenly he found himself telling his life story as a kind of running memoir, especially about what he referred to as "the bad patch that ruined his life."

"Ruined, Gordon? Come now, you are hardly a ruined man." She patted his flaccid penis and he felt the flicker of desire.

"Okay, then," he acknowledged. "A more accurate description would be revolutionized." He felt again the pain of that bad patch. Indeed, he thought he had put that to rest.

"We've all had bad patches, Gordon."

"Odd, how I still feel the ripples of the wake."

"How nautical you are, Gordon."

He enjoyed her creative sarcasm and told her so, which only encouraged her. Then he found himself running at the mouth, telling her all about the bad patch.

"I was fifty," he began, memory flooding back on a river of bitter bile. "I had worked for Fidelity Insurance for twenty-five years and was on the top rung of the executive suite by then. Good job. House in Huntington, Long Island, traditional wife, son ten years old, a latecomer, but my wife was twelve years younger. Two cars. Vacations in Florida in winter, beaches in summer, the whole nine yards. I was a company man. Then they hired this fellow, Thomas J. Phelan, the name is engraved in my brain. He got it into his head and the board agreed that people over fifty . . . imagine, over fifty. Hell, that's practically a teenager in today's calculus. Anyway they were determined to get rid of everyone over fifty. Phelan's strategy was to worry them out, torture them until they squealed and quit. You know how they did it. Move them from a three-window office to a broom closet, humiliate them at meetings, drive them mad with useless paperwork, ignore them, and when they complain, promise recompense but do nothing. Oh, Phelan was a clever bastard. He was a true sadist. He showed no mercy, but was relentless in his subtle persecutions. The idea was to make you quit, to harass you until your nervous system broke down and you had to quit or have a breakdown."

"I get the picture."

"He was one son of a bitch. He just wore us out and the over-fifties started to fade away. I hung on for months. I felt hollowed out. The son of a bitch broke my spirit. It was subtle, but he was effective. The idea was to move you out without legal ramifications. You couldn't prove that it was deliberate. I was not easy to live with. My wife was sympathetic to my plight, but my home life was beginning to wear thin. I was short-tempered, hard to live with. Every day at work was hell. Phelan reveled in it. He had ice in his veins."

"How old was he?"

"Under forty."

"Why didn't they just pay you off with early retirement or some such?"

"Bad for the numbers. He wanted to show the board how clever he was. Those who quit got three months' severance, which he thought was generous. He was ruthless. Hell, jobs for people over fifty didn't grow on trees. He was, in effect, murdering our career chances. Phelan was a monster. God, I haven't thought about him for years. I hated that man. Finally, I buckled. Quit cold. Just walked out. The company sent me the three-month check and that was that. My life was ruined by that man."

"Revolutionized, Gordon."

"Okay, revolutionized. My wife left me, got custody of my son, and I went personally bankrupt, all because of Thomas J. Phelan. Just mentioning his name still gives me heartburn. I wanted to kill him. I dreamed of torturing him, tearing him limb from limb. Sometimes I still do. I have never hated a man more than I hated him. He was my Hitler, the scumbag son-of-a-bitch bastard cocksucker."

"My, my. That last epithet I would take as a compliment."

Her remark broke the tension of the memory and he laughed, but he could not completely dispel the old hatred.

"It took a while, but I did recover, at least partially. I drove a cab for a while. I had these alimony payments. It was awful."

"They say adversity builds character."

His comeback was, to his own surprise, agreement.

"It does. One does learn to cope. In time I got a sales job and it kept me going."

"And here you are," Sylvia said. "A survivor of all the bad patches with a great bathtub—with a comfortable king-size bed, a great tennis strategy, mobility and all your marbles and," she winked, "with help and inspiration, you are a reasonably adequate sexual partner."

"Is that a compliment or an insult?" he laughed, poking her playfully in the ribs.

"There is a lot to say for adequate if it does the job." She looked about the room, her eyes resting on the window air conditioner. "Like that antique of a device." She pointed with her chin, "Makes a racket, huffs and puffs and squeaks, but it does the job." She giggled and kissed him on the cheek.

"So now I'm an antique."

"Antiques have value. And wine grows better with age."

He laughed and embraced her, feeling better, memories of Thomas J. Phelan and his bad patch starting to fade from memory.

Still, he realized, it could never fully disappear. It was always there, locked in his brain cells, reacting to the summons of the old hatred. Weeks later, perhaps longer, he was heading to his daily luncheon at the Madison Restaurant when he noticed one of the walking wounded, a man being led by the hand by a black female caretaker. The man walked haltingly, each step an obviously difficult chore. His face was distorted by a frozen expression and his eyes looked lifeless and glazed. Still, Gordon sensed some vague familiarity as the man was led into the Madison Restaurant and maneuvered into a booth.

Gordon, seated in a small table facing the booth, studied the man, searching his memory. He watched as the caretaker looked over the menu and gave the order to the young waiter. He had his usual white mushroom omelet and coffee and continued to observe the man, much to the chagrin of the caretaker who offered annoyed glances in answer to his curiosity.

A large salad was placed before the man and he picked at it without appetite, sometimes spilling the contents on his shirt, again to the chagrin of the caretaker who had ordered a hamburger and a large order of French fries, which she proceeded to dip into a large pool of ketchup and eat with greedy relish while the old man suffered through his meal with difficulty.

Gordon had barely finished his omelet when his memory kicked in. Sitting across from him was the wreck of a man who had once been his nemesis. Thomas J. Phelan, the bastard who had ruined, no, revolutionized, his life; the demon that had made his last days at the company after twenty-five years a living hell; the son of a bitch who had helped break up his marriage, contributed to his bankruptcy, helped alienate his only son. Invective crowded into his mind. His stomach knotted and he could feel the backwash of the omelet in his throat. He tamped down the urge to vomit.

How many times had he imagined confronting this monster, this evil sadist? How many times had he wished for the man's slow and painful demise? Now, at last, here was his chance to confront him, curse him out, tell him how happy he was to see him in this condition, getting his just deserts. He fantasized the speech he would make, bending low over the table, whispering his tale of vengeance into the man's ear, gloating over his condition, salivating over this rare opportunity for payback.

Picking up his check, he rose and approached the table. He hovered over it for a moment, watching the man pick at his food, while the black lady was absorbed in dipping her French fries in the ketchup. She looked up as he came forward. Phelan, his head bent over his salad, attempted without success to get a bit of tomato on his fork. As Gordon watched him, he felt his words congeal on his tongue and suddenly he sensed a vast inner deflation, as if, in one big spurt, he was being sapped of some poisonous venom.

What a sad prick, he told himself, this once-evil man who was the principal motivator of his bad patch. Everything ends, he thought suddenly, the bad, the good, the indifferent, hate, love, anger, despair, every human condition. Life flows, ebbs and ends. Even for this miserable bastard. And here I am, he screamed within himself. Still standing.

"Sorry," he said to the caretaker, smiling broadly. "He reminded me of someone."

Phelan paid no attention, remaining bent over his salad, barely able to maneuver any part of it to his mouth.

The caretaker poked at the man's arm and he looked up at Gordon with rheumy eyes, then turned downward toward his salad.

"Not one of his good days," the caretaker said, shrugging, then returning to the process of dipping the fries into the ketchup.

Gordon paid the check and walked away. He felt neither exhilaration or pity or any sense of vindication, but he knew that, once and for all, this motivator of his bad patch was no longer of consequence to him. He felt energized as he walked quickly to his apartment and called Sylvia on her cell phone.

"What is it?" she said with a degree of concern since his call was unexpected.

"I need your ministrations. I am badly in need of manly validation."

"Why, Gordy, I never thought you'd ask."

He hung up, took a deep breath and popped a Viagra.

A STRING OF PEARLS

Planning a mad act was a lot easier than its execution. This was Helen's third attempt and no amount of reasonable self-argument could dissuade her.

The maître d', greeting the known female patrons of his establishment with double kisses, offered her discreet welcoming smiles and nods now that she was recognizable, although as merely a bar fly.

"I just love the way Larry makes martinis," she told him, loud enough for Larry the bartender to hear as he stood in front of his display of shiny bottles. She sat down on one of the stools, crossed her legs, put down the pocketbook in which she carried, as she had dubbed it, the swag, her ill-gotten gains, and waited for the right moment. Peripherally, she could see him at his regular Wednesday table holding court. They owned tables at Le Cirque, and Jock apparently owned this one, left of the entrance, once removed, visible, status blessed.

The martini came, straight up Bombay Sapphire gin with a twist, ice cold and she sipped, slyly observing him in full charming mode. At the very least, she would need two this time, she had determined. One had not, on two previous occasions, been enough to provide the Dutch courage required for her to perform this marvelously conceived and deliciously creative act of vengeance.

While her two earlier attempts had ended in cowardice and inaction, she did discover how much irony goes on in these pricey dining palaces where the charmed circle of what passes for New York elite goes to be seen and reassured that they reside within its circumference. The very name of the restaurant, "Le Cirque," implied it was at the very center of moneyed opulence and social cachet.

It was, after all, the splashy golden wallpaper of Jock Frazer's real world. There he sat, her dashing, much adored and worshipped former lover, over whom the sun had once rose and set. She defined him now as her liar lover, the great pretender, the master betrayer who had gifted her with everything but his future.

In the pocketbook that lay on the floor beside the barstool was a string of pearls in its velvet purse, one orb for every time they had made love, he told her. Times six, she had countered. It would have taken bushels of oysters piled as high as Jack's beanstalk, he had quipped. There were actually sixty-three in the string, enough for twice around. She had had it appraised for north of a hundred thousand. It astounded her. She thought it was paste and enamel. The affair had lasted eleven months.

At the table for six, spouses separated and placed by gender, Jock's wife, the frigid clotheshorse, the selfish, status-obsessed, social hustling, mean-minded bitch, as he had characterized her again and again, played hostess with what seemed like great charm and animation. She was definitely not recognizable as the character in Jock's repetitively embellished portrayal. But then he had needed to make her the heavy to embroider the fantasy and keep Helen going for the carrot.

Throughout it all, she had been a true believer. The yarn he spun was so incredibly real, complete with tangible evidence of his zeal, the lavish gifts, the lease on the west side apartment and the promised divorce from the harridan. Poor man, she had once thought. So abused.

So badly treated. So unloved.

Then, after their eleven-month affair, he had made his retreat unscathed or so he thought. He had let her keep the pearls and the other jewelry he had given her, enough to carry the lease of her west side apartment for another year, and ready cash of twenty-five thousand that he had managed to find in his own piggy bank non-joint account that he kept for emergencies like this one. All in all, a good haul, he led her to believe.

Her investment in his promise was yet another form of madness. She had given up her financial research job in the hedge firm in which Jock was a partner, taking a less lucrative independent contractor assignment for another firm so that she would be available to him on his secret schedule. They would see each other a few times a week in her apartment, mornings usually, or late afternoons.

On occasional evenings they would have dinner in neighborhood restaurants off the beaten path of his regular life. Once he had let slip that Wednesday was Le Cirque night for entertaining clients.

They were in love, head over heels, as they say. There was no denying her part in it. She hadn't suspected that his commitment had been transient, believing hers to be permanent. It had all the elements; the overwhelming sexual frenzy, the deeply transparent conversational transparency, an avalanche of inner thoughts, secrets, feelings, the hidden fears and, inevitably, the promises of eternal fealty. She really, really believed that "this was it," the girl's romantic dream come true, the soul mate found.

And the promises, the plans glibly spun, usually in post-coital intimacy. Of course, he would leave his wife. She was a frigid shrew, a gossipmonger, a superficial, empty-headed, one-dimensional fool. She was spoiled rotten, threw temper tantrums, was an indifferent mother to his only child who spent most of her time in boarding school. He hated her. He could not stand any proximity to her flesh. They hadn't made love for years. She was physically revolting, a slob, cruel, deceitful, mean-minded, grotesque, shallow, selfish. He needed to escape her and Helen was his designated escape hatch. She believed it implicitly. Not a doubt intruded.

Grudgingly, she would later acknowledge the creativity of his spousal descriptions. She supposed he needed the vituperation to keep the fire going. Apparently, it turned him on. And her. She put extra effort in making the pain disappear. Seeing his wife for the first time during her initial revenge attempt was a shock. She looked quite lovely, beautiful, self-assured, even regal. Even in his physical description he was a liar. Worse, seeing them at the table, the manner in which they interacted seemed respectful, even loving.

After he was divorced, he promised, they would live in Manhattan, become West Siders, first-class culture consumers, enjoy the opera, plays, concerts, lectures, live life to the fullest in the greatest city on earth. Together. Forever. He would wipe away his foolish past.

What he told her, finally, with that sad frat boy expression of remorse, was that he couldn't see her any more. That was after they had sex twice in her apartment one morning in the eleventh month of their affair made in heaven.

She was stunned, unbelieving, searching his face for some sign of satire, a big joke.

"It's a long story," he said.

"A long story?" She could barely find words.

"I'm trapped. She would crucify me financially, take away my kid. I'd be finished." He rolled over on his side and looked at her face. "God, I love you."

"You promised . . . " Her heart was beating so fast she could barely breathe. "What am I?"

"Somebody very special," he whispered. "Somebody who brought joy into my life."

Inexplicably, he reached out and traced his finger from her nipple to the inner crease between her legs.

"I don't believe this," she cried.

"There are ways to say goodbye."

"A farewell fuck. How gross."

She had jumped out of bed, staggered by the revelation, the humiliation. She went into the bathroom and studied her blotched face in the mirror, her features scrunched into a silent cry. The tears rolled down her cheeks.

"You've been screwed," she bleated to her ugly image in the mirror, shaking her head in disbelief. Then she washed her face and came back in her robe. He was already dressed.

"I don't want to give you one moment of hardship or pain."

"You're kidding," she sneered. By then she had recovered and was determined to retrieve her dignity. "I won't take this sitting down," she whispered, watching as the blood drained out of his face.

"What does that mean?" he asked, suddenly needing to clear his throat.

"You figure it out."

"I wouldn't do anything crazy," he warned.

"I would."

Ideas of vengeance filled her mind. She would confront the terrible wife, reveal the terrible truth, tell his partners how he had seduced her in on the firm's premises, how their first fuck was on the desk in his office, how they had carried on together until she finally left the firm. She would bring charges.

"Look, baby, I'm so sorry. I so much wanted this to work out."

"Bullshit."

"But wasn't it great between us?"

"All I was . . . " she fumed. " . . . was a mistress. I was never anything more. A damned mistress."

"You knew I was married," he said, his cheekbones reddening. "You knew the score."

"I was a naïve fool," she whispered. "You said things. You made promises, commitments."

"And wanted to keep them. Really," he said.

"Really?"

"This is painful for me, Helen."

"Painful for you?"

"Believe me. I wanted to find a way. She has me nailed. Maybe some day," he sighed.

"Some day?"

She felt herself reduced to repetition, unable to find words.

"Nothing is forever," he said. "Not even life. Most people never have what we had."

"I believed you," she said. It came out as a whine, a pitiful bleat. Anger had paralyzed her.

"And I believed it was possible."

A wave of nausea seized her. She ran again to the bathroom and hunched over the toilet, producing dry heaves. Then he was knocking on the door, which she had locked.

"Don't do anything foolish, Helen," she heard him say.

"Go away," she cried.

"Open up, Helen, please," he begged.

"Go away, you shit."

There was a long silence. Finally he said, "Can you hear me through the door?"

"Go fuck yourself," she cried.

"I've made arrangements," he said, telling her about the lease, the check for twenty-five thousand. And the pearls. "The pearls alone . . . "

It crossed her mind that they could be fakes like everything else.

"Just don't do anything foolish," he said again.

She put fingers in her ears, shutting him out.

"Go away," she screamed, falling on her knees, shoulders shaking with hysterical sobs, which she stilled with a fist. She did not want him to hear.

After a long silence, she heard the door to the apartment close.

For three weeks, she moped around the apartment, lying in bed, crying. What did he mean by something foolish? Suicide perhaps? Or what? It took her awhile to figure out the "or what." Now that she was on to it, she felt about to be redeemed.

One was supposed to learn lessons from such abortive adventures, from failure. She had misread all the signals, mistaken hope for reality. Every element of the affair became like digital chapters in her mind, played back and forth, again and again, mining for signs. Was it desperation? She had just turned thirty when she and Jock began. Was that some sort of dividing line, self-confidence turning into vulnerability, optimism becoming fear?

Perhaps she was living in some time warp. Marriage was not the Holy Grail it was for her mother's generation, except for gays and lesbians who wanted legal protection. She might have been quite content, over time, to live as a mistress. Hell, it wasn't such a bad life. Longing and expectation could be exhilarating. Had she been too needy, too pushy? Yet she hadn't pressed him.

In her digital memory, he was the one who concocted their future. Like that Second Life website in which you could reinvent a parallel life. For her, the problem was that he had never told her that he was living this parallel life, never hinted at it. She had consorted with an invented character, an avatar.

What was galling was that she was not an invented character, not by a long shot. She was real, flesh and blood, and Jock had slipped across the line to play his little game, then slipped back to his own reality. That was what it had boiled down to. Now it was her turn to confront his world, enter it and make him pay the price for the use of her flesh and emotions.

She upended the second martini and felt the flattening effect on her inhibitions. She uncrossed her legs, looked toward his table, then turned to Larry. Not quite ready, she told herself.

"Just a smidgeon more," she told him, holding up a finger and thumb to designate the size. He made it quickly, about half the usual, which she downed in one gulp.

She was fearless now, slightly unsteady, but certain she was in control.

This was the moment she had rehearsed again and again in her mind. She took a deep breath, smiled coyly at Larry, then lifted her pocketbook from the floor and opening it on the bar, she removed the large soft pouch containing the pearls, smiled at Larry who was watching her, and holding the velvet purse, started toward the dining room.

Jock turned his eyes from his table companions as she approached. She was holding the velvet purse by its neck. Then her head began to spin and she found she had lost control of her legs. She opened her mouth to speak, but could not get the words out.

Whatever words she had rehearsed disappeared from memory and she staggered against a chair, falling. The velvet purse banged hard against the floor, opening at its neck, breaking the string. The pearls rolled out. She heard ticking sounds as the white orbs unraveled, rolling under tables, chairs, under feet.

Strong hands lifted her to her feet. People seemed to saunter everywhere searching for the pearls. She heard astonished voices. Finally upright, she struggled with her handlers, forcing them to halt in front of Jock's table. Through the glazed drunken haze, she saw his face, their eyes met, and she tried to say his name, but couldn't get it out.

She had carefully rehearsed her speech, garbled in her mind now.

"You can keep . . . " she began, but nothing followed.

"You know her, Jock?" she heard the harridan say.

"I don't think so," she heard him say, just as she was hustled away. "Poor thing."

A cab had been called. Someone helped her into the cab and got in beside her.

"Help her get home," she heard the maître d' say. "We'll send her what we find."

After she had gone, a man at Jock's table bent over, picked up a pearl, and held it to the light.

"Probably a fake," he said.

"Probably," Jock said.

HOW CAN I POSSIBLY
MAKE YOU UNDERSTAND?

"Guilt," Anne's husband said.

"In a way," Anne agreed. "But he has been our neighbor for how long?"

"Ten years at least."

"We do share a landing."

What she meant was that there were two apartments on their floor, the twelfth on Madison and 75th. Such proximity did not mean that there was any requirement to be neighborly. In Manhattan apartments, people might live next door for a lifetime and never socialize, other than to offer a polite greeting or confer on the décor of their joint landing. The Sanborns had supplied a pleasant painting of a sea scene and the Bentons had contributed a copy of an antique table and a vase that was filled with flowers when a social occasion arose, like now for the Bentons' dinner party.

One or twice over the years Anne and Jack had the Sanborns in for cocktails, and the Sanborns had politely reciprocated, but it was all pro forma and quite stiff socially since they had little in common. Arnold Sanborn was a Wall Street corporate lawyer and his wife was, according to Anne's assessment, one of those WASP garden club type ladies who talked funny and seemed distant and superior.

Besides, Anne, a pediatrician, and Jack, a manufacturer's rep, were at least a generation younger. Their only child was working on the West Coast. The Sanborns apparently had grown grandchildren. Except for an occasional greeting and polite pleasantry when they met in the elevator or on the landing, neither family showed any personal curiosity about the other. There was no animosity between them, just disinterest. Actually, it was typical of New York apartment dwellers.

Mrs. Sanborn had been dead nearly a year and although the Bentons expressed their condolences to Mr. Sanborn, they did not attend the funeral. They did, however, note that Mr. Sanborn apparently had retired from law practice. They saw him rarely.

"I thought it would be a nice gesture," Anne said when she tendered the invitation to Mr. Sanborn, sending the formal printed invitation through the mail when she could have simply slipped it under the door of his apartment. Mr. Sanborn accepted, responding through the mail as well.

The Bentons had invited two other couples along with Mr. Sanborn, Sam and Mary Connors and Charley and Susan Lieberman. All were longtime friends; the wives were sorority sisters who graduated from Brown. The husbands had bonded through the women. They all shared similar views on most things including politics, although while nominal Democrats, both Connors couldn't care less.

"They're all a bunch of phonies, the lot of the them," Sam Connors was fond of saying, always with a crooked boyish grin. "It's a question of choosing between a rotten apple and one with a worm living inside."

Anne, who was the most activist about her politics, thought him cynical and indifferent and had told him so on numerous occasions. Both Liebermans were as passionate as she on the subject, but all four considered themselves confirmed Democrats, and agreed on all the hot button issues of the day, including the right to choose, school prayer, expanding stem cell research and reining in what they deemed threats to their civil liberties.

All four were unalterably opposed to the war in Iraq and, while supporting the war on terror, they thought it was being exaggerated and used for political advantage by the Republicans. In general Republicans were anathema and, in their minds, manipulated by right-wing fanatics as exemplified by the sitting president. In fact, these were the views held by almost everyone in their social circle. Birds of a feather, one might say. But then this was, after all, New York and the old gray lady of the New York Times was their principal informational outlet. They considered themselves acutely aware, informed, wise, knowing, liberal, tolerant and open-minded.

Since Anne liked things especially festive, she wanted the girls to dress in cocktail dresses and the men in jackets, although she allowed they could eschew ties, which they did.

Arnold Sanborn arrived precisely on time, which was somewhat earlier than the Connors and the Liebermans. He wore a double-breasted pin-striped formal suit with a handkerchief carefully folded in his jacket pocket and a dressy gray and blue tie which adorned a white on white shirt that looked slightly ill fitting, as if he had lost weight since she had last seen him. His shoes were shined to mirror brightness and his pinkish face was freshly shaven. Anne noted that he seemed somewhat shrunken in stature than she remembered, but then she had hardly observed him the last time she stood next to him in the elevator.

"He seemed to have aged since his wife died," Jack whispered to Anne as he poked around the refrigerator for a lemon to slice a peel for Arnold Sanborn's gin martini straight up.

"I guess tragedy shows more when you pass eighty."

Arnold accepted his martini, lifted his glass in an imaginary toast, and took a sip.

"Excellent," he said with a half smile. He looked about the apartment, perhaps seeking some focal point to use as an entry into conversation.

Anne noted that he was not exactly a loquacious personality and was already regretting having invited him. She was concerned suddenly how she would make him part of the dinner group. Clearly, observing Mr. Sanborn, it was going to be a challenge. The man seemed stiff and overly formal.

While waiting for the others, Anne and Jack felt obliged to entertain their guest.

"So how is the legal eagle business doing these days?" Jack asked, determined to bridge the silence with light small talk.

"Oh, I've been retired, put out to pasture a few years ago."

"Really. And now?"

Thankfully, they were interrupted before Sanborn could answer by the simultaneous arrival of the Connors and Liebermans.

"We met in the lobby," Mary Connors said as they hugged and chattered in the manner of old friends comfortable with each other and happy to be together.

Anne took great pains to introduce Arnold Sanborn, who did indeed, much to her dismay, look totally out of place. If there was any discomfort on his part, he did not show it, even as the conversation swirled around him. The Connors and the Liebermans chatted among themselves, mostly about their children and their various activities and the usual New York small talk about shows and movies they had seen.

"Have you seen any good plays recently, Arnold?" Anne asked deliberately trying to shoehorn Sanborn into the conversation.

"Not really," Sanborn replied. "Elizabeth was the playgoer of the family."

"His wife passed on," Anne explained using a euphemism she had rarely used before, hoping he would consider it appropriate.

"I'm so sorry," Mary Connors said. The others nodded or whispered condolences.

"How long were you married?" Susan Lieberman asked, her large brown eyes under a shelf of bangs expressing obviously sincere sympathetic feelings. Of the three women, she was the one most easily moved, always the first to cry and the first to vocally defend the downtrodden.

"Fifty-three years," Sanborn said, casting his eyes downward for a brief moment, before looking up again.

"How wonderful," Susan said. "A most unusual situation these days." She glanced toward her husband who shrugged. It was the second marriage for both of them. Sam Connors had been married before and had a son by his first wife. He exchanged glances with his wife but made no comment.

"You must miss her," Susan pressed.

Anne could see that Sanborn was slightly discomfited by the remark. "I do," he whispered, turning away. It was obviously a subject not open for discussion. Seeing his reaction, Susan desisted and turned the conversation to other matters. Again, Anne noted that Sanborn drifted out of the social chitchat. He still held his now-empty martini glass. Noting this, Jack asked if he wanted a refill. He looked blankly at the diminished liquid.

"A splash," he nodded. Ann surmised his consent to have another martini was an escape from his ostracism. He was quite definitely a fish out of water. Before calling them all into dinner, Anne, who liked to place her guests carefully, switched place cards and put Arnold Sanborn next to her, mostly to spare Susan his company or, she chuckled to herself, vice versa.

Making conversation with Sanborn was more than a challenge. It was a chore. She steered away from personal matters reasoning that perhaps, in his obviously WASPish corporate culture, the very personal might be a restricted subject. Not that she ever thought in these terms since she, as a white Anglo-Saxon Protestant herself, might qualify for such an appellation. But then, she was from the Midwest originally and Sanborn, with his noticeable broad "A," was obviously from Boston or somewhere in the New England area. She was, of course, well aware that she was reacting to a stereotype, but he did seem so typical of the genre.

Jack over-generously poured the wine and by dessert time rolled around, the conversation of the well-oiled guests shifted to politics.

"We have got to dump this administration," Sam Connors said. "Aside from bankrupting us, they have totally screwed up our foreign policy. They hate us all over the world now."

"It is beyond belief," Mary chimed in. "Our president is an idiot. I mean, really, how could we have possibly elected such a blundering incompetent fool. Never mind that we're going broke, that damned useless war was the biggest blunder in history."

"Those kids are dying for nothing, absolutely nothing," Susan said. "I can barely read the papers and watch the news on television. I want to cry. We have got to get rid of these people before it's too late."

"And this war on terrorism," Jack chimed in. "It's being used as a political ploy. I tell you it is being deliberately used to keep these sons of bitches in power, scaring the hell out of all of us. We should pull out of that fucking Iraq hellhole and let the bastards kill each other."

"I'm for that," Charley Lieberman said, his tongue slightly slurred but still coherent, his anger well stoked. "Let them all behead each other. We'll stand by and watch."

"That's so bloodthirsty, Charley," Susan said, berating her husband. "You sound like some right-wing nut."

"Don't tell me you feel sorry for those monsters?" Charley said.

"They're human beings," Susan said emphatically.

"Well, why don't they act that way?" Mary said.

"One thing I know," Charley said. "War is never the answer."

"Not with the weapons available today," Sam Connors said, as if he were the voice of reason.

"This administration keeps it up, we're all going to be pulverized," Jack said. "Kaput. One little bomb right here and it knocks out the whole East Coast."

"And all of us," Susan said. "And our kids."

"Now there's a gloomy prospect," Sam Connors said.

"That man in the White House thinks he has a pipeline to God. He's absolutely convinced he's on the right path," Charley said.

"Yeah, the path to hell," Jack muttered. "Shoot first. Ask questions later."

"We should never stop talking to our enemies," Anne said joining in. "Diplomacy is the only civilized way." From the corner of her eye she observed Arnold Sanborn, who had remained silent, although she did note that his cheeks were beginning to flush. Suddenly, she realized that he had been totally left out of the conversation.

"Bottom line," Charley said, "we have got to get rid of the idiots running things. They have to go and the faster the better. They have made all the wrong decisions. The war was stupid. And this terrorism scare. Sure, there is terrorism, but why should they use it to scare us?"

"Because it's true," Arnold Sanborn said suddenly.

He reached for his wineglass, sipped and studied the faces around the table as the looked toward him, then exchanged glances with each other. Anne felt her stomach lurch.

"I'm sorry," Sanborn said quietly, "but mine is not the prevailing view around the table."

"Really," Charlie began. Anne could sense the beginning of belligerence.

"Don't tell me," Sam said, his words more slurred than ever. "A Republican."

"An American," Sanborn said. His remark seemed measured, without any hint of belligerence.

"We're all Americans," Charlie said nervously playing with the stem of his wineglass, then emptying it. Jack filled his glass again.

"Are you saying you agree with . . . " she paused," . . . with them?" Susan began, then exchanged glances with Anne, who was getting agitated.

"Everyone is entitled to their view," Anne said, taking a deep breath. She could sense the hostility rising in her guests.

"War is not always the answer," Sanborn said quietly, his speech cadence lawyerly. The flush in his cheeks had spread further. "Although it was in my day." He nodded as if receiving some information by a voice inside of him. "If we hadn't gotten rid of Hitler, we would all be watching goose-stepping parades up Fifth Avenue."

"That chestnut again," Charley said, his tongue making a hissing sound.

"Four hundred thousand brave men died to make that so-called chestnut a reality," Sanborn countered politely.

"So what are you saying?" Charley asked.

There was a long pause as all eyes turned toward Arnold Sanborn. Anne, although aware of the hostility, felt herself siding with her other guests and not with Sanborn, who struck her now as a self-satisfied sanctimonious right-wing prig. But he is a guest in my house, she asserted to herself and for a brief moment she weighed the consequences of propriety. The hell with him, she decided. He's on his own.

"I'm saying that the president and his team are the canary in the mine shaft," Sanborn said. "It is the early warning of things to come. The Sudetenland, Spain, Czechoslovakia. As it was then, so it is today. Those people, in this case the radical Moslems out there, like the Nazis, want to kill us. They want to crush our civilization, establish a Caliphate and reduce our way of life to the level of the Taliban."

Although his words were militant, he was surprisingly calm and measured.

"Word for word," Sam said. "Right from the bully pulpit."

"The fact cannot be contested," Sanborn said. "The war has been going on for years and we are losing it. We are not heeding the tea leaves. We are still asleep. We are on the verge of a cataclysm."

"War-mongering," Charlie sneered.

"How can I possibly make you understand?" Sanborn said.

"You can't," Susan said.

"You know what I think?" Charley said. Anne could see he was winding up for a blow. Although the conversation still verged on the cusp of politeness, she could sense it was about to be getting out of hand and she was becoming slightly panicked. There was no point in having a confrontation, especially with a neighbor, whom she would inevitably have to face. But it was too late.

"I think you're one of those right-wing nuts we were just talking about."

Anne could feel everyone in the room bracing themselves. Goose pimples broke out on her skin.

"More wine, anybody?" Jack said, a futile gesture, although he did pour more wine into those glasses that were empty.

"Do you really?" Sanborn said calmly.

"How can you support those fools?" Susan said.

"Everyone is entitled . . . " Anne began, but by then Charley was revved up.

"It's people like you that are bring down our country. People like you who are choking off our civil liberties, our freedoms, everything we stand for as a people. That idiot in Washington is bringing ruin on our country." His eyes reflected his rising hostility. "It's you and your ilk that are killing us as a people."

Ilk? Anne thought. It was getting nasty.

"I have to agree with you, Charley," Sam said. "At some point you have to make a choice."

"I have," Sanborn said, rising, still calm.

He is leaving in a huff, Anne thought, wondering if she would be regretful and embarrassed when she met him on their joint landing.

"May I beg your indulgence?" he said, folding his napkin and putting it beside his dessert plate. "I'll be right back."

He left the room and they heard the door to the landing open. They looked at each other stunned.

"What is that all about?" Charley asked.

"He's gone into his apartment," Jack said. He had gone to check.

"Typical right-wing moron," Charley said.

"Sanctimonious prick," Sam chimed in.

"I'd say people like him are more a threat to our way of life than the terrorists," Susan said.

"She felt guilty," Jack said. "Him having lost his wife and we not having anything to do with him."

"Guilt will do it every time," Mary said.

"No matter what, Anne did the right thing," Susan said.

"With the wrong outcome," Charley said.

Anne sucked in a deep breath.

"Please, no clichés about what the road to hell is paved with."

"Okay then," Mary giggled. "How about no good deed goes unpunished."

"It's like relatives," Jack said smirking. "You can't choose your neighbors."

"But you can bar the door, Bill Bailey," Sam chuckled.

They heard movement across the hall and Arnold Sanborn was back. He was holding something in his hand.

"What is that?" Sam asked.

"A CD. It was a tape and I had it converted."

"A CD of what? Some propaganda bullshit," Charley said.

"You'll see," Sanborn said looking at Jack. He handed him the CD.

"Really Sanborn, if this is some scammy right-wing crap, forget it. We're not stupid."

"You won't change any of our minds," Charlie said.

"How can I possibly convince you?" Sanborn said.

Sanborn exchanged glances with Jack. Then shifted his gaze to Anne.

"What's on it?" Anne asked.

"Some pictures I took," Sanborn said.

"Of what?" Jack asked.

"You'll see. I watch them again and again."

"Hell, why not?" Sam said.

"What harm is there? I took the pictures myself. By coincidence. My office was just across the street and I had taken my video camera to work. We needed it for some case we were working on."

"Across from what?"

"Across from the World Trade Center," Sanborn said calmly.

"That again," Charley said. "How many times do we have to see those images?"

"Over and over again," Sam said. "Repetition. Burn the idea home. Haven't you squeezed enough mileage from that one?"

"Could you slip it into your player?" Sanborn pressed, ignoring the comments. Anne noted that he was single-minded now, commanding. None of the insults flung his way seemed to penetrate. If he was agitated, he did not show it.

"Must we?" Mary said.

"Yes," Sanborn said. "I don't know any other way to convince you."

For a moment there was silence as Jack looked at the CD in his hand.

"Maybe we should have another drink first," he said, picking up an opened bottle and pouring wine into each glass. Sanborn declined, watching them patiently. Drinks in hand, they all went into the living room where there was a large flat screen. Outside, through French doors that opened to a tiny narrow balcony, was a commanding view of the pulsating city, sparkling with lights and energy.

"I feel creepy," Sam said, taking a deep sip of his wine.

"Is there a point to this, Sanborn?" Charley asked. "We know where you stand."

"Yes. There is a point," Sanborn nodded, calm with certainty.

"Nothing will ever convince us of your position," Charlie said. "Whatever is on that CD?"

"Nothing," Susan said.

"You people . . . " Mary said smugly, directing her comment to Sanborn.

"Well, here goes," Jack said, slipping the CD into its slot. The screen morphed to moving images.

Anne watched the flat screen for a brief moment then caught the eye of Arnold Sanborn. For some reason his glance chilled her. He moved away from the screen to afford the others a better view.

There was no sound, only an eerie silence. On the screen, they saw the smoke rising from one of the towers as the camera slowly panned along the glass surface of the building. Occasionally the camera would stop moving and caught images of people huddled against the glass looking outward, their faces panic-stricken, their mouths open in silent screams. Then suddenly they saw windows broken by chairs flung through the glass. It was hard to tell how far up the tower the images were.

Then suddenly, as if on cue, bodies began hurtling out of the broken windows, like discarded plastic toys being thrown away, a small avalanche of human discards. The images jiggled as if the video operator, apparently Sanborn, could not keep his hands steady. There was an attempt by the operator to follow the bodies downward as they fell, but it apparently was futile. For a long time the camera concentrated on the incredible sight of the bodies falling, some holding hands for a brief moment. Shoes fell off the feet of the flying people. Blurred faces in imagined panic moved to certain death thousands of feet below. Not a sound was heard in the room.

Anne was stunned into both disbelief and denial. This could not be real, she assured herself. Plastic toys falling. This is a camera trick. These are not live bodies falling. No way.

Before the screen went blank, a sudden chill filled the room and all eyes turned to the opened French doors. For a moment, all movement was suspended. Life was standing still.

All eyes searched the room for Sanborn. He had disappeared. In the distance, the heard sirens, which was not unusual for the bustling city. They exchanged glances.

"I guess he needed to convince us," Charley said.

No one laughed.

FIRST RITES

You don't hear much these days about what they used to call the "rites of passage into manhood." It was a big deal back when I was a kid. Men wrote about the so-called moment when they first became a man, when they suddenly acquired this secret knowledge that propelled them in one quick hop from a boy to a man.

Some said it was when they shot their first bear or had their first piece of ass. Because we had so many damned wars in this century, some said it came the first time they walked into combat, or killed their first enemy soldier or saw their buddy lying dead with his guts spilled all over terra firma.

Others told of more subtle causes, like having their first broken heart or screwing someone over because they were trying to get ahead of the game or telling their first big whopper of a lie or suddenly being blasted into manhood while being called names by mean-minded people, names like kike or nigger or spic or wop or chink.

There were also a lot of family-inspired rites of passage stuff, too, like discovering good old Dad was a philandering son-of-a-bitch, or finding out that dear old Mom was drunk on vodka all day long.

It always struck me that this idea of becoming a man was always portrayed as a sudden experience, like walking out of a black tunnel into a bright sun or . . . vice versa? Did it mean that you were suddenly thrown into some kind of a jungle, discovering the hostile real world where you had to spend the rest of your life dealing with and trying to avoid predators and pain? Did it come at that moment when you knew that you couldn't depend on Mommy and Daddy any more, that you were stuck out there all alone to make your way and suffer all those slings and arrows or find some defense against them?

Maybe we don't hear too much about this aspect of a man's life anymore because the age of women has dawned. The philosophy of womanhood is center stage now. Hell, we had a tough enough time dealing with the hardship of being a man, making a living, being the protector and breadwinner, fighting the wars, taking the blows from bosses or competitors and, sometimes, even women. Now you've got to apologize even when you call them anything but person.

I'm not saying they don't have a point. All I'm saying is that it was tough enough becoming a man in the first place without having to hassle with one of the few things that gave a man a comfort, a woman. Having a good woman to love made a man feel safe, gave him a back to the womb feeling, made him feel like a boy again.

So we have this dichotomy of a boy wanting to become a man and a man wanting to become a boy and finally knowing that, in the end, there's no controlling either transformation. The fact is, though, that there is probably a point, a moment, when a boy does become a man and you'll only know that when you're about to become a boy again.

I know now when I became a man.

I was twelve, which seems a bit early now, but it really wasn't. Bobby, my brother, was eleven and I know that he, too, became a man at the same time. But Bobby died in Korea, another one of those stupid wars and, unless there's an afterlife, which I doubt, we'll never have the opportunity to compare notes.

We slept in the same bedroom in those days in our parent's' apartment in Brooklyn's Crown Heights. You can probably pinpoint it geographically, but don't think you can ever see it as it was. Today it's an old broken-down neighborhood, shared, if that's the operative word, by blacks, Hispanics and Lubuvitch's. I'm not saying we were better. But it was different then, really different.

My mother's folks, our grandparents, lived in Brownsville in a row house paid for by my mother's brothers who had made a few bucks and gone off to live in either Manhattan or Queens, which in those days was a step up the ladder of success. Every week, she would make us all go to my grandparent's' house in Brownsville for Friday night dinner. Sometimes my uncles were there with their wives and kids. There were never fewer than ten or fifteen people and we all made a lot of noise. But the food was great, old-fashioned Jewish cooking, a lost art now.

The important thing to know was that my grandfather was a man who really believed he was boss, the head of the house. Grandma called him The Papa, which implied that he was the boss, but everybody knew that it was really Grandma who was the boss. Grampa was a stern religious man who took himself very seriously. He could cut you dead with a look and I was a little afraid of him, although I had seen his good side often enough. Once he bought me a sled for my birthday, which I thought was a neat gesture, since I was never sure whether or not he ever noticed me.

Oh, he let me kiss him, of course, although his face, with its Van Dyke, always felt scratchy to the touch and made me itch. He was a very solemn man, who spoke mostly Yiddish, and although I rarely understood every word I sure as hell knew what he wanted when he wanted it. He was also a big man, well over six feet, and he carried with him what they called in those days, a huge "corporation."

Maybe because he was so big and bulky, I thought of him as a kind of monument. To me he was a person of awesome dignity. When he walked down a street, even going off to the grocery store, he looked like a man on his way to keep an important appointment, a man on a mission that would decide the fate of the world. I think I loved him. I certainly loved Grandma. Bobby also loved her, but I'm not sure how he felt about Grampa. That's another thing I don't think I'll ever know.

My mother, being their daughter, loved them both very much or seemed to. In those days, duty to one's parents was paramount, especially for an only daughter. Sons sent money. Daughters gave themselves. Having never had daughters, I'm not sure how it's supposed to work these days.

At that time I truly believe that everyone in my family loved each other. Nor do I have any evidence to the contrary that this was untrue. It was taken for granted. In families, everybody loved each other.

This one night back in the winter of 1947, Bobby and I were sleeping in our bedroom when the jangling of the telephone awakened us. In those days there was only one telephone in the house and it made a real racket when it rang, not like those new electronic jobs.

Bobby and I were old enough to know that no good ever came from a telephone call in the middle of the night. Not long after the ring my mother burst into our room and in a high shrill voice announced that Grampa had died and we had to hurry up and get over to the house. Of course, she was sniveling and crying like a baby and both Bobby and I knew what to do in those circumstances. We hugged her, told her we were sorry and that we loved her and Grampa and then we got the hell out of her way.

It was a cold night. Apartment owners in those days shut down the heat after eleven at night. We got dressed, shivering and feeling rotten, and then we all went downstairs and froze for about a half hour until we got a cab. It was one gloomy trip with Mom hysterical and Dad trying to soothe her.

We boys really had no idea what to expect. We had only seen death in the movies, nice clean death. People either died in big beds or in people's arms or in the gutter after being plugged neatly to death with bullets or stabbed with knives or swords and when they died, especially if they were stars, they usually made a speech.

"Is Grampa dead already?" Bobby managed to ask. Maybe he was thinking the same thoughts I was. We were going to miss the deathbed speech.

It was still dark and very cold when we got to my grandparents' house. My mother fell into my grandmother's arms and they were both hysterical. This happened in the living room. By then, they lived mostly on the ground floor since it was too much for them to be going up and down the stairs. In the adjacent bedroom Grampa lay dead in bed, his eyes closed. He had high cheekbones and in death he looked a little Chinese.

My father told us to get out of the bedroom where my dead grandfather lay and then went to talk on the telephone. We heard his calm voice as it spoke, but we didn't get out of the bedroom. Instead we both went close to the body. Bobby touched it.

"Don't," I said.

"Why not?" Bobby asked.

I wasn't sure, but I was also curious to touch it and reached out to feel Grampa's dead hand.

"I thought it would be much colder," I said.

"Maybe he's still alive," Bobby said.

It was then that I touched Grampa's face. It was colder than his hand. Then we both watched his face for a long time for any sign of life.

"There," Bobby said. "I saw him move."

"You're crazy."

"I saw him move. I swear it."

At that point I poked Grampa in the upper arm and got no reaction. Then I bent over and whispered in his ear.

"Grampa."

No answer. Then louder.

"Grampa."

Still no answer.

"Let me try," Bobby said. He whispered into Grampa's ear, louder still. Naturally, there was no answer.

"He's dead as a doornail," I said.

"I wouldn't be so sure about that," Bobby said.

After that, we stood and watched him again for a long time. I heard breathing and it startled me at first, but it was only Bobby's. Grampa didn't move.

"He moved that first time," Bobby swore.

My father came back in the room after the telephone call.

"I told you boys to leave this room," he said.

"We wanted to stay here with Grampa. We didn't want to leave him alone," Bobby said.

"Believe me," my father said. "He won't know the difference."

My father explained that he had called my mother's brothers and he was now going to Grampa's synagogue to "make the arrangements." He would have to talk to the shamus, or caretaker, he told us.

"I also called the funeral parlor," he said. "They're sending someone to take Grampa's body. You stay here with your mother and your Gramma."

We followed him out to the hallway and he waved goodbye. Our mother and grandmother were wailing to beat the band and Bobby and I went back to the bedroom to see more of our Grampa's body.

"He's getting colder," Bobby said touching his cheeks with the back of his hand as he had probably seen a doctor do. I felt my Grampa's face again and confirmed his judgment.

"Is this all there is to it?" Bobby asked.

"I'm not sure."

Remember that neither of us had ever seen a dead person in the flesh.

"He looks so different," Bobby said.

No question about that. His face had yellowed, which made him look even more Chinese. He seemed to be changing rapidly.

"Maybe there's some mistake," Bobby said. "Maybe he's really not Grampa, but somebody else who died in his bed."

He kept looking at Grampa's face, concentrating hard as he could, trying to be sure that this was, indeed, Grampa.

"Boo," I said, startling him. He shrank back as if I had stung him.

"You scared the shit out of me," he said.

"Think I was Grampa's ghost or something?" At that moment the possibility certainly existed.

After a while the doorbell rang and we went downstairs to answer it.

"I'm here from the funeral parlor," a man said. He was a small pale man, hunched over and unhealthy-looking. "Where is the deceased?"

We assumed he meant Grampa and led him to the bedroom. On his back he carried an ominous-looking rolled-up canvas thing. We passed the living room where Grandma and our mother were huddled together and hysterical. They barely glanced our way.

We could hear the man from the funeral parlor wheezing and muttering behind us, complaining about how he had to park his truck down near the corner instead of in front of the house. There was a hydrant on the curb in front of the house.

He came into the bedroom behind us and looked at Grampa. He was still changing and no longer looked anything like himself.

"Big one," the man whistled. He unrolled the canvas he was carrying and laid it out on the floor beside the bed. We could see what he had in mind then. He was going to get Grampa off the bed and zipper him into that bag.

"Charlie never showed up. Gotta do this myself," he mumbled, then looked at us. "You boys may have to help." I've always wondered what he would have done if we weren't there. He had no way of knowing that grown men wouldn't be around and the wailing women would sure as hell be of no help to him.

Grampa had died under the quilt and the man from the funeral parlor turned it aside. Grampa was wearing striped pajamas and the man took his

arms and stretched them out along his sides and then took him by the
ankles and put his legs together. He knew what he was doing, all right.

Then he tugged at Grampa, wheezing like hell all the time, and
edged him to the very edge of the bed.

"Think you can grab his legs?" he asked us.

We looked at each other and shrugged, then I guess we nodded or
gave him some sign of our consent. He slid one arm under Grampa's
shoulders and got a good grip on him, then he turned to us and instructed Bobby to grab him around the ankles and me to grab him behind the knees.

We did as he asked. I looked down at Bobby and he looked up at
me, both of us, I'm sure, wondering what we were doing here grabbing
at Grampa's body.

"When I say three, you boys just move him easy over the edge so that
he don't fall too hard."

We clutched at Grampa and waited for him to count to three and at
three we tugged until he gave way and moved over the edge. Only he
was too heavy for us to carry. Hell, deadweight he must have weighed
nearly three hundred pounds. It sure as hell seemed like it.

He had barely cleared the edge when we dropped him. Even the
man from the funeral parlor lost his grip and Grampa fell like a ton of
bricks on the floor of his bedroom. I won't ever forget that sound. It was
like a bomb went off in the house. Everything shook. Things fell off the
dresser including a glass vase that Grandma had. It was smashed to
smithereens.

One thing was sure. Grampa wasn't going quietly. Even the wailing
women must have sensed that, because at the sound of his fall, after a
dead silence, they wailed even louder than before. They knew it was
him that had fallen and they knew, like us, that he wasn't going to make
it easy for any of us.

He hadn't even fallen dead center on the canvas bag and we had to
really tug and sweat until we got him into position. The man from the

funeral parlor had to really work to get Grampa zipped into the bag. With a wheezing effort he stood up and looked at the bag for a minute while he caught his breath.

"He was big, all right." He turned toward us boys and it seemed that he was really seeing us for the first time.

"Your Grampa?" he asked.

We nodded.

"I'll tell you this. He was one big man."

Then he shook his head.

"I'm afraid you boys are going to have to help me get him into the truck."

We looked at each other and shrugged again. There was no point in arguing since there was no way this unhealthy-looking man was going to get that body through the downstairs hall and down the flight of stairs from the porch to the street without help.

It was getting light by then and from the front window of the bedroom we could see people already on the street hurrying to the Saratoga Avenue El station around the corner. My grandparents' house was just across the street from a park and people would cut across the park as a shortcut and pass right in front of the house to get to the station. Morning and night during rush hour it looked like a parade passing the house.

It didn't mean a damn thing to this man that the body in that bag was our Grampa and we were supposed to be grieving and crying and not carrying his body out of the house into the street. This is not to say that we were not grieving in our own way.

We must have both sensed that we had lost something, something very important, and after this things were definitely not going to be the same as they were. Don't think it didn't hurt deep inside both of us to see my mother and my Grandma beside themselves with grief and unhappiness. As I said, we all loved each other in those days.

There were four canvas handles on the body bag, two at one end and two at the other. The man told us to crouch and grab the two at the foot end, which we did while he crouched at the head and grabbed the canvas handles at that end. Once again it was one, two, three, lift and we did.

Grampa was heavy as hell. His weight staggered us, but we managed to straighten up our legs and get enough leverage to take a step at a time without dropping him. We were two determined boys. Bobby had tightened his lips together with absolute determination and I was showing him mine in my own way. We were not going to drop Grampa's body. No way.

We took cautious steps, straining and huffing, hearing the man from the funeral parlor wheeze like a tire with a bad leak. Step by step we moved Grampa's body through the bedroom doorway, down the narrow hall, past the room where my mother and Gramma were crying. We didn't want them to see us and, for some reason, found the strength to pick up a bit of speed.

"Papa. Papa," I heard Gramma scream as we passed the living room. "My Papa." I also heard my mother's loud sobs. God, my heart was breaking for them. Suddenly tears streamed down my cheeks and I couldn't see a thing and started bumping into walls and nearly dropped Grampa.

"Be careful," Bobby said, and his voice sounded like he, too, was crying behind the words.

I thought my arms would break. I could barely catch my breath. My legs ached under the weight. Bobby huffed beside me. He was younger and, I suppose, weaker which prompted me to somehow assume more of the burden that he had. I knew I was way beyond my strength. Under normal circumstances there was no way I could have lifted that weight. Even the man from the funeral parlor was having a bad time.

Somehow we managed to get Grampa through the front door. The sun was up by then. Of all days it had to be clear and crisp with nowhere to hide. The parade had begun in front of the house, but I refused to look at any of the faces of the passing people. I'm not even sure whether they even knew what was happening. I didn't even look at Bobby, although I could hear him groaning with every step we took.

Getting down the front steps was torture. At every step I felt like my insides would fall out. Still, under no circumstances was I going to drop Grampa, especially now, in front of all those people heading to work. It became in my mind an article of faith and I'm sure Bobby felt the same way. No way I was going to humiliate Grampa in front of all those people by dropping his body on the front stairs where it was sure to slide down into the street.

"Don't worry, Grampa," I remember saying to myself. "I will not let that happen." I might not have actually said it to myself at that moment, but I knew in my heart that it had become a matter of preserving his dignity and under no circumstances was I going to desecrate his body and, therefore, his symbolic spirit by allowing him to unceremoniously touch the ground.

This may sound a bit high falutin' for a twelve-year-old, especially in hindsight, but I have never doubted that description of my resolve in all the years since.

We reached the street without a mishap. Bobby's eyes were closed with pain and his face was red with effort, causing me to shift even more of the burden to myself. The man from the funeral parlor was also having a real rough time, walking backwards once we hit the pavement.

As he had said the truck was parked near the corner, which meant that we still had to carry Grampa nearly half a block. This was the worst part of all. It was not just the burden. We were numb by then and, as they say, running on fumes, but we moved along at a snail's pace. The pavement was narrow and by inserting ourselves into the crowd of people rushing for the subway, we slowed things down a bit.

I had the feeling that people knew what was happening, that a dead man was being taken out of the world while they were still scurrying about like ants, surviving, working, worrying, but knowing that someday even they could not avoid being carried out of their homes just like Grampa.

As we carried Grampa along the busy Brooklyn street, slowing down the crowd, I remember suddenly feeling a certain weightlessness take over. Grampa stopped being heavy. I looked over at Bobby wondering whether he was feeling the same thing and, by God, he was smiling, happy, too, that we were moving Grampa with dignity along that sidewalk with people slowing down respectfully knowing what was happening. He wasn't going feet-first either, since we were carrying the feet end, but going headfirst into what I once heard called the long night. I always felt, and still feel, that to Grampa, human dignity always came first and he had miraculously made himself light so that he would not be humiliated on his final journey.

We reached the truck and almost without effort hoisted Grampa and slid him into the back.

"Thank you, boys," the man said and without another word got into the truck and drove away.

We boys looked after him as the crowd passed us by, not looking at each other. It was, at that moment, as the truck disappeared around the corner that I knew . . . I'm sure of it now . . . forty years later . . . that I had left boyhood behind and had become a man.

And in the telling of this, I am also sure that it has given me what I crave at this moment in the hushed twilight of manhood.

To be a boy again.

THEIR GREATEST
ACHIEVEMENT

"I want this to be a real tribute to your mom, Barry, a real tribute," Marvin Stewart told his son. "A 50th birthday is a real milestone. Above all, I want it to be a surprise, a wow surprise."

Barry had come down to Manhattan from Boston where he was working for a software company. This was a business trip, but his father had corralled him for a coffee at a Starbucks on Third Avenue.

"She'll get a kick out of that," Barry said, studying his father across the little table. The man was clearly excited, enjoying the idea, smiling broadly, patting his son's hand. He had begun to gray around the temples, but his bright blue eyes still had the comforting intensity of his earliest memories.

"I think that's great, Dad," Barry said, feeling the old tightness growing in his stomach.

"Remember. Not a word. All the invitations are prepared and ready to go. Your mom, as you know, has lots of friends. Aunt Alice is coming in from Charlestown with all the kids and Uncle Mike and his brood will be coming in from Milwaukee. All her close friends from the store where she works will be there. It will be one hell of a bash, one hell of bash. I've booked the ballroom at the Lotos Club. I'm hoping for a hundred people."

"That will set you back a pretty penny, Dad," Barry said.

"Your mom is worth every cent," his father said. His vocal admiration of his mother was, as always, boundless. Considering what Barry knew, it had always struck him as an exercise in extreme denial. Or blindness. Or both.

Living with the pressing burden of what he characterized as "the great secret" was the hardest task he had ever had to deal with in his life. It's effect on his feelings for both his father and his mother, despite his love for them, was corrosive. In his heart he could find no residue of respect or admiration for them. As much as he had tried, he was unable to define his father as anything but a blind fool and his mother as a whore.

As an only child, he was adored by each of them. They had been devoted, dedicated to his well-being, cheering him on as he moved ahead in his studies and his career. No parents could be more loving, more respectful, avoiding any temptation to be cloying or interfering.

"You are our greatest achievement" had become their mantra. It distorted everything he tried to do, as if he had to continue to top himself, fearful that he would dilute their "greatest achievement" by any misstep or failure or, worse, that his actions might lead to the explosive revelation that would cause the rupture of his parents' marriage.

At the first opportunity after graduating college, he had jumped ship, gone to Boston to work. Of course, he called them frequently, but at that distance he could avoid face-to-face meetings like the one he was currently enduring.

Soon, he knew, he would jump again, further and further away from Manhattan, leaving them both in his wake. He berated himself for not having the stomach to make the move in one long jump.

Still, he could not find the courage to reject the role of devoted and loving son. For more than twenty years, he calculated, he had turned the matter over in his mind and as it matured he grew more and more resentful. It was becoming increasingly difficult to keep it bottled up, and he was fearful that one day he would slip and all he knew would inadvertently come out.

Worse, he was discovering as he grew older that such a possibility had become a terrible barely endurable temptation and keeping it inside himself was increasingly difficult. Even now, as he sat at the little round table at Starbucks, sipping his coffee and listening to his father enthuse over the coming birthday party, he felt the scalding words forming just below the level of articulation. He wanted to say it, shout it, scream out the truth.

"You fool, Dad. Don't you know that your wife has been making a monkey out of you for years, that she has had a string of lovers, that she has betrayed you numerous times?" In this fantasy revelation, he never referred to his mother as anything but his father's wife. How do you tell your own father that your mother is an adulterous whore?

It was the same with his mother and had destroyed any real intimacy between them, although he walked the walk, as he told himself, showing the façade of a loving son. If his mother recognized the gap between them, she never let on, never whined about his lack of candor about his life, about his relationships, about the lack of explanation about his various activities.

His communication with both his parents was merely reporting, mostly about his advancing career. If they inquired about his personal life, he offered little by way of information. For whatever reason, they never probed or interrogated him. The fact was that holding the big secret within himself had stultified his relationships with both men and women. He was, he knew, inhibited by distrust and the source of this attitude was no mystery to him.

He was five years old that first time and his father was out of town on one of his thrice-yearly selling trips flogging a line of men's suits. His territory was the northeast, all the way up to Bangor with as he put it "with a smile and a shoeshine," once a baffling reference. Later the image and the words would make sense when he finally saw the play "Death of a Salesman" and understood what it meant. Seeing the revival of the play, he was stunned by it. It shook him to the core.

In Arthur Miller's scenario, it was the father who was the adulterer, and it had a profound effect on one of his sons who had discovered it when he unexpectedly showed up in his father's hotel room. The role reversal in his real life did not make the play any less affecting and powerful.

They lived then in a small apartment on the West Side then. His father had left for the road the day before. For some reason, he was awakened. He would never know why except that perhaps a strange disruption in the nightly routine of the household had interfered with his sleep. He had crept out of bed. It was not uncommon for him creep into his parents' bed and snuggle between them during the night when bad dreams made him fearful. When his father was away, he continued to seek comfort and solace during the night in his mother's bed when childish fears afflicted him.

At the entrance to his parents' bedroom that night, he heard noises and peeking in, saw two bodies joined like wrestlers, which frightened him so much that he went back into his own bed and drew the covers over his head. Eventually when he awoke to the affectionate ministrations of his mother, he told her he had a dream about Mommy and Daddy fighting in bed.

"Just a bad dream, baby," his mother told him. It did have its effect. When a male visitor was present, his parents' bedroom door remained locked. Not that it mattered, since he was too fearful to approach it.

Even then he knew it was not a dream. Other men were paying his mother visits when his father was on the road. Occasionally, if they appeared at the apartment prior to his bedtime, his mother would introduce him to her pals, as she called them. In his child's mind, he did not think twice about her so-called pals. They seemed a normal part of his mother's life. Nor did he think it amiss that they appeared mostly during his father's absences, although sometimes they were familiar to him as "pals" of his father.

As he grew older, his mother seemed to change the routine of interaction with her men pals. They would take him on country outings and while he played with other children, his mother and her pal would drift away to some secluded spot. Sometimes he might come across them doing what he then thought were strange things together, but it was years before he determined the truth of those strange things.

When his father returned from his trip, life went on as before, although sometimes one or another of his mother's pals came to visit with his spouse, and they seemed happy and content to be with each other. By the time he was twelve and had learned from his friends what sex was all about, the truth began to dawn on him.

But while he was troubled by the knowledge of his mother's infidelity, he was baffled by the lack of reaction on his father's part. Life at home for his parents was tranquil and loving, and he basked in the warmth of their affection. Even then, he feared that the big secret that he harbored would be fatal to what appeared to be his parents' loving relationship.

"I want this surprise to knock her for a loop. A birthday celebration like no other birthday celebration. The works," his father said.

"Sounds like you're going over the top."

"Absolutely. And remember, not a word. But keep September 25th open. You've got to be there. Naturally we expect you to say a few words."

Back in Boston, Barry could not shake the idea that his father was a bigger fool than he originally thought. He wished he could find the courage not to show up, but, of course, that was out of the question. He would have to steel himself against the platitudes that he would hear about his mother, particularly the grand adoring speech his father was sure to make and his mother's saccharine and phony response.

As for his own speech, he fantasized what he might say. How his mother had cheated, had affairs, humiliated his father. It had occurred to him many times that his father might be having affairs himself, just like Willy Loman in Arthur Miller's play, and that all this show of devotion on his part was a ruse, playing the role of the good and faithful husband to keep the peace. Perhaps the idea was to keep the marriage going for the sake of "their greatest achievement," another nail in the coffin of his guilt.

Yet the fact that when they were together, his parents showed no signs of resentment or bitterness, never said an unkind word to each other and seemed as loving and affectionate as ever, continued to baffle him. There were never accusations between them, nor arguments, nor the slightest sign of discord. He concluded that his father was spineless and henpecked and his mother a clever liar.

In his mind, he made up nasty little birthday speeches bluntly accusing his mother of hypocrisy, dissimulation and sanctimonious duplicity and his father of obtuse ignorance and cupidity. While such a public accusation might lift the burden that he carried on his back like a heavy stone, he doubted he could face the aftermath of incrimination and alienation. To be certain he would not stray from the expected ritual, he wrote a toast, traditional, expected, and brief, that he would read to the assemblage.

The birthday party celebration was amazingly close to what his father had envisioned. Relatives came from long distances. He saw cousins he had not seen in years. An elegant and elaborate sit-down dinner was arranged, complete with a continuous video show of his mother's days before and after her marriage with pictures taken years ago that he had no idea still existed.

His mother, looking lovely, slim and marvelously preserved for her fifty years appeared dutifully surprised and blushingly kissed everyone she greeted, repeating over and over again to every well-wisher: "I was completely fooled. I can't believe it." In surveying the guests, Barry noted that one or two of them, his father's colleagues, looked excruciatingly familiar. By then, his mother, who worked as a salesperson at a Madison Avenue boutique, had surely acquired some new pals who passed unrecognizable among the many guests.

With trepidation, Barry waited for the inevitable toasts. He sat at the table in the center of the room next to his father, who sat next to his mother, her two sisters and their husbands. Suddenly the clang of a spoon against a champagne glass slowly quieted the celebrating crowd and his father rose to speak. He thanked everyone for coming and then began an emotional speech about his wife.

"We were just kids when we got married, two foolish children barely out of their teens and here we are years later still married, still very much in love, still happy campers, with a marvelous successful son. I thank God every day for the gift of Cecile, who has stood by me, through thick and thin, enduring the long absences of my work as a traveling man. But whenever I returned from a trip I knew she would be waiting, open-armed, devoted, her pretty face smiling and happy to receive me. Cecile is my one and only, my true love, a fabulous wife and mother and I cannot tell you how happy I am to pay her this tribute on her 50th."

Barry noted that there were tears in his eyes and in those of many of the guests. Despite his cynicism, he felt a lump begin to grow in his throat and a tiny sob bubble up from his chest. His father turned to his mother and lifted his champagne glass.

"I raise my glass to you, my lovely sweetheart, who I fell in love with at first sight and will love until my eyes look into the final darkness." His wife rose and they embraced and kissed.

The assembled guests voiced their approval and sipped their champagne. Then his mother rose, after dabbing her tear-filled eyes. She seemed radiantly happy and, clearing her throat, said, "This is one of the happiest days of my life, second only to the day Barry was born and my marriage to Marv. God has indeed blessed us with a happy marriage and a great son. I too fell in love with this guy at first sight and that love has sustained me through all the years of my marriage. He is my rock, my sweetheart and my best pal. Normally, we are not demonstrative people . . . " She turned to his father. "But I have to say that my husband is a most wonderful and saintly human being. I cannot imagine a life without him. He has been everything I ever fantasized when I consented to be his wife: Kindly, honest, faithful, decent and above all, loving. I love you, darling. I love you with all my heart and soul."

The entire room stood up and cheered. My father held up his arms to silence the crowd and turned to Barry, who felt weak in the knees as he rose. His parents' words had stunned and confused him. Were they acting or did they really believe their words? He seemed caught in a riddle. How was it possible for his mother to have been so unfaithful to his father and still mouth what at first he believed were contrived platitudes? And how could his father, the cuckolded and betrayed husband, make such moving statements about his wife?

Forgetting to take the card on which he had written his toast from his pocket, he managed to remain steady and for a long moment his tongue could not find words. Finally, he cleared his throat and clenched his fists, digging his nails into his palms.

"My parents," he began haltingly. The room was dead quiet and yet he felt very much alone. "I just want to say . . . " He paused cleared his throat again. "I just want to say that my parents are remarkable people. They have always told me that they think I am their greatest achievement. I think they're wrong." He felt suddenly emboldened, his eyes washing over his parents' uplifted faces. "I am not their greatest achievement. Their greatest achievement is their marriage, this bond between them that is the most important priority in their lives. No matter what. It has sustained them and us as a family. I have to say . . . " He felt a sudden surge of strength and deep loving genuine affection for them, something that he had never before felt with such power and sincerity. "Yes, I love them and, above all, I am honored to be their son."

Tears ran down his parents' cheeks as they stood up and embraced him. For a brief moment he felt the power of the old memory, when he had snuggled between them in their bed. It was no longer his business to probe the mysteries of their marriage. But he knew that the burden that had plagued him most of his life had disappeared.

LOOKING FOR AL

"Class reunions are like the picture of Dorian Gray. The image of the picture is on the guest list and that painting in the basement is the old you."

"Profound," Cathy Barnes chuckled, winking at her old classmate, Vivien Silver, who had uttered the so-called profundity. Vivien had panned the group, Columbia College Class of 1984, and pronounced them dreary, acknowledging that it could be the weather, which was rainy and dark.

Cathy had found Vivien a few years after graduation and, although they had not been friendly in their undergraduate years, the fact that they had both been Class of 1984 had provided the cement that bonded them. It was Cathy who had persuaded Vivien to attend.

In preparation and to chase her reluctance, Vivien had recycled all she could remember of those days, an exercise of selective recall. She had majored in English lit and philosophy, which was reasonably involving and somewhat entertaining, while secretly yearning for some occupational path that would light the way to a satisfying future.

While interning for a publishing house, George had come along with an offer of marriage, which she accepted out of fear that such a proposal might never come around again. That event was followed two years later by divorce, followed by years of therapy, followed by a slow climb up the ladder of self-esteem, followed by a growing realization of self-worth. Of all things, she was now a public relations executive advising people how to improve their public persona.

Those undergraduate years at Columbia had been a dark blur and she was having a hard time coming up with any happy moment worth cherishing.

"I was like a speck of dust," Vivien had confessed to Cathy. "You were the big cheese on campus."

"How are the mighty fallen."

Cathy's self-effacement was charming. From an unpromising beginning, they had bonded and Cathy had lured her into this new world of achieving single women, many of whom had struggled through the same early torments and insecurities that had made her post-adolescent life a nightmare.

"Do you good to compare yourself to your peers," Cathy told her. "That's what college reunions are all about."

"Will I come out win, place, or show?" Vivien asked fishing for a compliment. She got it.

"Winner's circle, baby."

"Okay then. I'll make the bet."

There was one undergraduate moment, a brief flicker of pleasure that did emerge from the mud of memory. To force herself out of a sense of deep dislocation and shyness, she had joined the drama club, which put on plays by Shakespeare. She was usually cast in secondary roles, waiting ladies mostly, the playwright's clever devices for exposition.

She had been cast as Nerissa, the waiting lady to Portia in "The Merchant of Venice," not exactly a star vehicle, but with one good scene in which she was the instrument in getting Portia to comment on the suitors that are after her hand in marriage and, of course, her wealth. She could still remember a single line.

"He, of all men that ever my foolish eyes looked upon, was the best deserving a fair lady."

For some reason the line was always associated in her mind with the heavy crush she had on Al Ackerman, the student director. She remembered him as dashing, beautiful, godlike. He had become the leading man in her fantasy life, an erotic obsession. Of course, he barely noticed she was alive, except when he provided her with notes on her performance, which were always critical. Nevertheless it was the only thing about her undergraduate years that had stirred her emotionally.

"Have you any recollection of Al Ackerman?" she asked Cathy on the way to the reunion.

"Ackerman? Ackerman? Yeah. I remember. Pretty boy."

"Very," Vivien acknowledged. "I would have parked my shoes under his bed in a New York minute."

Actually, she hadn't done much shoe-parking in those days. Throughout her college years, she was still a virgin, though not because of a vow of abstinence. No one had ever stepped up to the plate to do the deed and she had actually come to the marriage bed pure and inexperienced. She seemed to have left it in the same condition and it was only in her second chapter single life that she had uncovered the mysteries of adventurous sex and it was now a bedrock condition of her relationships.

"I think I had carnal knowledge of the dude," Cathy giggled. "In those days I was considered a manhood validator for those dear confused boys still in the closet. Sometimes it worked. Sometimes not."

"Did it work for Al?"

"I think he was a hard case." She giggled. "My memory is a bit fuzzy. In retrospect they all seem like Chinese waiters. Anyway, we'll soon see which pew they chose."

Vivien hadn't thought about Al for years, but the press of the coming reunion had wetted her recall, although she could summon up little nostalgic sentiment about any other relationship or incident. A partial cause of this sense of alienation, her shrink and she had determined, was that during her entire four-year college career she had lived with her overly possessive parents in their Brooklyn apartment and she was not really part of the extracurricular life on the campus. This geographic and psychological divide shrank the social possibilities considerably. Other students lived on or near the campus in apartments and dormitories, and partied and socialized practically around the clock.

Nor was she a distinguished student, her marks in mid range. The truth of it was that in those days, whatever the cause, she was nerdy, bashful, clumsy, insecure and boring. Be honest, she told herself. That was then. You've come a long way, baby.

Cathy, on the other hand, was one of those super-achiever out-of-town girls who was popular with everyone. Cathy was a motivator and had pushed Vivien to transform herself, goading her into a more socially active circle.

Cathy had never married, preferred partnerships without legal complications, and had been in and out of relationships for years.

"When what I throw out on the stoop gets stale, I'll opt for the road to compromise," she had averred, but it seemed to Vivien that Cathy's innate allure, that certain something she possessed, would far outlive her looks.

"I'd follow you anywhere, Cath, even to this boring reunion," she told her friend as they sipped Chardonnay and studied the other guests for signs of recognition. More people recognized Cathy and she was quickly engaged in conversation while Vivien circulated, on the prowl for familiar faces, particularly the one owned by Al Ackerman.

She did find a few faces vaguely recognizable. Few found her and she roamed through the crowded room, stopping to converse and offering her own brief history while listening to others who seemed to have operated on a faster track. She was not in the least intimidated by their stated achievements or the etchings of the aging process. Her sense of diminishment had long disappeared. On this test she gave herself high marks.

Comparing herself physically with the others, she noted that she had done extremely well in that department. Once, she had been a frizzy-haired girl with big glasses, bad skin and teeth that needed work. After her divorce she had, with Cathy's prodding, taken corrective action. Skin, teeth, hair had been redone. Dark circles and puffy bags had been removed from her eyes and a personal trainer had helped flatten her tummy. She was contemplating a boob job to enhance the improvement.

She was a blonde now, hardly the plain Jane of her college days, which was probably the real reason that few had recognized her. It was, of course, comforting to tell herself that. She did have to introduce herself to some people who she vaguely recognized and it pleased her to see their admiring glances.

About an hour into the event, she noted that a well-dressed woman with long dark hair, a good figure, skillfully groomed and dressed, seemed to be observing her with more than passing interest. The woman kept her distance and since Vivien could not muster a spark of recognition, she ignored the woman's interest.

At one point, she caught up with Cathy and asked a question, motioning with her head.

"You know her?"

Cathy eyed the woman surreptitiously and shrugged.

"Not on my dance card."

Vivien shrugged and moved on, realizing that she was pointedly searching for Al Ackerman. As more wine was imbibed, she had the feeling that the attendees were getting bolder and more and more people were introducing themselves. People struck up conversations and told stories of their experiences with various professors, few of whom she remembered. Business cards were exchanged. Many former students embraced each other.

As she moved through the crowd, getting wine refills and nibbling on finger foods, she could find no trace of Al Ackerman. It became increasingly clear that the woman was following her, although keeping her distance. For some reason, it seemed out of character for the event. Surely there was some connective memory between the woman and herself. Why, then, was she being followed? Why didn't the woman step forward and introduce herself?

Finally, Vivien turned, walked over to the woman and addressed her.

"Do we know each other?" Vivien asked, studying the woman's face. It reminded her of someone, an actress perhaps. With her long black hair, sculpted cheekbones, and sensual lips, she was quite beautiful. She wore a simple black dress and a double strand of pearls and had a fashion model's height.

"I certainly would like to," the woman said, her voice low and, Vivien thought, smoky and seductive.

"I assume you're part of the reunion, Class of 1984," Vivien said.

"Yes, I am. I hope you don't think I'm rude, but I can't take my eyes off you."

Vivien wasn't sure whether to be flattered or guarded. She had not quite reached that level of sophistication that allowed her to sense when she was being solicited. Blatant approaches had happened before and she was quite tolerant about it and wasn't about to be impolite or insulting. Thus far, she had never experimented in that area and felt neither tempted nor threatened.

"I'm genuinely flattered," she said, as the woman continued to assess and inspect her. In fact, she enjoyed the assessment.

"It takes a woman to truly appreciate another woman."

"So they say," she said casually, oddly titillated, wondering if she was throwing out some signal about which Vivien was oblivious.

"Are you free after the event?" the woman asked.

"I did come with someone," Vivien said.

"I don't want to intrude."

"I think we made plans," Vivien said. They hadn't, but it seemed sensible to leave the option open.

"Maybe we can meet somewhere," the woman said. Her persistence was becoming somewhat aggressive. Some deflection seemed appropriate.

"What was your major?" Vivien asked.

"Drama."

"Really. I was a member of the drama club. We put on plays by Shakespeare."

The woman laughed showing beautiful white teeth. "I was a member myself."

"Now that is really a coincidence. I can't believe it. I played Nerissa in *The Merchant of Venice*."

"Did you?"

Delighted, Vivien repeated the one line she remembered. "'I remember him well and I remember him worthy of thy praise.'"

"My God, Portia's response. I can't believe this."

She studied the woman's face. "Were you in it? I can't seem to place you."

"No," the woman said. There was something both playful and mysterious in her tone. Vivien became flustered.

"Do you remember the director, Al Ackerman? I had this mad crush on him."

"Did you?"

"He was so popular. He barely noticed me. I was looking for him here."

The woman smiled and tapped her chin, looking into Vivien's eyes with laser-like intensity.

"Well, you found her," the woman said. She held out her hand. Confused, Vivien reached out, felt the unmistakable and meaningful pressure of affection and seduction. "'She, of all the women that ever my foolish eyes looked upon, was the best deserving a fair lady.'"

"But the line . . . the gender is reversed," Vivien whispered, totally confused.

"I'm Alice Ackerman," the woman said.

Vivien felt her knees wobble and her breath came in short gasps. She could not find the words to respond.

"I'm me now," Alice said.

Vivien allowed her hand to linger, then withdrew it.

"I'm . . . I'm stunned."

"Most people are," Alice said smiling.

She opened her pocketbook and took out a card.

"Call me," she said. "I'll be happy to make amends for my earlier neglect."

She moved away while Vivien watched her, frozen with disbelief.

"You look like you've seen a ghost," Cathy said, approaching her.

"I have," she said, after a long pause. "I have."

A SMALL PRICE TO PAY

"And to you, Dimitri," Doris Henderson intoned, raising her glass of red, as the eight dinner guests and Gary looked on approvingly as she came to the end of her toast. "Your coming into our lives has been a highlight of the last couple of years. We have warmed ourselves on the open hearth of your personality, your wonderful sense of humor, graciousness and sincerity. We salute you, Dimitri."

"Hear, hear," one of guests, a director of one of New York's premier banks said enthusiastically, clinking her glass with that of her neighbors. "Beautifully said."

The others nodded or mumbled agreement as Dimitri Pappas rose to observe the tradition of answering his hostess' toast.

"I thank you, dear Doris," Dimitri exclaimed, his slim figure swathed in a cummerbund, the knot of his black tie plump against the high winged collar, his gleaming silver sideburns richly contrasting with his jet black hair. In a sonorous voice, his Greek origins clearly accented, he properly returned the toast. "I thank you, dear Doris, for your most loving friendship. We have bonded with strong cement and I am hopeful that such largesse will continue through the coming years. Your friendship and your hospitality have been a most extraordinary asset. I welcome it with an open heart and am proud to call you and Gary true friends."

Gary Henderson appeared to be listening, but he was thinking more practical thoughts, not without a hint of impatience.

"It's been months of promises," he had said to Doris as she had arranged the place cards, putting Dimitri's on the honored position on her right. On his right was Margaret Canfield, a trustee of the Met, an important cog in the visible machine of New York social life who appeared frequently on Joe Cunningham's charity ball page in the Sunday Times and David Patrick Columbia's website tracking the doings of New York's plummy social set. In fact everyone at the dinner party, including Doris and Gary Henderson, appeared regularly in the various media outlets that chronicled the heady socialite class that made up the so-called upper crust of the city.

Cadging Dimitri Pappas as an "honored guest" at a dinner party was considered a coup for the Henderson's, who had previously spread the word via the golden social virus network that Pappas was a Greek in shipping, a combination certain to stir memories of other celebrity Greeks in the shipping business and their fabulous and well-documented adventures. Reflected glory was a staple of acclaim in the head-of-the-pin social world that the Henderson's inhabited.

"Beyond mere money," Doris Henderson described Dimitri in carefully placed whispers at cocktail soirees and intimate ladies' luncheons. "You simply must meet him."

"His profile's invisible," Gary told the distaff side at various board meetings of the right non-profits. Such anonymity hinted at vast subterranean activities and fabulous hidden wealth.

For the Hendersons, both lawyers, getting to the exalted position of attending the best balls, a matter of giving, and the best dinner parties, a matter of notoriety, was an important element of their general business acquisition program. In polite circles, such acquisition was called "rainmaking," a semi-respectable name for the practice of monetizing contacts and connections. Others of a more cynical bent characterized the effort as "hustling."

Whatever it was called, the practice was prevalent and tolerated only when it was not obvious, often a difficult observation to quantify. Nevertheless, in the rarified super-wealthy precincts of the city's elite, fueled by the fact that New York was the anointed international capital of finance and culture, the covert operation was hand-in-glove. In this charmed tight circle, the possibility of great reward offered predatory temptations to professional fee and commission seekers, like lawyers, real estate, insurance and stock brokers, investment bankers as well as various philanthropic trustees and executives, especially in the arts and disease categories.

In this exalted environment, the moneyed meritocracy merged with the so-called entitled elite, which included inheritors of name-brand fortunes, descendants of an earlier generation of aristocrats or deceased royalty, political stars of yesteryear, and various living celebrities of the higher arts. To many observers, this was the absolute top of the greasy pole of high society acceptance and often took hard work, people-collecting skills, reciprocal dinner parties and extraordinary outreach and follow-up to ascend to the slippery pinnacle and stay there.

The Hendersons, both sixty-ish, were charter members of the meritocracy and absolute masters of the business-getting art, totally focused on its various manipulations required to bring home the bacon. "We are what we seem," was their mantra and they assiduously built this image, brick by translucent brick. They had far more misses than hits but when they did make a score, they provided excellent legal services at exceptional fees, highly profitable to them and, when all was said and done, reasonably effective for their living clients.

In those circles, wrapped in an aura of affluence and excess, higher fees were expected. This did not mean that the Henderson's were as rich as their counterparts in such heady company. Their predatory lifestyle, constant entertaining and necessary giving kept them on the raw edges of financial insecurity. Thus, they were always on the prowl for business opportunities.

If the Henderson's took ethical liberties in their practice, they were extraordinarily discreet. While they engaged in general legal work for selective clients as a kind of loss leader, their real specialty was in estate and inheritance law, preferring situations in which the client was of advanced age with no heirs, giving them sole discretion over of the deceased's cash and property dispositions. Of course there were whispers of impropriety, but they remained barely audible, despite rumors from competitors that hinted of less than ethical schemes to enrich themselves from the coffers of their dead clientele.

To Gary and Doris, Dimitri Pappas was a targeted potential asset. He was a man on the darker side of 60, who when asked, referred vaguely to having shipping interests in the global economy. When googled, nothing came up, and the assumption, shrewdly disseminated by the Hendersons, was that he was paranoid about any revelations about his business or his fortunes.

"I keep a very low profile," Dimitri would often tell anybody who was curious, reinforcing the contention. "I don't want people to know my business."

The remark hinted at nefarious doings, which did not deter the Henderson's pursuit. In fact, it increased its energy since the lawyering possibilities were multiplied by the implication and there was much gold to be mined in defense litigation. By his demeanor, his discretion and personal presentation, the idea of a Greek in the shipping business, as everyone knew, referenced the late tycoons Onassis and Niarchos.

Apparently Dimitri spent a great deal of his time on the go and his availability for the social whirl was limited. The Hendersons, however, managed to zero in on these time slots, capturing him exclusively when he arrived in Manhattan and showing him off like a prized racing stallion. He was always sure to call and his presence was, to the Henderson's, a great social enhancement.

"You do get around," Gary would say during the usual camaraderie of the greeting. "I guess commerce on the high seas beckons." Clearly it was a probe which was never embellished by Dimitri.

"The nature of the business," Dimitri would comment. Nothing more.

Dimitri appeared in public, mostly accompanied by his girlfriend, Netta, who was forty-ish and beautifully coifed and always fashionable. She spoke with a lilting accent difficult to identify, but her complexion hinted at Indian antecedents. She and Dimitri were affectionate to each other and well versed in many subjects, including politics and finance. By any measure they were urbane, sophisticated, able to converse on all levels and. largely owing to the Henderson's assiduous efforts at promotion, were the kind of social companions that inspired envy among their peers.

Frequently invited to the Henderson's country home in the Hampton's, Dimitri and Netta shared a bedroom and throughout the well-programmed weekend activities, the Henderson's subtly probed Dimitri's legal possibilities.

"Surely you have an estate plan?" Gary would interject periodically during their private conversations, heavily larded with the usual gossip about people in their circle.

"Not really," Dimitri revealed. "I have no children, no wives or ex-wives, no close relatives."

"No favorite charities?"

"None." Dimitri chuckled.

"No heirs. No favorite charities. No place to leave your assets when the time comes. Dimitri, that is idiotic. Your inheritance will be rifled by predators. And the government will swoop down for their share. Surely you've talked about this with your current legal counsel."

"I never mix business with personal matters."

"I'm not saying you should. But certainly they owe it to you to raise the issue. Apparently you're not getting the best legal advice, especially on estate matters. What you need is overall legal "representation.""

Gary was cautious, merely raising the question, never making an obviously self-serving direct pitch.

"I have thought of it, Gary. Often at night when I can't sleep."

"But the world goes on, Dimitri, and money has a life beyond the
grave."

Dimitri would shrug, smile and grunt.

"Maybe some day," he mumbled.

"We can analyze this, Dimitri," Gary would answer offhandedly, as if
it were a gesture of magnanimity, with an air of indifference. "It is the
business of trusted friends."

"I will consider this, Gary. You make perfect sense. Yes, I will definitely consider this."

The statement, offered at various times on numerous occasions, appeared to keep the idea alive in Dimitri's mind. It was encouraging
enough, as well, to keep the hospitality spigot open and encourage the
Hendersons to continue to invest their time and money in pursuit.

Doris concentrated on developing a bonding relationship with
Netta, burrowing in on intimacy, invoking the gender alliance. Netta
had reiterated the fact that she and Dimitri had been companions for a
dozen years, although she confessed that they kept separate residences.
The Henderson's had not been to any of them. On the infrequent occasions when Dimitri and Netta entertained, it was often at a Greek restaurant on First Avenue where Dimitri, considering all the hugs and kisses
of the proprietor, had celebrity status with the owner providing a traditional Greek feast fueled by vast amounts of Greek wine and yogurt.

"Why don't you get married?" Doris would ask.

"Dimitri does not believe in marriage."

"And you?"

"I married once long ago. It was not fruitful."

"Meaning no kids?"

"No kids. No chemistry. A disaster. I have wiped the experience from
my mind."

"Many of my clients have accepted that kind of arrangement you have with Dimitri." She would lower her voice. "With strings." Then after a pause. "Has he provided?"

When Netta hesitated, Doris nodded knowingly, her voice offered at a lower decibel.

"We see things in our practice. The woman gets short shrift. You should urge him to think about it."

"Believe me, I have. Dimitri promises to be generous."

"Verbally or on paper?"

"He says his word is his bond."

"Isn't that naïve, Netta? He has no heirs and made no provisions. Apparently, as he told Gary, not for anyone. You should urge him to codify any bequests, especially to you."

Netta looked confused

"It's all over my head."

"You have got to protect yourself."

"The problem, you see, is that Greek men do not want to appear to be dominated by their women. It's a macho thing, part of the masculine culture. I have to be discreet."

"Are you . . . ?" Doris hesitated. She had waited patiently for the right moment to inject the idea. Netta was ahead of her.

"Exclusive?" Netta said "I have no reason to think otherwise." She hesitated. "Of course, if he has sudden needs, you know what I mean. As long as he brings me no trouble and returns without scars."

"How generous. I would not stand for it with Gary. Marriage, you see, creates legal boundaries. There are consequences, especially monetarily. That is why a legal framework is essential."

"I suppose you're right."

"Then really, Netta, you should be directing him to the nearest lawyer, those you can trust. Believe me, Netta, as friends we are ready to help. Just remember we are here for you, Netta dear. For you and Dimitri."

"I feel that in my heart."

"We have more than enough on our plates. Nevertheless, we stand ready to help either of you if you should need us." She paused, then added. "God put us on earth to help each other."

"Yes. I believe that implicitly."

"You really owe it to yourself, if you get my drift. Believe me I am making these suggestions out of real affection." Doris persisted.

"I know."

When they compared notes, Gary and Doris were encouraged, but impatient. Both agreed that the man was a natural client. But they instinctively knew the limits of persuasion and they carefully chose intimate moments to make their pitches.

"The man's a fool," Gary told Doris. "He needs us more than he knows."

"She's a bigger fool. She relies on his promises."

"Is she of independent means?"

"It doesn't sound like it. She seemed completely dependent on him and invokes the image of Greek men who need to feel dominant."

"Not like us pussy-whipped American males," Gary snickered.

"That's a laugh."

"Is it? Remember, Doris baby, you're a Johnny-come-lately to this business. I've been in it from the get-go."

That was true. Gary had been the estate expert with a major law firm until forced retirement at sixty caused him to retire. Planning for this eventuality, Doris had gone to law school, passing the bar at the first try after a career in fashion. They had become Henderson and Henderson and discovered the social scene as the golden path to new clients. Their marriage, second for each, had morphed into more of a business arrangement than a loving cohabitation. But they had found that they made a good team of rainmakers and were cautious to keep any personal hostility between them a private matter. Both were well aware of the monetary boundaries of their marriage. When an argument ensued, Doris' response to any conflict was invariably the same.

"Let's stay focused on the matter at hand."

That had a calming effect on Gary.

"I'm trying to, Doris. Dimitri is a tough nut to crack."

"I think I've planted a seed in his squeeze. She's naïve and not very smart about these things.

Besides, she thinks she's his one and only. I have my doubts. He's quite sexy."

"Now there's an idea," Gary said. "Call it Plan B."

"It had occurred to me," Doris replied.

"Might even stoke the dying embers," Gary muttered. Sex had not been part of their marriage agenda for years.

"Fire needs oxygen," Doris shot back. It was a familiar back and forth verbal sparring.

"It's a hairsbreadth separation between frigid and rigid."

"It takes two to tango."

"Sometimes. But there there's a lot to say for soloing."

They had learned in their rainmaking the essence of obliqueness.

"Never mind all that," Doris scolded. "What now in the case of Monsieur Pappas?"

"We let it simmer," Gary said with some conviction. "At least the seeds are planted."

"In her, as well," Doris assured him.

They persevered in their pursuit. When Dimitri was in town they swooped over him like vultures on carrion.

Then, unannounced, Netta appeared in their office. She seemed greatly upset, her usual well-groomed exterior badly flawed, her voice agitated.

"You said you will help when I need you," she told Doris, who was the first to see her. Doris double-kissed her, summoned her secretary to offer coffee, which she refused, then she excused herself and looked in on Gary in the adjoining office.

"Pay dirt," she whispered, winking, waving him to follow her. He rose quickly and soon they were sitting at the small conference table in

Doris's office. Netta's skin looked a shade darker than usual and her eyes seemed fired with anger.

"The bastard." She spit out the words through pursed lips.

"Who?" Gary asked.

"Him. Pappas. Sumbitch."

Gary and Doris exchanged glances. This did not augur well for their overall plan.

"I told him." Netta waved a finger in the air. "I warned him." She made a slicing motion with her hands. "He threw me out. You can't do that, I told him. The stupid fool."

"Just like that?" Gary asked.

She was starting to calm, suddenly taking a mirror out of her purse and peering into it.

"Good God, look at me." She fixed her hair.

"Can't say I didn't warn you, Netta," Doris said. Like Gary, she knew the implications of this visit and was less than comforting. Apparently, Netta had not noticed the subtle change in attitude.

"Believe me, I didn't take this lightly. I told him. Okay, you have a new heartthrob, so what do I get out of all those years? He told me and I laughed in his face."

"He made you an offer?" Doris asked.

"Ten," Netta said. "Actually, he wrote out a check. I told him to go eff himself. That's why I'm here. I told him I would. He threatened me. The bastard threatened me. I ran like hell. Believe me he's capable. He once beat me black and blue. You don't know him like I do."

"And the check?"

"I deposited it. What else? What I want is what I deserve. That's why I'm here."

Again Gary and Doris exchanged glances. Gary shrugged. He was thinking that ten million was a nice settlement for a mistress being sent out to pasture. Of course, he was thinking, we could go for more and get a tidy fee to the bargain, thinking in terms of tax consequences and percentages of any futures sums they could obtain from Dimitri. There was, of course, a risk in that. Representing Netta would certainly mean that they would probably have to forgo any hope of handling Dimitri's estate, which might net them a much higher number than what they would get out of representing Netta."

"What do you think would be a fairer settlement, Netta?"

"Five times at least. You cannot imagine what I have sacrificed for this man."

"Can he handle that?" Gary asked.

"Yes." She paused and gazed at each of them in turn. "You said come to you whenever I needed you. Well here I am."

"This requires some thought, Netta," Doris said.

"Yes, it does," Gary said. Further discussion was obviously in order.

Netta narrowed her eyes and her complexion suddenly faded to dull beige.

"You're kidding?" she said, turning to Doris. "You said anytime I needed you. Well I need you now. I thought you were my friends."

"We are, Netta. We most certainly are," Doris said. At that time Gary had decided in favor of Dimitri and he knew Doris would accede. Dimitri was a far bigger catch monetarily and socially. He was certainly worth the gamble.

"Take the money and run." Gary said.

"Good advice," Doris agreed.

"Settle for ten thousand dollars?"

Gary felt a sudden sense of panic. Beside him, Doris had turned ashen.

"Thousand?" Gary managed to say, his voice constricted.

"I wanted fifty. He could pay me in installments. Like twenty-five down and five a year. I would not have been completely satisfied, but at least it would be fair."

Both Gary and Doris looked at her in horror. Thousands? The word hung in the air. Gary felt his stomach lurch.

"Is that your advice? Take peanuts?" Netta asked visibly astonished.

"He wasn't in shipping?" Doris said, clearing her throat, barely able to talk.

Netta smiled and shrugged.

"In a way, I suppose. He was a maître d' on a cruise ship. That's how I met him. I was a waitress. I still am, in a very fine restaurant in Westchester. Who did you think he was, Onassis? God, are you people naïve! Okay, maybe he exaggerated. I'll say this for him. He can charm the pants off anyone. Me, for starters. So we were a little bit theatrical. Actually, he never really lied, did he? So he didn't say cruise shipping. Neither did I. You fussed over us so much. Tell you the truth, we thought you had become our true friends. Really true friends. That's why I'm here."

"I don't believe this," Doris muttered.

"I guess I came to the wrong place for help," Netta said, glancing from face to face.

Gary had been too stunned to offer any comment. Finally, when he was able to speak, he turned toward Netta.

"Would you mind, Netta, if Doris and I consulted privately for a moment?"

Netta shrugged and nodded.

"Have I a choice?"

Closing the door to Gary's office, they stood stiffly, facing each other, contemplating the potential consequences.

"This mustn't get out," Doris said, the first to speak. "We'll look like idiots."

"Down the chute." Gary said, then paused, contemplating their potential exile.

"They were good. Smooth as silk," Doris sighed.

"Con artists," Gary said, shaking his head.

"Hustlers."

"She's got us over a barrel," Gary said.

"I suppose in the scheme of things it's a small price to pay."

They came back to Doris' office. Netta looked up. She had freshened her makeup and combed her hair.

"You are absolutely right," Doris said. "After all, there is nothing more powerful than friendship. We will negotiate with Dimitri and take no fee for our services. Moreover we will guarantee the settlement. Ten thousand more today and six thousand a year for five years. We believe we have the negotiating skills to get Dimitri to agree."

"Really, Doris." Netta protested, although lightly. "I hadn't expected such generosity."

Oh, yes, you did, Gary thought. In his mind, he was already composing the paperwork. Still, he told himself, it was a small price to pay for silence.

"We were duped," Gary said. "You were a couple of phonies."

Netta stood up and looked at them with what Gary saw as naked contempt.

"Okay, I'll buy that. And you?"

"We are lawyers," Doris said indignantly, looking at her with clear contempt.

"So who are' the bigger phonies? You or us?"

She offered a hollow laugh and left the office.

When she had left, Doris and Gary stared at each other in stunned silence.

"We are," Gary muttered hoarsely after awhile.

"We are what?"

"The bigger phonies."

"We're lawyers," Doris repeated.

"Maybe we should take a cruise on his ship?"

"We could use a vacation."

"At least we might get a good table."

They looked at each other and smiled grimly. Gary went back to his office.

A LITTLE WHITE LIE

They were six women sitting at a round table at Michael's where they lunched together every week. Not everyone showed up each week. Some were still working women. Sara owned an art gallery. Karen designed jewelry at home. Joy was on a number of business boards. Pat was a freelance editor, Barbara wrote children's books and Susan was on a number of non-profit boards.

What they had in common was that all were single and over sixty, self-supporting through inheritance or their own entrepreneurial skills. All were well coiffed and dressed, articulate, witty and bonded mostly by the luncheon group, which had been Pat's idea. All agreed it was an important event in their lives and regretted when they missed a session.

As Joy defined it, they were not the "Ladies who Lunched" of the Sondheim lyric, a mostly sad commentary about women who had nothing "meaningful" to do in their lives. Two of the women were widowed, two had never married, and two had been divorced multiple times. The widows and divorcees had children and grandchildren, but they had agreed never to let that enter the conversation.

Although they socialized through the medium of this weekly lunch-eon, they did not socialize exclusively together in the evenings. They did meet sporadically at various events that punctuated New York's busy social agenda. Susan, who had been a corporate wife almost all of her adult years, considered this luncheon group the absolute highlight of her present life.

Of all the women around the table she considered herself the least interesting. She had been married for thirty-seven years when her hus-band had died suddenly. Having grown up in Washington D.C., she had married a young Marine who had been a ceremonial attendant at the Kennedy White House and who later joined a multi-national corpo-ration serving mostly in Washington, then New York.

She had been devoted and supportive of her husband's career and had willingly accepted the role as wife, mother, organizer of their home life and social world, the latter built largely around her husband's busi-ness environment and mostly for the purpose of his career advancement. She had pursued her role cheerfully, believing that she and her husband were a team and feeling no sense of remorse, jealousy or disappointment that she had missed out on not doing "her own thing." She had been quite content in her role.

"My own thing is "you," Susan had told her husband numerous times. He often acknowledged his dependence on her and by any meas-ure she was convinced she had a wonderful marriage. She adored her husband, had come to the marriage a virgin and had never been with another man.

His sudden death two years before had left her bereft but financially secure, and after a long mourning period she began to realize that she had to build a single life from scratch. She had been active in philan-thropies, mostly because it helped advance her husband's profile in the very competitive corporate world, and retained her ties to two non-profits, where she served in a largely honorary capacity on their boards. Although a doting mother in her early years, her two children lived in other parts of the country, and, although dutiful and affectionate, pursued their lives independent of hers.

From her years as a corporate wife, Susan had learned how to socialize, work a room and engage in small talk. She knew people characterized her as vivacious and chirpy. She had long ago conquered her innate shyness and reserve and had developed an outgoing personality that made her popular among her husband's colleagues and their wives. Now that that life was over, she realized how narrow it had been and she was forced to confront the fact that she had better develop a persona that was individualized for her own benefit as a single woman. After all, she could no longer be an adjunct and helpmate for a deceased husband. For the first time in her life, she realized the narrowness of her range of experience compared to the other women around the table.

Their lives had been far more adventurous and creative than her own. They had had lovers and multiple husbands. Even her sister in widowhood had been married before. They told wonderful stories, some quite racy, about their lives, sparing no details. She would listen to them intently, secretly shocked by their titillating details. It was hardly the conversation of the corporate community which she had inhabited. She loved hearing these stories and although she managed to appear equally "interesting" by the force of her outgoing personality and enthusiastic and perky charm, she felt intimidated by a feeling of inadequacy in comparison.

What she feared most was that these lively, intelligent and experienced women would ultimately discover that her life had been one big yawn and ultimately reject her from the group. Even the designation "corporate wife" was considered, in this company, a contemptuous slur, one rung below prostitution. Behind her façade of smiles, she was terrified that her luncheon companions would intuit the truth, her guilty secret. The fact was that deep in her soul she could define herself only as a once-loyal corporate wife with no compelling narrative that would interest and or engage her luncheon companions.

Being asked to be part of this luncheon group by her friend Karen from whom she had bought jewelry was on the one hand a fantastic stroke of luck, but on the other hand it revealed her own sense of inferiority. Compared to them, I am a nothing, she told herself. Not that she regretted her earlier life. It did have its compensations. She had been secure, comfortable and, by the standards of her middle class upbringing, happy, even in retrospect. Despite this private rationalization, she could not chase away the thought that she was, by comparison, lesser, a crashing bore, not only in her own eyes but in theirs.

She would think about this often, recalling scattered mini-monologues of revelation from her tablemates. Like what Sara had told them at one of the lunches.

"I was broke and going to the Art Students League, hoping to be a female Picasso one day. There was a rich guy in my art class who had his own dreams of greatness. So I made this deal. You pay my tuition and the rent in my apartment and I'll provide your sexual comfort. Like in Japan during the war, they called these little girls comfort maidens or some such, for the sexual gratification of the soldiers in the Japanese Army. All I had to do was put out for one guy. It was a good deal for both of us. To tell you the truth I got the better of the deal. He was really good in the sack, which was a bonus. The arrangement lasted for four years and got me through a real rough patch. Talk about unintended consequences. He was the best lover I ever had."

"Of how many?" someone had asked.

"After the first dozen I stopped counting," Sara answered laughing, completely at ease in the telling. It was just one of many stories that peppered Sara's conversation about her life. They were always breezy, matter of fact, full of humor and irony.

Even in her widowhood, Susan had remained chaste, having still not found the courage to sleep with another man. She'd have to work that out one day, she promised herself. Her sex life with George had become more duty than pleasure. The truth was that even the pleasure was sporadic.

Joy, too, told some hair-raising stories of her own experiences. What struck Susan as unique about these luncheons was that there was no holding back, as if some mysterious confessional was taking place between the participants. She wished she had something juicy to confess.

"You can't imagine what my early life was like," Joy had told them in her soft lilting Southern accent. "I was abused by my stepfather. It wasn't as if we were dirt poor scratching for money. My stepfather was a banker, pillar of the community, a man of parts he was called by the newspapers. I sure can tell you about one part. Can you imagine, he would slip into my room after my mother was asleep and force me, ask, cajole, whatever you call it, to kiss his thing. Hell, I was eleven years old and I had never seen a club-like thing like that. To me it was like a baseball bat. It was awesome. I thought he would slam me with it and I was too scared to refuse. After awhile he got bolder and asked me to do a lot more than kiss the damned thing. I refused and told my mother and she shot him. Imagine that. We lived in a little town not far from Birmingham and it did make the papers and Mom got two years and I went to live with an aunt up north. But it did lead to a lifetime distrust of men. Now don't get me wrong. I like men. I like the whole nine yards, even that. I just can't trust the bastards, which may account for my three divorces. All in all, though, I have no real regrets. Hell, I'm a rich woman because of them. And the first one was a great dad to my kids. But it does color one's view of life, let me tell you."

"So there are now no more men in your life?" someone asked. "You know what I mean."

"Hell, I've got a stable. Just as long as I don't have to live with them. I'm from the 'bang bang thank you kind sir' school."

"Do they know your story?" another asked.

"Sure do. Turns them on."

Susan would listen and search her own life for an episode, an incident, some narrative that might make her more interesting but always with little success. The inner search stimulated memories of her husband who had been a fly fisherman, a sport that had never interested her. In life as in fly-fishing, the reward comes only to those "who match the hatch." Find the right fly to attract the fish. For this situation, the metaphor was certainly apt, only she couldn't find the right fly.

Barbara, who wrote children's books, told them what got her started on that career. She had a twin sister who was, as it was now described, mentally challenged with a span of concentration that hardly lasted for more than a minute or two. That is, until Barbara had discovered that her twin would respond to her made-up stories, always asking after almost every sentence of the story: "And then what happened?" It turned out that telling stories was the only way Barbara's twin could be pacified and calmed.

"I would invent characters, many of them animals, since Stacy, my twin, had many stuffed animals and could relate to the stories. Although it was very trying and rather sad for me, I dug deep into myself and came up with these stories that later on I recycled and published. My contracts with my publisher were set up to share any royalties with her and to this day they pay for her to be well cared for. In many ways I owe my career to her. To this day when I see her, and she's my age, remember, I still go through that routine. It's as if God had ordained this to be. Can you imagine?"

"One never knows," someone said.

Susan had seconded the comment, but she was even then thinking that she had nothing to tell that could possibly match such stories. Besides, she was an only child and had grown up in a very conventional and loving household. Her mother was a schoolteacher and her father was an accountant who worked for the Department of the Interior in Washington D.C. and her childhood and adolescence were hardly of interest to this group. Child abuse? Sibling problems? Sexual scandal? Personal achievement? Creative activity? She could not come up with anything unusual and certainly not bizarre. Her life was not remotely within the parameters of interest to these ladies.

Pat, too, had her stories. She had begun her career writing features for movie fan magazines and had interviewed many of the stars in the waning days of Hollywood's golden years. She could spin yarns about the sexual orientation of Hollywood greats and keep the group mesmerized with tidbits about Cary Grant and Randolph Scott, who were supposedly lovers in Hollywood's early days, and Paulette Goddard's penchant for performing oral sex under tables in nightclubs. She could reel off names of stars and stories of famous Hollywood executives that could singe one's scalp with hot material and keep her fellow diners glued to the edge of their seats in astonishment. In her repertoire were stories about backyard orgies and drunken and dope-drenched Hollywood parties that she had attended and whatever other intimate details she could dredge up about the stars in the golden age of tinsel land.

Susan listened to all these stories mesmerized and grew more and more depressed, although she was careful never to reveal the dark mood that often assailed her. Even her friend Karen, whose friendship she cherished and who had brought her into the group, had come up with life experiences that mustered the group's concentration and interest.

Karen's story was bizarre, even by the standards of the luncheon group. She had been married for a number of years when her husband had left her for another man.

"I knew he was bisexual since he had persuaded me to engage in threesome sex, meaning two males, a number of times. You see, I would have done anything to keep that marriage together. What tripped me up was that he fell in love with one of the participants and that was the end of the marriage. We're still great friends. "

Aside from the nature of Karen's story, what bothered Susan most was that Karen had never confided it to her alone, but provided it readily when the group was together at the weekly luncheon. She continued to live in dread that one day her luncheon companions would turn to her to confide her own intimate narrative. Her fear grew into an obsession. She would lie awake nights trying to concoct a story that would prove her bond with these women, illustrate her equality, prove her bona fides.

Her mind spun with possibilities. For a long time, she eschewed the idea of creating a fictional account. No one questioned the accuracy of her companion's' stories. Perhaps they had taken a core of truth and embellished it with a bit of blarney to give it more heft, more interest. Wasn't it the story itself that mattered? Did it really matter whether it was true or not? Just as long as it held the interest of the others in the group.

Susan ran through a number of possible scenarios in her mind, rejecting each one in turn. She needed a big idea, something that resonated, something that would earn her instant respect, something so original and compelling it would earn her permanent credibility and once and for all foreclose on her own feelings of inferiority. After weeks of fretting, a story began to emerge in her mind. She remembered her husband George's tales emanating from the Kennedy White House where he had been enlisted as a "walker," an escort and dancing partner for the single ladies invited to White House dinners. The stories were filled with rumors that implicated Kennedy in numerous extramarital affairs. In time, the stories became lore and passed into history, their truth validated in numerous memoirs. It was these stories that triggered her big idea.

She had always had difficulty with not being able to tell a lie with a straight face. Everyone knew, as her husband George had told her many times, that with Susan, "What you get is what you see." He had actually made such a comment as the centerpiece of any compliment he would give her and often share with others. Integrity. Honesty. Fidelity. Once she had reveled in such praise. Not anymore. It did not have the same currency that it had when she was a protected species living on what seemed another planet.

It took her weeks to perfect the story she had concocted to tell her luncheon companions. She knew it required a sense of performance and the absolute appearance of truth. Then suddenly, her moment came.

"I had just graduated from Georgetown and was recruited for the typing pool at the Kennedy White House. It was a lot different in those days, before computers, before security paranoia, before political correctness. Things were informal, easygoing. Jack Kennedy would often nod and wink at us as he passed through the corridors. We knew there were two girls in the typing pool, dubbed Fiddle and Faddle, who were invited to go swimming with Kennedy when Jackie was on the road. Everyone, including the Secret Service, was in on the ploy. We all knew. And Fiddle and Faddle were quite proud of their activity although they did not speak about it, not to us at any rate. Heck, it was a feather in their cap."

She noted that the women around the table seemed more alert and concentrated than usual. She was on stage and she loved it.

"Yes, one day I was recruited. Faddle was home with the flu and Fiddle asked if I wouldn't mind. Mind? Would any of you mind? I did have some experience and knew my way around the maypole." She thought she would choke on that remark, which she had thought up the night before. "Yes, I went. Jack, I mean the President, was there with one of his intimate buddies and we skinny dipped and played around, then later we dried off and Jack and I paired off and you know . . . " She paused. Too long.

"You're leaving us hanging?" Pat cried.

"How come you never told me this?" Karen asked.

"I never told anybody." She laughed, feeling suddenly powerful. "I saved it all for you guys."

"So what happened?" Sara pressed.

"What happened? What do you think happened?"

"Oh my God. I'm going to pee in my pants," Barbara squealed.

"All I'll say is that it was rather quick."

"I've heard that," Joy said.

"Did it happen again?" Sara asked.

Susan nodded.

"How many times?" Barbara asked.

"Who counted?" Susan giggled.

"Come on, Susan. More details." Joy said.

"Sometimes we did it in the Oval Office. In that little private room where he would take naps. Only sometimes he didn't," Susan said.

"Like Monica," Pat said.

"No cigars," Susan said, laughing.

"And the real thing." Susan said.

"Did you . . . " Karen asked.

"Not in that time frame."

"Did you feel anything?" Sara asked eagerly.

"Proud," Susan winked.

"My God," Pat said. "And you kept all this under your hat all this time?"

"Now that all the participants are gone . . . " Susan said.

"You're not, Susie. You're here to bear witness." Barbara said.

"And I have," Susan said.

She could sense that they wanted more, but she had the good sense to stop when she was ahead.

"That is an unbelievable story," Sara said.

"Looking back," Susan said, "I can hardly believe it myself."

For the first time since she had joined the group, she felt fully accepted. After all, it was only a little white lie.

REMEMBRANCE
OF THINGS PAST

Of course it was her. He knew immediately. He had, by any measure, raped her sixty years ago.

They were sitting on the same bench in the little private park outside the apartment building on Sutton Place, where he lived, enjoying the view of the East River in the late afternoon of summer. He went there almost daily to smoke one of his prized Cuban cigars and read a chapter of one of the books he was rereading.

"You don't mind?" he asked her.

He could have taken one of the empty benches, but this one had the best view of the river and, besides, it was part of his regular routine. For some reason, at his age routine was comforting and important.

"Not at all," she replied, casting a sideward glance over her reading glasses. She was reading the business section of that day's New York Times.

All it had taken was one glance at her in profile. Adrienne Frank. He was dead certain. She would be his age, or close to it, by one or two years, part of their old crowd at Rockaway Beach where their parent's went summers. He could remember the beach party, the blankets circling the bonfire, the smell of potatoes, spuds they called them, still baking under the fire, the glowing ashes, the tang of ocean salt and the sound of the waves slapping against the beach, the vast canopy of stars twinkling in the cloudless sky.

His memory was specific to that event, although their crowd often frequently built bonfires during those summers. Beach bonfires, burning old crates, were part of the ritual of their crowd, perhaps twenty of them, teenage boys and girls, who necked and petted as body contact was called in those days. During the afternoons, they stretched across a spot along the beach at 63rd Street, heads on stomachs and thighs, like some erector set built of teenage flesh.

He had little doubt it was her. He could see the old outlines of youth hidden behind the wrinkles and the loose flesh around the mouth and neck. She had been a brunette. Now she was blonde, but that could not hide her identity from him. There was the same nose, which seemed slightly elongated, the chin with the vague cleft. He remembered a dimple.

"Actually, I don't mind the smell of cigars. Reminds me of my father."

She had turned to him full face, offering a smile, and, sure enough the dimple creased. He even remembered her father, a kind of roly-poly balding fellow who always winked at him when he saw him on the porch of that big converted Victorian-type house in which their parents rented rooms in those days to get away from the blazing non-air-conditioned sweltering New York summers.

Memory had become his proudest possession, both long and short term. Those of his friends who were his age now, late seventies, would often claim lost memory, especially short term. Senior moment, they called it.

With some pride he would often cite what to him was a phenomenon, the memory of his days in his baby carriage. He was dead certain that he could recall the smell, a powdery scent of his toddler's clothes, the leathery smell of the carriage and the straps that held him secure, even the movement of the wheels as his mother pushed it from behind. And the feel of his baby clothes, soft and wooly.

He could remember the exact layout of his parent's apartment on Eastern Parkway, and could walk it through his mind as if it were yesterday. They hadn't lived there long since it had been a step up at the time, but the depression had been cruel and by the time he was three they had moved back to his grandparents house.

Perhaps it was his accountant's training, since he could add numbers in his head and could remember old telephone numbers and addresses despite moving frequently in those days. Retired now, living alone in the apartment he had shared with Betty, who had died four years ago, he followed the routine of a relaxed widower who had come to terms with his new singleness. He wondered if that, too, had to be with memory, since he could relive his entire life, almost. At least seventy-five years of it. Maybe, he wondered laughingly, the attraction to the East River had something to do with sloshing around in his mother's womb.

"Are you visiting?" he asked politely, not having seen her in the little park before.

"Not officially," she said. It was uncanny, he thought. Even the voice seemed the same. "I've moved in with my sister-in-law. Birds of a feather. We're both widows. Call us roommates." She laughed, the same laugh then put out her hand. He took it, even the touch of her flesh had a familiar feel to it.

"I'm Adrienne Bartow."

"Oh yes. Sybil Bartow."

"Her husband, my brother, was on the board."

"Yes, that one. Poor fellow."

"He had a good life."

She looked at him, smiling but without curiosity. There was not the slightest sign of recognition. In the process of nodding, his gaze swept her figure, greatly expanded from what he remembered. For a brief moment, he held back offering his name, but then, he decided, to test the waters, tamping down trepidation.

"I'm Herbert Bass," he said.

He watched her face for even the slightest flicker of curiosity. None was visible.

"Nice meeting you," she said, looking out across the river, his name quite obviously barely a blip on her memory, then her interest turned elsewhere. "Great view." Had he expected recognition? The thing he had noticed with older people, they had varying degrees of long-term memory.

Then he recalled that most kids of that era were prone to nicknames. He was Beebee, which came from Bertie, which was his parents' name for him. Bertie Bass. She was Addy, short for Adrienne. He could reel off many of the nicknames of their crowd. Immie and Fritz and Smitty and Hesh, Solly and Moe. Harry for Harriet. Cholly for Charlene. And on and on.

They came together summers only, dispersing when it was over. They lived in different places in the city. In those days neighborhoods had preset boundaries, mostly connected to school districts under the city public school plan. High school expanded the territory. Addy lived in the Bronx and went to Evander Childs. Beebee lived in Brooklyn and went to Erasmus. Summers they all lived in Rockaway, one block from the gorgeous white beaches and the ocean, another bounded territory.

They were part of the crowd that congregated just off the boardwalk on Beach 64th Street. Each crowd was self-contained. They came together by some mysterious process. Crowds never crossed boundaries. They were planted on a specific spot on the beach. At night they gathered at a specific spot on the boardwalk and moved together like a dog pack.

It was, of course, a lost world, long gone, although it lived vividly in his persistently accurate memory. He considered such recall a gift. He felt enormously lucky to be able to relive his life to its nether reaches and revisit places and moments in his long history like an endlessly spinning movie reel. Grandparents, parents, siblings, aunts, uncles, cousins, schoolmates, girlfriends, boyfriends, business acquaintances, places where he had lived or visited came alive again under every fresh spell of memory, recalled by sheer willpower. It gave him the insight to tell himself the truth.

He opened his book and pretended to be reading, but he was really going over that moment with Addy. The book was the third volume of Marcel Proust's "Remembrance of Times Past," which seemed oddly appropriate. He spent most of his time these days reading classics of literature and it was ironic that of all things he was reading Proust, the translation's title based upon the Shakespeare quotation, also remembered. "When to the sessions of sweet silent thought, we summon up remembrances of times past." Sitting next to Addy Frank, the irony sent chills throughout his body.

They had been as the expression went, "going steady," meaning that they had staked out a definite pairing, since the crowd settled into couples during the first weeks of the summer. It was more than puppy love, since by then the hormones were charging and the first clumsy sexual couplings were taking place.

The sexual rituals of those days were a far cry from today's anything goes activity. Fear of pregnancy, instilled by worried mothers of that era, was the dominating inhibition of the girls. The boys were perpetually horny, grappling with their masturbatory fantasies and frequent self-induced emissions.

Everyone knew the boundaries, although some were more adventuresome than others. He smiled at the language one used to describe their sexual exploits. Getting bare tit was a big step in climbing the ladder of sexual prowess and stinky pinky was almost like winning the sweepstakes. A hand job was nirvana and actually getting laid was an achievement that went beyond the pale of accomplishment. As for a blowjob, that was something so unattainable that it was barely mentioned in the mix of conquests.

Most of this hot sex was achieved under the blankets lying around the beach bonfire.

"You won't respect me," was the girl's perpetual plaint as the boys grappled with the forbidding elastic underwear of the day and the tricky catches that fastened brassieres.

He and Addy were mad for each other that summer. He hung around her like a moth around a flame and the flame seemed to give off a lot more heat than light. They could not keep their hands off each other. They graduated from bare tit to stinky pinky and a hand job in what was a short period of time.

They swore undying love to each other. He could think of nothing else that summer. Being with Addy was like breathing. He needed the oxygen of her presence. He wrote her passionate love letters, which she returned in kind. She had given him a lock of her hair, which he carried around in his wallet, along with the just-in-case condom which left its impression on the surface of his leather wallet and which he never used.

Not a day passed when they were not together during that summer. Others, too, among their crowd had also coupled in that manner. Necking and petting was a daily ritual, more intense at night, especially under the blankets around the bonfire on the beach.

That night, after the fire had died down and they had eaten their semi-burnt spuds and roasted marshmallows, they retired, along with the others, under their individual blankets and began the nightly coupling ritual. She wore loose cotton shorts over her panties and once under the blankets, her brassiere came off and he kissed her nipples and kneaded her breasts while she stroked his erection over his pants.

The details of the memory did not surprise him, although until that moment in the park, he had not thought about it for least nearly the six full decades of its happening. Emboldened by his and her passion, he opened his pants and exposed the flesh of his penis to her ministrations.

What he did then was to slip it between her legs where it rubbed against her clitoris through the loose bottom of her shorts.

"Please, no," she whispered, her breath coming in short gasps. In those days, he was never certain whether or not she had an orgasm, probably thinking that once he had come that was the end of the sexual experience, something that had to be re-taught as he grew older and more experienced with the other gender.

"Let me, sweetheart. I love you."

"No, you mustn't."

"Don't you love me?"

"With all my heart and soul."

"Then let me," he pleaded. "Just a little bit. Not all the way."

"No, its wrong."

"Please darling, prove your love. Just for a second, just a little bit. I promise I won't do it all the way."

Her breath was coming in short gasps. She tried to push him away, but he was adamant, getting his erected penis to the entrance of her vagina through her loose shorts. He had pulled her panties aside and was positioning his body so that he could provide enough purchase to get his penis through the tight opening.

"No. No. Please, Beebee, please."

It was a heavy whisper, half drowned out by the sound of waves slapping against the beach. She was pushing him away, trying to close her legs, but he had her bested. He was stronger than her and was pushing his body with all his might, getting his penis through the opening of her vagina in one giant thrust. She gasped, but did not cry out and he pulled himself out of her after a spine-shuddering orgasm. Clearly, in retrospect, by any present definition, it was forced rape. He felt a sudden thrill of shame, but it quickly passed.

"See, I kept my promise," he said when he had calmed.

"I'm wet," she whispered.

He kept her in a tight loving embrace.

"I love you," he said. "And you proved to me how much you love me."

They continued to lie together for some time. The fire slowly dwindled and they got up, folded the blankets and started homeward, hands around each other's waists. In the streetlight she looked down at her crotch and she could see the blood and the greasy stain of his semen.

"Oh my God. Oh my God," she cried. "What have you done?"

"It's okay," he said. "It will be fine."

"No, it won't. My mother will find out. You made me pregnant."

A stab of fear shot through him. For her, the shame of such an outcome was a fate worse than death. For him, it was an equal disaster, but in a different way. They truly believed that if she were pregnant their lives would be ruined. Perhaps they would have been.

She told him that she had disposed of her panties and washed out her shorts and told her mother she was having her period, which did come after about a week, a week of agony for both of them. It was near the end of the summer by then, and a couple of weeks later, the crowd broke up and everyone went back to the city.

For some reason, they assumed their separate city lives and he did see her a couple of times during the winter, but it was never the same again. It was as if a fault line had opened between them allowing other things to intervene. Sitting on the bench, smoking his cigar, the event came back vividly and, he was certain, that it was graphically and emotionally accurate.

Considering that this event was a defining moment for both of them, he was oddly disappointed that she did not recognize him, although he was relieved. Pure and simple, it was rape and he could not know how the event was characterized in her mind. Nor, at this stage, did he wish to know.

It was the very first time he had gone all the way with a lady and for her, however she reflected on its consequences, he would always and forever be counted as her first lover. In the crude vernacular of the day, he had popped her cherry.

"Isn't this a great time of day?" she said suddenly. She was silent for a long time, watching the river and the boats lazily floating past. Then she got up and looked down at him.

"Nice meeting you, Mr . . . "

He hesitated for a moment, tempted. "It's Beebee," he nearly said.

"Bass," he said. "Herbert."

"Oh yes," she said smiling, showing her dimple.

"I'm sure we'll meet again."

"I'm sure," he said.

He watched her back recede as she entered the apartment house, marveling at the extent and vividness of his memory.

To his great surprise, he discovered he had an erection.

IN GOD'S NAME

The neighborhood, west of Sixth Avenue, a few blocks from the cusp of gentrification, was rundown, a relic of the twenties. Rows of tenement-type four-story walk-up apartments lined both sides of the street. Garbage cans, secured by chains, sat beside the narrow entrances of the buildings.

Consulting his little notebook, Carey checked Father Joseph's address, and shook his head as he confirmed it. Not very pleasant, he thought, but then the man was in a kind of forced purgatory, out on bail and awaiting the result of an appeal that seemed bound to be denied. He faced the remainder of his life in prison.

He had followed the case in the newspapers, at least at the beginning, until it had become too painful, especially when confronted by photos of the poor man, aged, blank of expression, empty-eyed and pitiful. An embarrassment to the Church, a pedophile, a seducer of young boys, he had been excoriated in the media, broken; his life as a priest, a shepherd to his flock, ruined.

Guilt-ridden by his own cowardice, Carey could not bring himself to step forward. Gilbert, his partner for a quarter of a century, his lover and true friend, had agonized with him, losing sleep, listening to Carey's litany of memories and, in the end, advising him to stay silent.

"Leave it alone. We have a good life." Gilbert told him. "There is no point in martyrdom," Gilbert advised. They were untroubled, respected, with a wide circle of friends of all genders and persuasions. Carey was a lawyer at a prestigious law firm and Gilbert a professor of English literature at NYU. To step forward was pointless. Whatever he would say would have no legal standing. Nothing could possibly change the relentless course of justice.

The law was the law and the vaunted self-righteous Catholic Church, which had long been a secret safe harbor for men of their persuasion, was being called to account and doomed to embarrassment and monetary loss. And the men caught in the trap of their sexual orientation who had crossed the legal line had to be prosecuted. It was a drama that was destined to be played out with a vengeance. Numerous witnesses who professed to have had sex with the priest had come forward, testifying how Father Joseph's seductions had impacted negatively on their lives.

"You would accomplish nothing," Gilbert pressed. "He has numerous accusers, people who allege that they have been damaged by the priest's conduct. Then there is the element of greed. The Church is a great money target. To assert publicly that the priest's illegal conduct was a boon to you would make you a laughing stock. Put it out of your mind."

"I won't act, of course. But it won't be easy getting it out of my mind."

"Try."

For Carey, the memory of his own experience was powerful, life-changing, and yes, wonderful, joyful. It was burned into his memory, contemplated obsessively, shared with Gilbert numerous times in their earlier days together. It was the quintessential watershed moment of his life. Years ago it had receded. Other events put it on the back burner of memory, exploding again when the situation was revealed and Father Joseph stood accused by boys now grown.

The notoriety of the trial had ignited his memory, bringing back the full untarnished narrative from the very moment the troubled twelve-year-old boy arrived in the confessional box with the words "Father, I have sinned."

"Tell me, my son," the priest beyond the grille had said in a kindly soothing voice. Carey was imbued with faith then, the recipient of a strict Catholic upbringing by good and caring parents, traditional, religious, believers with unquestioned alliance to the Church and all its rituals. Carey had been an altar boy, a devoted participant, and like his parents, a true believer.

It had seemed a terrible sin at the time. Carey had been attracted to a boy in his class and they had indulged in a number of episodes of mutual masturbation which had graduated into something worse. It was the "worse," meaning oral sex, that had driven the confused and guilt-obsessed Carey into the full confidence of the confessional. Up until then he had kept it concealed. Then it suddenly erupted in his mind as a full-blown sin. Not only the acts themselves, but the emotional component, the secret longings and desire to be with and please this other boy.

In the context of the time, the mutuality of the acts was considered merely sexual experimenting among boys, as normal as what was then described as a "circle jerk" which was accompanied by fantasies about girls, about whose parts he showed little interest, concentrating instead on the sight of the boy's' erections. But the newly practiced oral aspect and the sense of longing was a step beyond, especially since he had these odd romantic and obsessive feelings about the boy in question.

He was goaded by the priest on the other side of the grille, who he knew was Father Joseph, to supply precise details of the events and his reaction to them.

"How did you feel while you did this?" the priest asked gently. To lie, he knew then, was to compound the sin.

"I felt, well, good."

"Did you feel it was wrong while you did it?"

"Yes, Father, but it did not stop me from committing this sin."

"Did the other boy like it when you did it?"

"Yes, Father."

"Did he do it to you?"

"No Father."

"Why not?"

"I don't know, Father."

"How many times did you do it to him?"

"Many times, Father. He wanted me to do it again and again."

"And did you want to do it?"

"Yes Father, I am ashamed to say. How can I absolve myself in the eyes of God?"

What was particularly strange was that talking about the event was arousing and before he realized it, he found that he had begun to stroke himself and his breath was coming in little gasps. He had the sense that the priest was watching through the grille.

"What are you doing, my child?" the priest asked.

"Nothing, Father."

He had continued stroking and could hear strange sounds coming from the other side of the confessional.

"Are you certain?" the priest asked.

"I am sinning, Father," the young Carey said, lost in his culminating pleasure.

"Does it feel wonderful, my son?" the priest asked.

Not answering, he had rushed out of the confessional in embarrassment. That, of course, had been the beginning. In those days, Father Joseph was a young, quite handsome, popular figure in the parish. Parishioners of all ages and genders adored him.

"You must come to confession again, my son," Father Joseph told him every time they met. Carey had the impression that Father Joseph had singled him out, paying greater attention to him when he attended services and urging him to help in other ways. On those occasions when he entered the confessional box, the priest suggested that he tell that story again. He did and the same experience ensued. Oddly, he felt less and less embarrassed and would eagerly await the next session.

After a while, Father Joseph would invite him to church for what was termed special instruction. His parents were approving, thinking that perhaps Father Joseph would persuade him to enter the priesthood. Their extended family boasted two nephews who were attending a seminary and an aunt who had become a nun.

What was happening, he knew instinctively, although it was only later that he truly understood it, was that he was falling in love with Father Joseph. He could not wait until he saw him again. Although he attended the confessional frequently, he was beginning to prefer his face-to-face meetings with Father Joseph, who was always kindly, reassuring and overtly friendly. He was often invited to dinner in Carey's home, not far from the church. His parents adored him.

One evening Father Joseph arrived unexpectedly when Carey's parents were out to some function. By then his older siblings were living away from home attending college. Tim Carey was the youngest of three and he was then called Timmy.

He was elated to be alone with the priest, whom he offered drinks from the family liquor cupboard. They sat together on the couch. Carey would never be certain who made the first overt move, but before he realized it he was entwined in a deep embrace with the priest. Father Joseph's gentle caresses and sweet velvet-like kisses on his body were ecstatic, beyond any pleasure he had ever experienced before.

He reveled in its mutuality and he lovingly ministered to the priest in ways that he had fantasized over the months before this had happened. The fact was, he loved it and over the months of his affair, he realized the depth of his sexual orientation. He was a homosexual through and through.

"Feel no guilt, my son," Father Joseph cautioned. "We are what God made us."

He believed that implicitly to this day. Months later, Father Joseph was transferred to another parish and Carey went on to other pursuits. But he remained grateful to Father Joseph for defining what he was, opening the door to the truth of himself.

Still, he understood the trap that Father Joseph was in, having obviously set it for himself. He had entered the Church, certainly for reasons of religious conviction, but for a deeper reason as well. The cassock protected his sexual inclination which was strongly homosexual, powerfully so. His need was, as Carey remembered, very strong. Later, he would characterize it as insatiable. Father Joseph was at that point in his late thirties, making love to a boy that had just discovered his sexual preference and was reveling in the discovery. Their last moments together in a hotel room the priest had booked in an out-of-the-way motel under the West Side Highway were sad, tearful and repetitively sexual.

"I cannot see you anymore, my sweet darling, but I swear to you in God's name that I will love you forever," the priest had vowed. "You are my one true love."

Carey believed this implicitly. Perhaps he still believed it. "In God's name" was a powerful injunction. He could not remember whether he seconded the priest's assurance, but he felt certain that he had. His sadness at their final parting was profoundly heartbreaking for him, his grief overpowering. He had spent months in a deep depression.

Later he would wonder if Father Joseph had been transferred for having been found out, his sexual proclivity for young boys reported by other parishioners. Carey would not have believed it at the time. He was dead certain that Father Joseph had been a true and faithful lover.

Despite the absolute logic of his not stepping forward in defense of Father Joseph, the idea of his inaction gnawed at him and grew into an obsession that morphed into a compulsion, a deep need. He had to confront Father Joseph and offer him the gift of his gratitude, his humble thanks for defining him, for demonstrating his true nature, for giving him the courage to confront himself without guilt. Surely it would brighten the bleak moments that now afflicted the poor man.

Carey viewed such a face-to-face assertion as an act of mercy, an oasis of gratitude in a desert of excoriation and bitter accusation. What had happened between them was a good thing, not the bad thing that had been alleged by scores of others. In his heart, he was martyred by the idea that he was an exception and he wanted the priest to know this. Was there a biblical side to such an act? Familiar quotations from scripture rolled through his mind. Let he who was without sin cast the first stone? Was Carey the prodigal son returned? Or a rescued soul who had escaped the fate of Sodom?

A private detective who his law firm used extensively had come up with Father Joseph's address and apartment number in the dreary four-story walk-up. The buzzer system was not working and Carey was able to enter and find the apartment door on the fourth floor of the walkup. He felt a sense of heart-thumping fear grip him as he knocked on the door.

Chained from the inside, the door opened a crack and he could see a partial view of Father Joseph's face.

"Are you a reporter?" Father Joseph asked hoarsely.

"No, Father," Carey said shocked at the ravaged face that peered at him through the partially open door.

"Who are you?"

"An old friend," Carey said, hoping for some vestige of physical recognition.

He sensed that the priest's eyes scanned him.

"I don't believe you."

"I'm Tim Carey," Carey revealed, gazing into the troubled man's eyes, waiting for a response.

"I don't know you."

"May I come in?"

"No."

"We knew each other long ago," Carey said.

"Leave me alone. Haven't you all punished me enough?"

"I'm not here to punish you, Father."

"Don't call me Father. I have been defrocked."

"You will always be Father Joseph to me," Carey said, feeling foolish, standing in the badly lit hallway, talking to half a face.

"Go away."

There was a long silence as the priest's eyes contemplated Carey.

"You don't remember? I'm Tim Carey. We were . . . " Carey looked about him, as if searching for eavesdroppers. He lowered his voice. "We were great friends once." It shocked him suddenly to calculate the years, nearly forty.

"I don't know you," the older man said.

"I wanted to . . . " Carey felt choked for a moment. " . . . To show my gratitude."

"Gratitude?" Father Joseph snickered. "For what?"

"You really don't remember, do you?" Carey said after a long silence.

"I told you. I never saw you before in my life."

How could it be? Carey thought. The poor man could not remember what for Carey was the quintessential experience of his life. The words that Father Joseph had uttered many years before came back into his mind with perfect clarity. "I will love you forever. You are my one true love."

Suddenly Carey felt a sense of deep disappointment. He had expected the affair to be locked forever in Father Joseph's memory and in his heart, an enduring, ecstatic and precious moment to be protected and perpetually savored. The two men exchanged glances.

"Well then," Carey said, his plan in shambles. What Father Joseph had fallen in love with then was a young boy, perhaps nothing more than a symbol, a mere representation of all young boys whom he craved and coveted, one of many.

The older man who peeked at the priest through the opening of the chained door had no relevance to that craving. Carey was, he realized, hardly unique, merely disposable young flesh, not the one true love of his fantasy life. Still, the revelation did not tarnish his gratitude. Father Joseph had been the instrument of his self-knowledge.

"You were a great help to me, Father. I came to thank you."

"You're mocking me, mister," the old man responded. "I deserved what I got."

"I guess the only thing to do, then, is wish you good luck," Carey muttered.

"Luck," the old man croaked. "There is no luck in hell."

The door slammed shut and Carey stood there for a few moments in the dark hallway.

"Still a believer," Carey shrugged as he made his way downstairs.

THE LOVE OF HIS LIFE

"Could it be?" Jason Haskell thought, his eyes focused on his open laptop laid out in front of him on the tray of the business class seat. His reference was to the woman sitting beside him in the window seat, a gray-haired compact figure, already settled in and reading a paperback. He studied her peripherally, uncertain what fifty years of living might have wrought physically upon her and his own perception.

Such things had happened before. A gesture, an expression, a tone, some strange echo of the past, might trigger a tiny shard of memory, of vague recognition. Most of the time it amounted to nothing, a kind of false alarm, quickly dismissed.

He felt certain it was another one of those, although he had immediately put a name to the person imagined. Dotty Frank. He no longer concentrated on the figures on the computer screen. The laptop was merely a prop now. Still he dared not turn full face and assess the woman.

Was it fear of confronting the embarrassment of mistaken identity or the fact of true recognition? Why the odd reaction? He was, after all, a man of the world, a grandfather, married more than forty years, on the cusp of retirement, an accomplished and respected member of the accounting profession. He was coming home from a speaking engagement in Los Angeles where he had been properly applauded and honored by his peers. Then why the sudden nervousness? Perspiration was rolling down from his underarms. His stomach was in knots.

The stewardess came by and he ordered a double scotch, for him an unusual occurrence. Mostly he drank white wine these days, but suddenly the need for a jolt of what he characterized as Dutch courage assailed him. The memories of Dotty Frank flooded his mind, as if they had been pent up somewhere in his subconscious and were mysteriously uncorked.

Like a movie, the images rolled out with such strong fidelity that he felt actualized into the narrative of what had occurred nearly five decades before. How old was Dotty then? Sixteen, he remembered, and he was eighteen and it was summer and they had fallen in love. It came back to him now with all the power and ecstasy of what he felt at that period in his life, that maddeningly obsessive all-encompassing sensation of total possession and need.

How had it happened? He remembered only that she was there, a love object so profound that it crowded out everything else and fixated itself on this lovely blonde girl woman whose look and touch represented nirvana. It was summer and they lived, each with their parents, in Rockaway Beach in little bungalows, colonies of people escaping the city heat.

He and Dotty were part of what then was referred to as a "crowd," a group of like teenagers from middle-class families, mostly lower, who huddled together like a single species, staking their blanket territories on the beach and moving together like a single organism. Some, like he and Dotty, paired off as sweethearts. After a day at the beach they would gather on the boardwalk, still in staked-out territory, where they danced to nickel jukebox tunes and paired off later to, as they called it then, neck and pet.

Dotty was still in high school and he had just finished his first year at City College, having taken the obligatory liberal arts courses preparatory to choosing a major. That summer, he was enrolled in extra credit work but that only took two mornings a week, and he always made it back to Rockaway in time for lolling on the beach with the crowd and, of course, especially to be with Dotty.

They were inseparable, he remembered, as if they lived in a private paradise. He thought of nothing but Dotty. She was the epicenter of his world. He wrote her daily love notes, composed love poetry, bought her a "slave" bracelet to wear on her ankle, engraved with the words "forever yours." Thoughts of Dotty filled his mind whenever he opened his eyes in the morning until he closed them at night. He supposed she filled his dreams as well.

When the social part of the night was over, they would go to some secluded place, a corner of a bungalow porch somewhere, or on a blanket on the beach, wherever some semblance of privacy could be found. There they kissed, hands caressing body parts, and grew progressively bolder in their lovemaking until at some point very late in the summer they went, as they said in those days, "all the way."

It was the first time for both of them, a scary and somewhat clumsy experience, more bonding than pleasurable, but memorable and profound nonetheless. He recalled professions of eternal undying love, pledges of lifetime fealty. Each had the sense, he was certain, that that summer was to be the quintessential incandescent moment of their lives, the beginning of what would be forever. To hold Dotty in his arms, to kiss her, become part of her, was paradise found, unbounded joy for eternity. She was and would forever be the love of his life.

As the past reeled its way through his mind, he could not remember conversations between them, although he could recall the salt-tinged air and the soft feel and smell of her flesh and the taste of her lips. He supposed that, in retrospect, as time progressed, first loves were always like that, clichés of obsession, romantic love at white heat, fueled by stories and poems rendered by others who had experienced similar flights of ecstasy.

When the summer was over, the reality of geography and the routines and rituals of their lives kept them physically apart. Jason lived in Brooklyn and Dotty lived in the Bronx. This meant that Jason, on Saturday nights, which was the only courting time available to them in those days, had to take the more than hour-long trip by subway to be with Dotty.

Being completely alone was difficult. Dotty lived in a tiny apartment with her parents and slept on a studio bed in the living room. It was not exactly conducive to leisurely sexual congress and what little privacy they could get obliged them to either pursue their lovemaking in hurried encounters or postpone it for their next date. It did not diminish their ardor and he could never get through a day without at least two or three telephone conversations with Dotty. He continued to write his usual barrage of love notes and poems and her absence from his daily life made him crazy with longing. Being separated from her was agony.

There had been no doubt in his mind that their commitment to each other was total. She was never out of his thoughts and he assumed that such devotion was matched by her. Thinking about this now, decades later, it surprised him that these feelings returned with such power as if nothing had occurred in the intervening years, his subsequent courting of his wife, another experience of falling in love, the births of his children, his financial success, the multitude of incidents and the endless chain of events that constitute a life lived. Indeed, everything that had occurred to him in his life since his experience with Dotty fell into another category as the power of this memory of his teenage experience with Dotty dominated his thoughts.

Now the dark side intervened, cutting through the old scar tissue and recalling the pain.

One Saturday, he arrived in her neighborhood in the Bronx earlier than usual. As he approached her apartment building, he noticed a group of young people, as they did in those days, hanging out in front of a candy store. As always, his heart leaped at the sight of her. Suddenly he froze. She was being embraced by another boy, a tall boy in a leather jacket. He held her from the rear, arms around her waist, a gesture that declared easy and, as it registered on him, longstanding intimacy.

The effect on him was profound. His heartbeat accelerated, his breath came in short gasps, his legs grew wobbly. Even in memory, he could feel the pain of this revelation. He was consumed by what he supposed was jealous rage. He was certain that he was observing betrayal in its most basic guise.

How could she? The line became a repetitive refrain. He wanted to move forward in blind anger and fight the boy who had absconded with his girl. He wanted to conquer him, humiliate him, disgrace him. He felt diminished, intimidated, his self-respect and his honor besmirched.

Worse, he began to contemplate how deep the betrayal ran. Was Dotty having sex with him? By his lights at that moment in time no crime was greater than that. He felt himself suddenly afflicted with a monstrous plague. She had sullied their love, had lied to him, trampled on something so sacred and precious to him, that he suddenly felt worthless and suicidal.

He remembered watching the couple part with kisses and laughter and Dotty disappeared into the entrance to her apartment house. At that point, he saw no other choice than to proceed with their date. It was, of course, impossible to dismiss what he had seen, but then he allowed some rational thinking to intrude. Perhaps it was just innocent horseplay. Nothing serious. Maybe his imagination got the best of him. He forced himself to give Dotty the benefit of the doubt. Her life in the Bronx was different than her summer life in Rockaway. She had grown up here, had other friends, another crowd. He was jumping to conclusions.

Still, he knew he could not live without knowing the truth and he was determined to get it. As he moved up the stairs to her apartment, he met her parents.

"Hi, Jason," her mother said as they greeted him warmly.

"Off to the movies," her father said, smiling.

To him that meant that they would have the apartment to themselves for at least a couple of hours, a rare gift. In those days, parents felt somewhat certain that their teenage children were observing the proprieties and sexual conduct was regulated more by caution and discipline, since the consequences could bring disgrace and ostracism. These were the days before the pill and the sexual revolution was still far into the future.

Jason and Dotty had indeed crossed the line, rationalized by the intensity of their love for each other. They knew the risks. The condom was the accepted method of birth control, although that did not fully mitigate the anxiety of a missed period and the terrible fear of pregnancy.

Such thoughts, he was certain, did enter into the equation of his anger. What was worse than an unwanted pregnancy was being blamed for a conception that was not caused by him.

Immediately upon entering her apartment, the passion of possession moved him to fierce sexual aggression, which both surprised and delighted her. Calmer and more cerebral than he had been when he had first observed her with the other boy, he plotted his interrogation. He was determined to know the truth. However he tried to rationalize what he had seen, things had changed between them.

They lay together on the living room couch, tightly embraced. Suddenly he said. "I saw you with that boy." He felt her body stiffen.

"What boy?" she asked.

"The one in the leather jacket."

"Bobby?"

"That one. Yes, Bobby."

He watched her face. Her eyelids fluttered, betraying her sudden nervousness.

"He's a friend."

"Just a friend?"

"I saw you together. It seemed more than just a casual friendship."

"Who told you that?"

"Never mind."

He was relentless now. Nothing was going to stop him. He was willing to try anything, push ahead without mercy.

"They were lying," Dotty said, defensive now.

"Were they?"

"Yes, they were." He noted the first signs of hysteria. Clearly she was covering something up. He went further.

"I know the whole story."

"I don't know what you're talking about."

She had moved away from him, sitting upright now. Her face was flushed and he imagined that her guilt was palpable.

"You let him," he pressed.

"I did not," she said.

"Yes, you did. They told me."

"Who are they?"

"It's true, isn't it? You let him. You let him do it to you."

"I did not," she said again, but tears had welled in her eyes and were spilling over her cheeks.

"How could you?" he asked, his stomach in knots. He felt nauseous.

"I didn't . . . "

It was obvious to him now. Her certainty was collapsing.

"You did, didn't you?"

He was gentler now, acting as if he was ready to forgive her.

"It happened," she whispered.

"Many times," he said with certitude.

"I'm so sorry, Jason. I didn't mean to."

"How could you do this?" he asked, his throat constricting.

"It's you I love, Jason," she said. Tears came in gushes now. Her face contorted. "I'm so sorry, Jason. So sorry."

"I never want to see you again," he said.

He could remember leaving the apartment, standing outside in the street, leaning against a lamppost crying hysterically, but he could not recall the long subway ride home. Days of agony followed. He lost interest in school, in everything. His conduct alarmed his parents, although he tried valiantly to keep them from knowing the cause of his melancholy. He picked up the phone numerous times to call her, but he never did. Had she called? He couldn't remember.

He was not sure how long the effects of this trauma lasted, although the power of its recall brought back the pain despite the distance of time. He could not recall a single incident in his life since that had caused him such pain.

Finally, the Dutch courage kicked in and he was recalled to the present. He shut the computer, reattached the tray, and turned to the woman beside him. She was still concentrating on her book.

"Don't I know you?" he began, inspecting her now. Behind her glasses, he recognized her eyes, hazel, green in good light. She looked up and observed him.

"I'm not sure," she said. The voice, the tone. He was certain. His heart pumped and he felt his lip quiver.

"Jason Haskell," he said, forcing a smile.

She looked at him for a long moment, then recognition came.

"Oh my God, Jason." She smiled. That was different, he noted. Dental work. Implants, he decided.

"Hair gone, as you can see." He patted his bald head.

"I can't believe it. Jason Haskell."

"Dotty Frank," he said, his throat constricting.

"Gartenhaus now. Been for years."

She watched him and he wondered what she was recalling.

"So what have you been doing all these years?" she asked, casual, comfortable, bemused by the coincidence.

He related the bare facts, his occupation, his long marriage, his children, where he lived. It was brief, like a tight paragraph in Who's Who. She listened and smiled.

"How wonderful," she said, rubbing her chin. "Can't believe it.

Wait'll I tell Hal. That's my husband. We live in Westchester. I have five grandchildren and shuttle between them. That's where I was in California. Calabasas." She reached into her pocketbook and brought out a sheaf of pictures, and passed them one at a time to him. "That's Barry, my son-in-law, with Joanie my daughter and the kids. The children are amazing. You wouldn't believe how smart they are. Gladdie wants to be a doctor and Charles is a budding scientist. He wants to go to MIT and believe me, he has the marks." She pulled more pictures from her bag. "This is Larry and Sean, my grandkids that live in Boston. Could you imagine five grandchildren? I know. I know. I'm a professional grandmother, but I'm so proud, Jason, so proud."

It went on and on. There was no stopping her, as if a plug had been pulled. He must have seemed interested, since his look of concentration only encouraged her to tell more and more about the grandchildren. His thoughts were elsewhere, lost in memory of another time and, he was certain, another person. This could not be the Dotty Frank he knew and worshipped. Not this little compact gray-haired woman who obsessed about her grandchildren, about whom he had little interest.

He stole a glance at his watch. Three hours to go. He was trapped, his mind searching for excuses to end the conversation. The revelations of the trauma of the past disappeared from his thoughts, although he wondered if his own history struck her as dull. She was merely reporting her life, which had little emotional content worthy of conversation, one long monologue that, after a while, seemed distant and agonizingly, crushingly, boring.

From time to time, he interrupted politely.

"Sounds like you had quite a life."

"I've been very lucky, Jason," a comment which set her off again. It became increasingly apparent that she had no interest in his life, and was totally absorbed in her own.

The stewardess came by with their meals. The proximity was almost unendurable. He ordered two more scotches and a couple of glasses of wine and still the surge came. By the time, the plane landed he was lightheaded and very grateful that the ordeal had come to an end..

"Well, it was great bumping into you, Dotty," he said, as he unfastened his safety belt.

"Wonderful. I can't wait to tell Hal," she said.

He proceeded to the exit, relieved, swearing never again to trust nostalgia.

Suddenly, she tore off a partially blank page from her paperback and wrote her telephone number on it. He noted that it was the title page from a romance novel, *The Fatal Kiss*.

He rushed down the aisle, thankful that his rollaway on the overhead bin contained all his possessions and he did not have to endure her at the baggage claim. As he got into a cab to take him home to his Manhattan apartment, he rolled the title page into a ball and tossed it out the window.

JUST WILD ABOUT HARRY

"It seems so unfair to keep such a large dog in a New York apartment," Bud said. It was his regular role to walk Harry on the fringes of Central Park before he and Shirley went to bed. Their apartment was on Fifth Avenue overlooking the park on East 66th street.

"You always say that when you have to walk him."

Days, they had a regular walker who charged twenty-five dollars an hour. Shirley had insisted that the walker be exclusive to Harry every afternoon for at least two hours.

"Big dogs need lots of exercise," she had asserted, countering Bud's argument. The action neutralized Bud's contention, although he expressed annoyance at the expense.

Mornings, in all seasons, Shirley would rise at six to take Harry to the no-leash section of the park where he romped with the other dogs in the early morning group. On rare occasions when Shirley was sick, Bud would do the honors.

"All they do is chase around and hump each other," Bud told her. "Maybe we should have Harry fixed."

"No way, Bud. How would like someone to do that to you?"

"Ouch."

"They do fix the girls," Shirley informed him.

"Doesn't matter to Harry," he snickered.

"He has a very strong libido," Shirley said, winking.

He did not like to get up that early and was always grouchy when he returned. In fact, he was also grouchy when he took Harry out at night, confessing that it was scary duty and he could get mugged.

"Don't be silly. Giuliani fixed all that. The park is as safe at night as it is during the day."

"Then you do it." He paused and shrugged half-jokingly. "Afraid of getting raped?"

She always smirked at the comment. They had been married ten years, the second for both of them. They were in their early fifties and each had grown children from earlier marriages who lived in other parts of the country. On occasion the children visited, but Bud and Shirley rarely left the city to visit them. Shirley hated leaving Harry in a kennel, a condition that impacted on foreign travel as well. Bud, who worked as a salesman for a jewelry company, traveled four times a year for a couple of weeks to visit his clients.

Since he carried valuable merchandise, very expensive gold and diamond jewelry, Bud, by New York permit, carried a pistol for protection.

"I hate those things," Shirley told him whenever he inadvertently displayed it after a trip and slipped it into the table drawer beside his bed.

"So do I," he shrugged. He had once been robbed at gunpoint. "Just a precaution."

At the beginning of their marriage Shirley had accompanied Bud on these trips. But when they acquired Harry she preferred to stay home and not subject the dog to the vicissitudes of car travel. Besides, Harry would occasionally get nauseous during the long drives and she objected to his being caged when they stopped at motels.

Bud, although he barely tolerated the loneliness of these road trips as he grew older, did not openly protest. His first wife had divorced him because of his absences.

All in all, profiting from the problems inherent in their earlier marriages, they had negotiated the coping mechanisms that made them a reasonably contented couple. The hardest issue to compromise was Harry and Shirley's overweening affection for him. Shirley loved animals and in the early days of their marriage, Bud put pleasing his new wife as his number one priority. He had never expected her to be so overwhelmingly devoted and protective. It wasn't that he particularly disliked Harry. Indeed, he went out of his way to compliment Harry's good looks and intelligence.

"He's smart as a whip," Harry would say whenever Harry quickly obeyed a command.

"Brilliant," Shirley would agree, obviously loving any complimentary comments about Harry.

Harry was a white standard poodle. They had named him Harry after an old song that they had remembered. "I'm just wild about Harry," which she often hummed while running the wire brush through Harry's white coat. Coming from championship bloodlines, he was regularly groomed by expensive groomers.

When Bud was not on the road, Harry slept at the foot of their bed. But when Bud went away on his business trips, Shirley let him sleep with her, loving the feel of his furry body next to her bare flesh. Sleeping with Harry made her feel safe and protected when she was alone.

Once, when Bud was traveling and Harry was about four, she discovered that Harry's affectionate doggy lickings were so insistently pleasurable that his ministrations actually induced an intense orgasm. She had also discovered that during the process she had actually reached for Harry's underparts and stroked them, desisting when she realized that she had somehow crossed a forbidden line. Not that. Never that, she told herself. Besides, she had heard stories that such couplings could be dangerous and it was possible, someone had told her, to get attached in that

147

way, requiring outside help to tranquilize the dog. She knew she would never be able to bear the terrible shame of such a discovery.

But she felt no guilt at having her beautiful doggie offer his delicious tongue caresses. To be sure, there was some residual shame in the practice, which happened when Bud was at work and she was alone with Harry. It became a kind of ritual in her life and she assumed that this was one of those unspoken secret taboos that occurred frequently between other females and their beloved canines, but was always far too embarrassing to share with others.

Without her realizing it at first, her relationship with Harry had consequences in terms of her sex life with Bud. Once, they had been truly compatible in that regard. She had loved to have Bud make love to her, but, increasingly, she found less and less satisfaction in the process and she found herself making more and more excuses to keep that part of their domestic life to a minimum. Mostly, she feigned health reasons.

"I'm just not myself, Bud," she told him as she searched her mind for excuses. Headaches, nausea, a cold coming on, a sore throat and a host of women's ailments.

"You should see a doctor, Shirley," he advised.

"I will, Bud. I promise."

Of course, she knew she could not keep him at bay forever and on occasion would submit, although the activity left her cold, totally without feeling. But then, for that, she had Harry. He had never failed her.

There were other little moments of friction, mostly about leaving Harry in a kennel. Once when Bud's son, now living in San Francisco, invited them to Thanksgiving dinner, Shirley refused to go on the grounds of being unable to bear leaving Harry in a kennel.

"Well then, let's put him on a plane," Bud suggested.

"In the baggage compartment?"

"Why not? Others do it."

"Not for my Harry. No way. Besides, it's so far," she argued.

"He's only a dog, Shirley," Bud protested. "Then hire a dog sitter. There must be plenty around who would like to live in a Fifth Avenue apartment and take care of a dog."

A couple of years ago, they had tried such an arrangement, but, on their return, Harry looked grungy and unwell and Shirley vowed she would never let that happen again. There were other incidents as well. Shirley refused to go to an important dinner with Bud's boss because Harry was sick with one of the many dog ailments, real or imagined, that sent Shirley off to the vet.

"Do you realize how much Harry is costing at the vet?" Bud complained.

"Harry's well-being is very important," Shirley declared.

"His medical costs are more than both of ours combined."

"And well worth it."

"Those damned vets are robbers. They take advantage of your devotion."

"Harry is an important part of our lives."

"Maybe too important," Bud muttered.

"There is no substitute for the non-judgmental love of a dog."

It was a frequent and time-honored homily which Shirley uttered often.

As Bud's complaints escalated, this was always her first line of defense. The fact was that maintaining Harry was a costly enterprise, but when he referred to the expense, Shirley countered with anger and recrimination.

"All you think about these days is money," Shirley told him.

"Business stinks."

"Then we'll cut down," Shirley said, noting that the matter was getting out of hand. What she meant was that she was willing to cut down on anything but Harry's maintenance. Bud grew more and more persistent.

"Why does Harry need an exclusive dog walker? I see dog walkers schlepping sometimes eight dogs at a time. And is there any need of

Harry going every week to a groomer? Those are extras that we can do without."

"You hate him, Bud. That's what this is all about."

"I don't hate him. I only hate what he costs."

"He has needs. Besides, he's beautiful and loves to be well groomed."

"How do you know that? Does he talk?"

"He communicates in his own fashion."

As time went on, the discussions on the subject of Harry became more heated. Bud developed a cough that was persistent and resisted all medications.

"The doctor thinks it's an allergy," he told Shirley. "It could be something that has to do with Harry."

"That's ridiculous."

"Lots of people are allergic to dogs."

"Cats mostly."

Nevertheless Bud did go to an allergist. To his disappointment, the doctor found no allergies.

"I was hoping it was because of my dog," Bud told the allergist.

"Thank God," Shirley said when he reported the allergist's findings.

"Who would have had to leave?" Bud asked, making it sound like a joke. He was finding that, more and more, the dog was taking over Shirley's life.

"I believe you're jealous, Bud," Shirley told him during a particularly heated argument.

Bud flushed with anger. The implication had a telling effect on him.

"You seem to care more about him than you do about me."

It was true, she noted to herself. Harry's companionship, his non-judgmental affection, his sensual ministrations had, by then, become an essential part of her existence. She was, in fact, leading a double life, secretive, clandestine and, she admitted to herself, deliciously sensual and exciting and perfectly safe. It was not as if she was having a real affair.

She continued to rise early to take Harry to the park, where he could frolic in freedom and play with his four-legged friends during the period when the park allowed such activities in the early mornings in certain specified areas. She loved watching his sleek graceful body as he moved with aristocratic bearing among what she considered inferior specimens in the pecking order of canine beauty. In the course of these outings, she began to note that Harry was beginning to show a particular partiality to a female chocolate lab who he was perpetually trying to mount without much success.

At first it struck her as amusing, but when the exclusiveness of the friendship became more noticeable, she spoke to the owner, a dour man with a gray beard who rarely fraternized with the dog owners. His dog's name was Milly.

"I hope she's been spayed?" Shirley inquired pleasantly one morning.

"You think I want her to have a lot of bastard puppies," the man grunted, turning away.

But despite the lab's being neutered, Harry continued to run after her with predatory intent. Soon it became apparent that Harry was not interested in socializing with any other dog but Milly. At times, Shirley had to literally pull him away by releashing and scolding him. It did little good. As soon as he was unleashed he ran toward Milly, who, despite her reluctance to Harry's sexual desires, seemed to enjoy the process.

Finally, in a fit of pique, Shirley addressed Milly's owner.

"Your dog is annoying my Harry," she told him.

"Looks to me as if it's the other way around."

"She's deliberately baiting him," Shirley protested.

"She's a woman," the bearded man said, smiling, showing a line of browning teeth.

No matter how hard she tried to rebuke Harry for his interest in Milly, Harry would persist. It began to take away all the joy of the morning. As she grew more and more agitated, she tried to explain the situation to Bud.

"It's unhealthy. He should be socializing with the other dogs as well."

"Hell, he's got a crush on the lab. What's wrong with that? Besides, you say she's been neutered."

"Not as far as Harry is concerned."

"So where's the harm?"

"She's so beneath him," Shirley mumbled, as if to herself.

Bud dismissed her complaint with amusement.

"What are you, a dog dating service?" He chuckled and patted her cheek. She resented his indifference.

"I don't know what he sees in her."

For a few days, she kept Harry away from that area of the park. But every time she took him in another direction, he strained at the leash and she needed all her strength to keep him from leading her toward his favorite destination. When alone with Harry, she would whisper into his ear as he ministered to her.

"You mustn't go near that terrible Milly. She's bad medicine."

But the deprivation of keeping Harry away from his morning ritual in the park was having a noticeable effect on the dog. It was Bud who noticed it first.

"He looks, well, hangdog. And he's losing weight."

"I'll have to take him to the vet," Shirley told him. Of course, she knew the cause of his weight loss. She noticed something else as well. He was getting less affectionate.

She found herself losing sleep, unable to concentrate, paying less and less attention to Bud, who was becoming increasingly annoyed with her general lack of interest, especially in him. She was taking less care of herself, paying less attention to her own grooming and neglecting the most routine household chores.

"Is something wrong?" Bud asked. It became a persistent refrain.

"I'm fine. Just a bit under the weather."

"You seem depressed, Shirley," Bud told her. He advised her to see a shrink.

"Don't be silly," she assured him. She had enough self-awareness to understand the cause of her troubles. How could she possibly explain this to a psychiatrist?

Finally, noting the effect this forced deprivation was having on Harry, she took him once again to the dog run in the park. Harry made a beeline for Milly and they began to frolic in the usual way. She had never seen Harry more visibly excited. She grew angry at the sight and again accosted Milly's owner.

"You see the effect on him," she cried. "This must stop."

"What must stop?" the bearded man asked, his attitude as reactive as hers.

"Your dog is having a bad effect on mine."

"Doesn't look that way to me. Hell, she gives him a boner."

"I demand that you keep her away from him."

The bearded man shook his head and walked away from her. She followed.

"I don't want you to bring her here any more. Do I make myself clear?"

She was becoming increasingly agitated. She poked a finger close to the bearded man's face.

"I'm warning you," she said with obvious menace.

"Who the hell do you think you are?" the bearded man said, shaking his head. "You don't own this place. It belongs to all of us. You don't like it, keep your fancy mutt out of here."

"Your dog is a whoring bitch," she cried, raising her voice. Other dog owners turned around to stare. The bearded man looked at them, pointed to her with his thumb, then pointed to his forehead and made a twirling motion.

"And you're off your rocker, lady."

Furious and angry, she re-leashed Harry and dragged him away, snarling and resisting the pull on his leash. That day Bud was on the road and she was alone. In the apartment Harry was surly and disobedient and she tried everything she knew to calm him down. He would not touch any of the snacks she gave him and left his food untouched.

Later that night when she got into bed, she tried coaxing him up to join her. Instead he lay on the floor in front of the bed, his head in his paws.

"Please Harry," she whimpered. "Don't be like that. You know I love you. Please come to me. How can you do this? Haven't I been everything to you? What has she ever done for you?"

But no amount of sweet talk moved him and she cried herself to sleep.

When Bud got home three days later, he found ominous changes in the general atmosphere. Harry was confined to a cage in the middle of the living room and Shirley seemed angry and distracted. Her complexion was pasty and her hair unkempt. She looked like she hadn't slept for days.

"He's being punished," Shirley said, throwing the dog a menacing glance.

"For what?"

"He knows why," Shirley muttered.

"So you put him in prison," Bud said, trying to lighten the mood. It didn't help and he became worried that the dog was overwhelming her life and greatly impinging on his own. Worse, she seemed to direct all her attention to the dog, addressing him, mumbling epithets, threatening him with dire consequences and talking to him in increasingly angry tones. She did release him to take him outside, but always returned in short order.

"Let me take him," Bud protested. She was adamant.

"No way."

As soon as she returned from taking Harry for a brief walk, she would return and place him in his cage. He was no longer being regularly groomed and looked shabby and unkempt. He was not permitted in the bedroom but was kept in his cage whenever he returned to the apartment. Nor did Shirley rise early to take him to the park.

He wasn't quite certain how to handle the situation, but he feared that her obsession with Harry was having a dire effect on her mental health and, most of all, their marriage.

"This has got to stop, Shirley," he told her. "We have got to get rid of that dog. He's making you nuts."

"Oh no." She turned to Harry, who looked forlorn in his cage. "I'll show him who's boss. When I'm through he'll never go near that bitch again."

"You mean this is all about that other dog in the park?"

Bud was totally confused. It seemed such a trivial matter. He shook his head in despair.

It was becoming increasingly apparent to him that she was having some sort of mental crisis. He tried his best to be gentle and understanding, but nothing he did could direct her attention away from her fixation with Harry. Still, he postponed giving her an ultimatum, hoping that she might understand that her obsession with Harry was becoming too serious to ignore.

"You've got to get help, Shirley," he persisted.

"Stop making me out to be some kind of loony. Harry has got to learn how to conduct himself around here."

"But what has he actually done to make you so angry?"

"Believe me, he knows."

After he was home for a week, she seemed to be beginning to relent in her program of punishment for Harry. Perhaps, Bud thought, things might be getting back to normal. Maybe, Bud reasoned, he was overreacting. He had been on the verge of tossing his marriage, but suddenly she had turned reasonable.

"I think he's learned his lesson," Shirley said one evening.

In the morning when he awoke, she was gone. In the living room Harry's cage was empty. Obviously, she was taking Harry to the park. All would soon be well again, he thought.

Shirley approached the park with some trepidation. Harry was not straining on his leash. He was being patient and obedient, stopping along the way to sniff at a hydrant and patches of grass that surrounded some of the trees along the way. With growing optimism, she approached the park and soon found herself in the area where the dogs were unleashed.

She unfastened the hook that tethered Harry to his leash. For a long moment, he stood frozen, watching the other dogs.

"He's learned his lesson," she thought. A great burden seemed lifted from her heart. She bent down and whispered in his ear. "You see, my darling," she whispered. "Everything will be as it was."

At that moment, Harry stiffened, sniffed, then, like a bolt of lightning, ran toward Milly.

"Harry," Shirley screamed. "Don't you dare!"

She ran after him, opening her purse as she ran, catching up to the two dogs. Suddenly, she was brandishing a pistol.

"Lousy whore," she said, addressing the brown lab, who looked up at her with an uncomprehending gaze. She pointed the pistol directly between the dog's eyes and fired.

Then she looked down at Harry.

"You see what you made me do," she said, dropping to her knees and embracing her dog. Suddenly in a whispery voice she began to sing: "I'm just wild about Harry."

RISK AND REWARD

"He kept squeezing my thigh," Maureen said. "See, I have a mark."

She showed him, opening her robe. Josh looked at the faint imprint, bending over on the couch and kissing it.

"Poor baby," he said, then straightening and nodding. "A good sign."

"Easy for you to say," she mocked, winking. "He's awful, Josh."

You'll have to hold your nose and close your eyes," Josh said. "We need the son-of-a-bitch. He's the green-lighter with the purse strings and power. I really need this loan."

"I'm not into business, Josh. You know that," she said, haughtily, shaking her head. She studied him and saw the anguish and pain on his handsome features. She hadn't bargained for this. Not on my resumé, she thought, having grown accustomed to the lavish lifestyle he had given her for the past six months, the clothes, the travel by private jet, the apartment in which they lived, the furnished penthouse in the Bristol that he rented for thirty thousand a month.

She was nearly fifty now, a well-guarded secret, still fashion model exquisite, with a body carefully maintained for draping and showing off designer clothes. By every standard, she knew she could still turn an eye. In fact that was her occupation, to be stunning and statuesque. It took hard work, commitment and funding. While the paymasters had changed, the occupation persisted long after her modeling career had changed venues.

Josh was hardly the first of her devoted male worshippers, but she had decided that he had potential as a keeper. Hadn't he left his wife of ten years for her? The divorce was messy, the usual financial arguments. That wasn't her business, although she knew it would water down his personal net worth, which, was now, as he loudly proclaimed, at serious risk, a very worrisome condition. After all, she lived through the "generosity" of wealthy men and her value, she was well aware, would inevitably diminish with the passage of time.

Maureen was a realist. Her looks were her main asset and its presentation was her principal and only major concern. She was obsessively high maintenance and costly. As she aged, the price grew higher in time and money. She worked with her personal trainer three times a week and spent many hours with her hairdresser, make-up artist, manicurist, nutritionist, cosmetic dermatologist and a professional shopper to keep her wardrobe au courant with the latest designer clothes. She knew, of course, how to wear them, move in them, show herself off in the best light.

She had grown up, pampered in an upper-middle-class home in northern California, the youngest of three siblings. Pretty from birth, she was the favored child and had taken up modeling in high school. Instead of college, she went east and was quickly signed by one of the top model agencies and had had a good twenty-five year run. Her siblings were scattered now, having drifted away, and their communication with her relegated to occasional e-mails.

Both her parents were dead, having died early. She had been "on her own" for more than twenty-five years. She had earned enough for her elaborate personal maintenance, but as she grew older and the modeling jobs dwindled, she grew more and more dependent on other sources, mostly wealthy men.

To a number of them, she was "arm candy" and she knew it. Once she had actually been a "trophy wife," having married a much older man who was a serial groom. Unfortunately, the prenup she had signed left her with little to show for it. More and more, she was on the lookout for some permanent arrangement, a situation that came with a guarantee that would cover the cost of her maintenance and assure her lifestyle.

Marriage, of course, was an obvious option, but the requirement of catering to the needs of a wealthy husband with its heavy social obligations and intimate commitments was more of a fallback position, a compromise she was prepared to make as a last resort and Josh seemed a logical candidate. She would rather have preferred a situation in which she was merely required to appear, a presentation to be admired, spending her time preparing for a "showing," much like her days as a model.

Over the years, she had learned how to fully exploit her most valuable asset, her looks. To embellish them, she contrived a "look" and "persona" based on her modeling experience, a practiced coolness which made her seem deep and mysterious, although she knew she was neither. She had mastered the art of being a good listener and appearing intelligently engaged in discussions on most subjects, from politics to art to science, although she read only the gossip columns and those sections that dealt with clothes and beauty enhancement.

Men, she had discovered early on, were captivated by her looks and quickly professed their love for her. Although it had baffled her at first, she grew to accept the idea. Indeed, she had gotten used to it and she noted that it did give her a certain power, which she happily exploited.

At thirty-two she had her first facelift, at forty-three her second and, in between, surgical nips and tucks and Botox and Restylane injections. She likened these procedures to necessary maintenance, as if she were an operating railroad.

There was, of course, an obligatory sexual side and she had applied herself to learning all of the technical aspects of satisfying male needs in that area. She took little pleasure in the practice, but considered it a necessary condition of her lifestyle. She had learned, too, that no matter how adept she became in the process, sooner or later men, the kind of men in her target orbit, needed change and variety and she had learned all the little signs of eventual disinterest. In the heady Manhattan world of wealth and status in which she operated, the competition was fierce and battalions of younger and younger hopefuls were always entering the arena.

Being a realist, she knew there was a downside to her spectacular beauty . . . time. All of her energy was mounted to defend her against the encroachments of time, the ultimate enemy. Increasingly, she had become aware of her need for a more guaranteed arrangement.

Josh and she had been together for six months now and she had moved in with him to the Bristol, a super luxury complex on Lexington Avenue. Josh was not yet forty and she had passed herself off as the same age. To do so required hard work, money, commitment and time.

To hide her age, she had disposed of her driver's license years ago and used her subway fare card as her photo ID, although she never used the subway. Not ever. She had let her passport expire and told him she hated travel to foreign countries, which, at least temporarily, foreclosed on her getting another.

Like most of the others, Josh had fallen head over heels in love with her. For her part, he was very acceptable and projected style and money, although, as she had recently discovered, the money aspect was increasingly shaky and he was panicked over the possibility of bankruptcy.

Applying her sense of realism, she knew that the curtain was falling on her long run, although she continued to believe that she could pass as arm candy or a trophy wife for a few more years. What she needed now was security, real security, for the days when her assets, which were dimming, were completely gone. Unfortunately, the promised guarantees of her intended spouse were in immediate danger.

"This loan is a matter of life and death, baby," he told her, making it clear on numerous occasions that without this loan, he'd lose everything. His increasing whining was unnerving. Nevertheless, out of necessity, she reluctantly accepted her supportive role.

Her assigned mission that evening, was to charm the hell out of Myron Glass, the billionaire green-lighter for the bank loan that Josh needed desperately. At this point, he had been to every bank in New York and had been turned down by each of them, except Glass, whose rare privately owned bank was "considering" Josh's loan. The bank fees were out of sight, but Josh was as desperate as Glass and his bank were greedy.

"It's all over my head," she insisted.

They had dinner at Le Cirque, which was attached to the Bristol complex, one of Manhattan's most prestigious eateries, where they dined frequently and Mario always gave them a choice table. He made a huge fuss over Maureen, double-kissing her, and showering her with compliments. Maureen, used to such tributes, accepted it with a cool nod and a faint smile. It was, of course, expected and she knew Josh loved the performance. She was well aware that a man who appeared to possess a beautiful woman was envied for his imagined virility and superiority, a God among men.

Glass, pushing sixty, fat bald, and bathed in what Maureen thought was a sickening fragrance, was not averse to the attention. Like Maureen, he was used to it, but for different reasons. He controlled a lucrative money faucet and understood his prerogatives and his power.

Worse, he had opinions. He hated politicians, and blamed the poor, especially blacks and Mexicans, for their own plight. He was stubbornly obstinate about the rightness of his positions and all his supplicants knew better than to disagree with him.

In retrospect, as she lay beside Josh, she pondered what he had characterized as "a good sign." It wasn't just a squeezing. It was a stroking and it stopped just short of her panty line. With beaus and lovers she was tolerant and at times encouraging of such conduct and if the occasion called for it she reacted with mutuality. She woke Josh.

"A good sign, you said. His hand was headed north."

"It didn't," Josh muttered.

"What should I have done?"

"In this case?"

"You said charm him, Josh. This wasn't on the menu."

"You did exactly the right thing, baby. You didn't make a scene. Considering how important it is to both of us."

"I let him keep on stroking through dessert."

"When would he ever have such an opportunity to stroke one of the great beauties of New York?"

"The man's a pig."

"Yes he is. A greedy fat billionaire pig. But that pig stands between us and the abyss. He's our last chance and he knows "it.""

"And if his hand had headed further north, what was I supposed to do?"

"But it didn't," Josh mumbled, embracing her, leaving the question unanswered.

"Would it have made a difference?" she asked.

He didn't answer, having drifted to sleep or feigning it.

"He's making me jump through hoops," Josh said, a few days later. "More numbers. More accountant charges. More lawyers. I'm really feeling the pressure now. And he wants us to have dinner again."

They took him to La Grenouille and once again, he sat between them and put his hand on her thigh, stroking it. Her eyes met Josh's who received the signal and shrugged. But this time Glass devoted himself almost exclusively to Maureen, practically ignoring Josh, who sought an opening to get into the subject of his loan.

"It's looking good," Glass told him, "but you have to be patient."

"I'm being pressed, Myron," Josh said. "I guarantee you, though, with your loan, I'll pull through with flying colors."

"Will you?" Glass said with a cryptic smile. Josh had explained to her that if the loan defaulted, Glass and his bank would own everything.

Maureen felt Glass's hand go north, as she had put it to Josh. She froze but said nothing, although she did resist by putting her hand over Glass's to keep it from going further.

"He really needs this loan," Maureen said, interjecting, although she never had before. Josh nodded his approval of her remark. "It will be good business for your bank."

"You think so, little lady," Glass said, offering a big smile. His teeth, Maureen noted, were like Chiclets. Besides, she knew implants when she saw them.

"I do," Maureen said in a cool but emphatic tone. She exchanged glances with Josh, who blinked his eyes in approval.

"I really value your opinion, Maureen," Glass said, sliding his hand from under hers, then quickly embracing it and applying the pressure of familiarity and endorsement. "You say we should grant this loan?"

"Absolutely," Maureen said.

"She has a sixth sense about business matters," Josh said.

"A regular financial genius. I could tell the minute I laid eyes on her," Glass said, chuckling.

"Tell you the truth," Josh said. "I trust her gut reaction more than the numbers."

"Beauty and brains, a rare combination," Glass said smiling.

It was laughable, Maureen thought, since she hadn't a clue to any of the business implications. Nor was she interested, except for the negative impact it might have on her.

"So you think we should grant this loan?" Glass said, showing her his row of Chiclets. He squeezed her hand and she returned the squeeze, which she was certain he would interpret as a promising sign.

"Of course you should," Maureen purred.

"Tell you what," Glass said while Josh was signing the credit card receipt. "You both come to my office tomorrow and we'll see what we can do."

Both, she thought, amused and not surprised. When they parted outside the restaurant Glass gave her a strong hug and his thick lips sought hers in a goodbye kiss, but before it landed, she quickly turned her lips away.

"He's in love," Josh said, winking at her, playing the comment as a joke.

"Poor jerk," Maureen shrugged. Of course, she knew the signs. "But you did say charm him."

"You were brilliant," Josh said.

"Was I?" Maureen said, wondering where all this was going. She was silent for a while. "Suppose he makes it a condition of the loan?" Maureen asked. She had been picturing in her mind such a scenario.

"I don't understand."

"Yes, you do," Maureen said.

"There are laws against such things."

"Just suppose, then."

He turned his eyes away, thought a moment, then said:

"I would never let that happen. Never. I'd rather go bankrupt. No way. Nada. "

She knew better. Her experience with men had taught her where their priorities lay. Business was warfare and unforgiving. No holds barred. Anything to gain an advantage.

"Even if he says, no deal unless . . . "

"Then it would be no deal."

"Are you sure?"

"Beyond the shadow of a doubt. I would never subject you to such a humiliation. As if you were a piece of meat to be bartered around."

"Like a prostitute."

"I love you, darling. I couldn't bear it."

She wondered if she could, picturing the man, naked and ready, his big belly hanging low over his engorged thing. Actually, she thought, having been with many men in that way, doing it had been pro forma, a price one paid for the privileges of her lifestyle. Concentrating on the technical aspects only, it had become a kind of out-of-body experience. She chuckled.

"What's so funny?" Josh asked.

"Nothing, really," she said.

They showed up at the appointed time in Glass's elaborate antique-ornamented office, one wall filled with civic service plaques and pictures with Glass with various political leaders and celebrities. Another wall was festooned with what she knew were certain works of art by famous painters. The carved wooden desk was large, polished and totally clean of papers. Glass got up from behind the big desk and greeted her with a tight embrace and a handshake for Josh.

He took her hand and led them to a conversational grouping off to one side of the large office and he sat down across from her and Josh who sat on the facing couch.

"We're almost there, Josh," Glass said after some small talk about the weather. It was a sunny spring day and she wore a beautiful beige Valentino dress with a hemline that showed her long shapely legs, which she crossed with polished provocation. She knew exactly where the hem would fall. He could not keep his eyes off her crossed legs.

"Almost?" Josh asked.

"There are still some Ts to cross," Glass said, unable to keep his eyes averted from her legs. Occasionally she would reverse legs, offering a quick view of her inner thigh.

"Like what?" Josh asked, clearly disappointed, his expectations crushed. All morning, he had told her, he had called his creditors, promising that he was about to close his loan.

"So when can we expect the loan to go through?" Josh asked. "Surely you have all the guarantees." She noted that a film of perspiration had sprouted on his lip. "I'm up against certain deadlines that must be met."

"Yes, Josh," Glass said. "I'm well aware of that."

Glass could not pull his eyes away from Maureen's crossed legs.

WARREN ADLER

"But it still looks good?" Josh asked, unable to hide an air of desperation.

"We're just assessing the risks," Glass said. "You know this business, Josh. It's all about risk and reward." He turned to Maureen and winked. "Don't you agree, Maureen?"

"Risk and reward," she said coolly. "That about covers everything."

"I'm sure you've taken risks in your life," Glass said, addressing Maureen.

"It's the rewards that count," she said. Glass nodded as if she had said something profound. She met his glance, assessing him, remembering the image of him she had conjured earlier. At these close quarters she felt somewhat neutral, although his scent was still vile. Turning to Josh, she could see that he was suffering.

"The man's a sadist," Josh said when they had left the office. "He's playing games with us."

"Us?" Maureen said.

"It's pretty obvious," Josh muttered.

"Is it?"

Of course it was. She was, she knew, coveted. The signs were clear. She understood the role and how it should be played. Glass wanted to possess her like a prized show horse. Despite the fact that she was past her prime, she still had the right stuff. Certain men would give anything to be admired by her. It validated their manhood. To possess her and exhibit her as a private ornament was a victory of sorts and her contrived aloofness made the victory of possession all the sweeter. Josh had torn his life apart to possess her. Others had, as well. She had grown used to the temporary nature of their obsessions, and she was always on the lookout for the inevitable alternative.

When Glass kissed her goodbye, he whispered what she knew would come sooner or later.

"Call me," he said.

Back at their apartment, Josh paced the floors.

"It's pretty obvious what he wants," Josh said. "The fat bastard."

She deliberately did not comment.

"Will it make the difference?" she asked watching his face. His hesitation gave her his answer.

"Don't even think it," he said.

"Of course, there would be no guarantees."

"With that crud? No. No guarantees. He uses people. He tortures them. That's his modus operandi."

"Risk and reward," she said, a deliberate sigh riding in her tone.

"I won't hear of it," he muttered. She interpreted that to mean "don't tell me about it."

"He wants me to call him," she said, watching his face. He shook his head, his cheeks flushed.

"The bastard," he sneered. "The evil bastard."

He paced the room and muttered to himself. After a long pause, she said "I know how to handle these things."

He continued pacing, contemplating. Finally he stopped and looked at her.

"Are you sure?" he asked.

She nodded, offering a thin, cryptic smile. He had, she knew, given her carte blanche. Typical, she thought, hardly shocked. That night they made love. During the process her thoughts were elsewhere, contemplating the image of Glass that had again formed in her mind. What did it matter? she snickered to herself. They were all wired by nature to react in a similar way.

She met Glass in his office late the next day. He sat down beside her on the couch, then opened a bottle of Dom Perignon and poured the bubbling liquid into two crystal flutes. Her attendance at his office was an acknowledgment of a willingness to negotiate, an opening gambit.

"I drink to the most beautiful woman in New York," he said, his hand shaking slightly as he lifted his glass.

"Thank you, Myron," she said, barely smiling, taking a tiny sip. He drank half the glass.

"I can't keep my eyes off you," he said, showing his Chiclet teeth. She allowed her glance to meet his eyes and hold it there. Yes, she decided, he was hooked. She let her eyes drift and studied his office. She assumed that the wooden desk and other furnishings were antiques, although they could be faux, along with the paintings. The plaques and pictures of Glass with celebrities indicated a man eager to display his connections. His office was quite obviously an extension of his ego. Look at me, look what I have. It was the inevitable cry of the little man inside the façade of a big man.

She did note photographs in a silver frame of a heavy-set woman and two heavyset grown daughters who appeared in additional pictures with equally heavy men and well-nourished children. Family man, egocentric, show-off, manipulator. She knew the type well.

He put his hand on her thigh, but did not stroke it. She had gone over it in her mind, calculating how the event would begin and when the moment would come when she needed to react. She knew the drill and all the moves that would ensue. She put her hand on his, sending the signal that she was now open to negotiation.

"I could really take good care of you, Maureen," he whispered.

"Could you?"

"Anything you want."

"Really."

He moved her hand to his mouth and kissed it.

"I adore you."

"I don't know, Myron," she said in a way that she knew would move the matter along.

"I'm a very direct person, Maureen. I am a man of quick decisions. I want you to be my girl." He squeezed her hand. "You know what I mean."

"I'm flattered, Myron, really I am. But, as you know, I'm committed."

"So am I," Glass said.

"I noted that," Maureen said, waving her free hand toward the pictures.

"We could be, you know what I mean, exclusive friends. You know what I'm saying. I'll take care of you, soup to nuts."

"That's an odd way to put it, Myron."

"I know I'm not exactly Brad Pitt. And I'll admit I've got some rough edges. But I have the means to be very generous. Very, very generous."

"I'm not sure I understand," Maureen said. She had heard all this before.

"An arrangement," Myron said. "I'll set you up. Your own place in the best location. Anything you want. This is not about money, Maureen. The sky's the limit. Really."

"You've lost your mind, Myron," she said coyly as his hand began to stroke her. He bent over and kissed her neck.

"You smell so beautiful," he whispered. His lips moved toward hers and she let him kiss her. It was a chore, since she hated the scent he wore.

"You said arrangement," Maureen said. He kept her locked in his embrace, but she had turned her face when he attempted another kiss. She put her hand on his thigh and began to stroke.

"Anything you want," Myron said.

"Anything?"

"Absolutely," he whispered. "Anything."

It was now or never, Maureen thought, the moment.

"I need guarantees, Myron."

The word had resonated in her mind since the dinner at Le Cirque."

She listened carefully for a reaction, a change in breathing pattern, a sigh. She was certain she was speaking in a language he would understand.

"Whatever you want," he said as she stroked.

She had observed his obvious reaction. "I can see that you are a man that usually gets what he wants and will do whatever it takes to get it."

His answer was to be a bit more aggressive as he moved his hands over her body. She stiffened and stilled his hands.

"I have needs too, Myron."

"Name them," Glass said. She could tell that he had entered business mode.

Calculations had run through her mind ever since Josh had given her carte blanche.

"I have numbers, Myron. They are based on my needs."

"Of course. Everybody has numbers."

"I'm a realist, Myron."

"So am I."

Here it was then, the crucial moment. It was time to test her true value.

"Here are my conditions," she said, holding his glance, eye to eye. "An apartment in my name, fully furnished, a steady income, say $600,000 a year. A ten-year contract. Two years in advance. For you, an exclusive friendship. You set the schedule. On my part, absolute fidelity. I will honor my commitment to the letter. And I want it in writing."

"Such a gold digger," Glass said laughing. He thought for a moment. "Tell you what."

She had literally held her breath awaiting his answer. She had decided in advance that there was no point in beating about the bush. No risk. No reward.

"I'm all ears."

"The apartment of your choice, in a neighborhood of your choice. Whatever it costs to decorate. I'll go $500,000 and five years. My schedule agreed. If not exclusive and I find out, the deal ends. And only one year in advance." He smiled showing his Chiclet teeth. "One more thing."

"What?"

Actually, she had expected a counteroffer. And, after all, five years was not too bad. It would bring her to her middle fifties and she would have the security and value of the apartment and what she might save. All in all, it was a deal she could live with.

"I would like a sample. Right now."

She thought about that for a moment.

"No samples, Myron. Not until you get rid of that godawful cologne you wear and you have signed the agreement and deposited the money in my account."

"You don't like my scent."

"It's awful, Myron."

"Really."

He moved away from her and stood up.

"I'll have everything ready by tomorrow." He winked. "Same time. Same station."

She got up and smoothed her dress. She felt his eyes surveying her.

"I'll take a bath," he said.

"A good one."

She was pleased by his reaction. She had established a ground rule. In the future there would be others. It would help her retain some semblance of dignity.

"Tomorrow then."

She felt his gaze as she walked across the room. She was proud of herself, of her assertiveness. She had established her value and would, of course, honor her commitment.

"You are a piece of work, Maureen," he said.

But before she opened the door, he called to her.

"What about the loan?"

"Your call, Myron. I've made it a rule never to interfere in business."

She offered a haughty glance and let herself out the door.

THE THEATERGOERS

Sara Harris loved the Broadway theater. Along with her friends Charlotte Broad and Emily Gold, who she had met in Tilden High School when they were growing up in East Flatbush, they had attended every Broadway show for fifty years. For the three of them it was a passion that transcended everything in their personal lives, through marriage, raising children, employment, divorce and widowhood.

Whatever life handed them, tragedy, joy or disappointment, in good times or bad, they managed to ply their passion. The Broadway show and the legitimate theater in general, which included off-Broadway and scores of little theaters scattered throughout the city, was the focus of their lives, the center of their universe. They knew every actor and actress that ever graced a stage. They knew the names of singers, dancers, directors, producers, choreographers, even costume and lighting designers involved in the New York theater world.

They watched the Tony awards each year with rapt attention and remembered who had won in every category and they scrutinized every newspaper and magazine that covered the landscape of their theatrical obsession.

With the exception of anything that directly affected live theater, like 9/11 or the occasional strike, no other subject or event ever penetrated their interest. If it wasn't about live theater it simply didn't exist for them. It was as if any energy applied to events outside the realm of theater were irrelevant. If asked, they would react with blank stares to any question which involved terrorism, the middle east, Congress, the White House, political campaigns, wars in general, lurking dangers from nuclear prolif-eration, the stock market, the world financial situation, sports, medicine or any other subject that did not have a relationship with live theater.

They saved every playbill from every show they ever attended and had stood outside the stage doors in good weather and bad to get the autographs of any actor who appeared. Their consistency was awesome and a bafflement to their families, most of whom were relieved not to attend any shows, although each woman had tried valiantly to instill a love for live theater in their children with not even modest success. As a result, deep chasms had opened between them and their families.

When Sara Harris' husband died, she mourned him appropriately, but to her two friends she confessed that she was delighted that she would never again have to endure his vitriol about her obsession with the theater.

"He hated the whole process," Sara told her friends, cataloguing his many objections. He especially despised the seats, accusing the theater owners and producers of packing them in like sardines just to make a buck. He was bored at the performances, often dropping off to nap. In his later years he used a device to augment his hearing but never turned it on. "It's the tourists and suckers who enjoy that drivel," he had ranted. It was the one issue that divided them.

Her two divorced friends each had a similar experience with their cast-off husbands and often referred to the reasons for their divorce as "having nothing in common with their spouses" or more specifically, "he hated the theater." They were, however, more militant and coura-geous than Sara and dumped their husbands early on in their marriages.

With their husband's gone and their children grown, they were no longer constricted by criticism of their theatergoing.

"Free at last. Free at last," was now the operating motto of their lives. With the exception of a very occasional and tiny twinge of guilt about how their persistent theatergoing had undermined their family life, they felt no remorse. The theater transcended everything. As they grew older, they had graduated from the second balcony, to the mezzanine, to the orchestra prodded by a modest prosperity and the normal sensory declines associated with aging.

They knew the various strategies to get discount tickets, and balanced comfort with affordability, making the proper connections to get seating in the first dozen rows. When other responsibilities intervened, which was rare, they had opted for matinees on Wednesdays and Saturdays, but as their outside obligations ebbed, they preferred evening performances, believing that in the evening the actors and the audience were more responsive.

Their perspectives and opinions of the various shows they saw differed somewhat from each other, often resulting in extended discussions which served to further enhance the experience. Sara loved to analyze the skill of the director and the psychology of the characters, often citing how the element of plot surprises were so crucial in creating tension and suspense. Charlotte's focus was mostly on the believability of the actors and how cleverly they could enter the persona of the fictional characters. And while they all loved musical theater, Emily had the uncanny ability to remember every lyric and could accurately sing most of the songs created by the composers.

Their lives took a more dramatic turn when Charlotte and Emily were invited to move in with Sara after her husband died. At the time of his death, Sara lived in a large house in Forest Hills and her two friends were happy to accept the new living arrangement and share expenses. Each had her own bedroom and bathroom and happily worked out a plan to manage the housekeeping and generally maintain a comfortable and tension-free existence. Their children, who they rarely saw, thought the arrangement "peculiar" and wondered aloud whether there was a sexual component involved, much to the amusement of the three women.

The fact was, as they each knew, that they had much in common, but the essential glue that held them together was their passion for live theater which had dominated their lives for half a century. One of their first acts upon living together was to convert Sara's pine-paneled rec room to an archive of all the theater paraphernalia they had acquired throughout their lives. File cabinets were filled with playbills, autographed pictures and notes that they had received from various stage stars were lined up around the room. On the walls, they had hung numerous posters from past shows. Clearly they had created a shrine to live theater.

As for the disposal of this vast cache after they were gone, they consulted lawyers who prepared legal documents that gave the material to museums that preserved such archives and artifacts for future generations. They were determined that such a collection would not fall into the hands of their disinterested heirs.

They were remarkably compatible and, while it was not often expressed, could define their relationship as affectionate, caring and, yes, loving.

"We are so lucky," Sara would often tell her two friends. "How many people in this world can find others with such passionate common interests?"

"And in the theater capital of the world," Emily chimed.

They were well aware that there were others in the city with the same obsessive interests and would see them often in theaters and at the stage doors after the shows, seeking autographs or a few sacred words from their idols. Indeed, when they were not attending the shows themselves, they would show up at lectures in which producers, stars and playwrights would share their experiences with their dedicated acolytes.

As for attending the theater, they worked out a routine that suited their lifestyle and had conceived of ways to time themselves and use the subway system to avoid the nerve-wracking traffic jams that occurred around show time, especially in the major Broadway theaters.

They would have dinner at Joe Allen's on 46th Street, making a standing reservation, usually on Thursdays and timing their meal to arrive at the theater, depending on the walk, about fifteen minutes before curtain so that they could glance over the playbill. Of course, they knew all the salient facts about the show in advance. At Joe Allen's, the exposed brick walls were festooned with row after row of posters of shows that had flopped, an ironic satirical flourish that spoke to those who immersed themselves in such theatrical lore. Naturally, the three friends had seen every one of the shows. In their lexicon, however, there were no flops, only financial disasters, which had nothing to do with the quality of the offerings. To the three women every play was wonderful in its own way.

At dinner, they would often discuss the relative merits of each show identified by the posters, often disagreeing, sometimes loudly, with the critic's pans that had contributed to the play's failure to attract an audience.

"They are so cruel," one of them would say, usually Emily, who was the softer and more compassionate of the group. She was also, as Sara would often remind her, less discriminating and therefore more likely to praise every show on the basis of it being there at all as its prime achievement. In many ways her two friends agreed with her.

"Look how hard those people, on the stage and off, work to create these wonderful shows for our benefit. Why do people have to be so mean and harsh? There are plenty of folks out there who would enjoy the show, if only the critics would not express their biased opinions."

"You have a point," Charlotte was bound to say, trying to be a peacemaker between Sara, who had a tendency to be somewhat harsher in her criticism, and Emily, although they never allowed conflicting opinions to get out of hand. The fact was that all three of them were accepting of what they saw on the Broadway stages, valuing the experience itself above all. They often would see a play two or three times and, of course, would attend all revivals, comparing them, mostly unfavorably, to the originals.

After the show, they would invariably go to Sardi's where they would order champagne cocktails and a slice of cheesecake and revel in being in the society of many of the stage actors who would have dinner at Sardi's after their performances.

What was remarkable about their theatergoing was that the three of them would always attend together. If one was sick, the other two stayed home until the third recovered. It was as if, they often joked, they had become one person. They never ever addressed the subject of what might happen if one of them died.

Sara Harris was the first to encounter this inevitability. She was, by then, sixty-five years old and had been diagnosed with cancer. During the immediate aftermath of chemotherapy, she could not attend the theater outings and although she insisted that her two friends go by themselves, they refused.

"Look," she would remonstrate, "we all knew in back of our minds that something like this would happen some day. Be realistic."

"We are, Sara. Like the three musketeers. One for all and all for one."

"That is ridiculous," Sara would reply.

"Not to us," Charlotte agreed, winking at Emily. "The experience would never be the same."

As her illness progressed and it became more apparent to Sara that she would not recover, she continued to press the point that her two friends should not curtail their theatergoing life because of her illness.

"I'm dying, girls." She had chuckled. "How many death bed scenes have we seen together? How shall I play it? Noble? Fearful? Regretful? Drawn out like in Shakespeare? Cynical like in Shaw? Heck, I loved my life, especially with my dear friends. So the producers will have to sell my empty seat. Shall I cry for their loss? No way. About the only thing I would regret is that I'll miss out on the new plays."

"Don't talk like that, Sara," Emily would say, tears rolling down her cheeks. At tragedies she was always the first to cry.

"True to form," Sara snickered. "After all, it's only make-believe."

She knew this was an unusual comment for her to make. It was never make-believe. In fact, to all three of them, it was truer than life. Such a statement, Sara knew was a harbinger of her inevitable demise. She was preparing them in the only way she knew how, dismissing herself from their company, giving them permission to go on with their passionate obsession with live theater without her, diminishing her role. It was hard going to convince them.

Finally when it was obvious that the end was near, her two friends sat beside her. By then she was having difficulty breathing, but her mind was still operating and she had decided on a course of action for her ultimate disposal.

"I want to be cremated," she told them, "and I want my ashes to be scattered over Shubert Alley."

Emily and Charlotte exchanged puzzled glances.

"Can you promise me that, girls?" Sara said.

"Of course we can," Charlotte said, already contemplating the logistics of such an action.

"What a wonderful idea, Sara," Emily said. "Isn't it, Charlotte?"

"I love it," Charlotte exclaimed. "It is a perfect dramatic moment. Where else but Shubert Alley, right smack in the heart of the Broadway theater district. What an absolutely lovely idea!"

"Perfect," Emily agreed. "That's exactly what I want as well."

"And me," Charlotte said.

"I can go peacefully now," Sara whispered.

They were the last words Sara would speak.

Arrangements were made by the two friends, even above the somewhat ingenuous protestations of Sara's children, but in the end, knowing how their mother's passion for the theater had dominated her life, they agreed. By then, Sara had become irrelevant to her children's lives. It was a condition both of her friends knew well since it had impacted on their families in the same way.

On the day of the event, a bright sunny spring day, they carried the vase in which Sara's ashes were kept and had lunch at Sardi's where they ordered champagne cocktails for three. The waiter, who had known them for many years, understood the gesture. When he put the third cocktail down in front of the empty chair on which they had placed the vase of Sara's ashes, he crossed himself and nodded respectfully. Holding back their tears, they raised their glasses and clinked the third glass in memory of their absent friend.

"It will never be the same," Charlotte sighed.

"Never," Emily agreed.

Although they ordered cheesecake for old time's' sake, they had no appetite and did not touch it. In any event the Sardi management picked up their check and their waiter refused their tip.

"You see," Emily said. "They always considered us a member of the theatrical family."

"Without us, where would they be?" Charlotte replied.

They left the restaurant and carried the vase the short distance to Shubert Alley. A light breeze had risen and they attracted little attention from the people that milled around looking at the posters and shopping at the store that sold theatrical memorabilia. They had determined that they would scatter parts of the ashes at various points in the alley.

Charlotte tipped the vase and spilled a small amount of ashes into the breeze, watching the specks float away. Then they moved to the another part of the alley and repeated the process.

Suddenly, the sound of earsplitting sirens broke the street din and a phalanx of police cars approached the street at either end of the alley. People in orange protective gear descended on the alley and quickly relieved Charlotte of the vase. Then they swiftly handcuffed the two women and herded them to a waiting police vehicle and shoved them inside, slamming the door behind them. Two people in protective gear accompanied them into the vehicle.

Both women were too stunned to speak. Aghast and frightened, they exchanged glances of complete bafflement. They felt the vehicle move and heard the sirens screech above their heads. They heard the crackling sounds of walkie-talkies as the people in their orange gear spoke in hoarse whispers through their masks. Neither woman could make out the words being spoken.

Charlotte was the first of the two to muster some semblance of composure.

"What have we done?" she asked, perplexed, barely able to comprehend their situation.

Is there a law against spreading ashes?, she wondered. Did such a law warrant this bizarre response? She was too confused to ponder such questions and the people in the protective gear were not able to communicate due to the screeching noise of the siren.

After a while, the vehicle stopped. The door opened and the men in protective gear brought them into a building and led them to a room in which a table and two chairs were provided. The women's handcuffs were removed and they were ordered by a disembodied voice to be seated. They noted that there was a mirrored surface on one wall of the room from which they quickly deduced they were being observed.

"Why are we here?" Charlotte asked the disembodied voice.

"On suspicion of endangering the health and safety of our citizens," the voice said.

Again Charlotte and Emily exchanged confused glances.

"Are ashes of dead people lethal?" Charlotte asked. She was quickly gaining confidence.

"We are analyzing the material," the disembodied voice said. "You are being temporarily incarcerated for the protection of others."

"Why are you analyzing the ashes?" Emily suddenly interjected. She, too, was beginning to regain her equilibrium.

"We can't take chances," the disembodied voice said, although Charlotte could detect a kind of diminishment of authority. "Anthrax is a deadly poison and is transmitted through the air."

"Anthrax?" Charlotte cried, totally confused. She looked toward Emily, who shrugged.

"It can be deadly," the disembodied voice said. "There have been incidents. Don't you read the papers?"

"No," Charlotte said flatly and truthfully. It was, however, clear to her by now.

"You think Sara's ashes are anthrax?" she said to the disembodied voices.

"Idiots," Emily said, proud of her sudden militancy. "You thought our dear friend's ashes were anthrax."

There was a long silence at the other end. After a few moments the door was opened and a group of official-looking men and women entered. One of the party, obviously the person in charge, addressed the women.

"The preliminary analysis has confirmed that it was not anthrax, but human remains. Please accept our apologies, ladies. We were just doing our job."

The two women looked at the group confronting them.

"You people," she began, hesitating as she surveyed the faces. "Do you think . . . " She paused, embellishing the drama of the comment from years of viewing such an action on the stage. "Do you think we would endanger the lives of anyone in the theater district?" She looked toward Emily.

"These people just don't understand the joys of theater. Now if you can give us back Sara's ashes, we will proceed with fulfilling her last wishes."

They were handed back the vase.

"Sara would have really enjoyed this," Charlotte said as they passed through the crowd of officials.

"She loved surprises," Emily agreed.

BIG JUDY

That summer we rented Mrs. Miller's garage in Long Beach, Long Island. It had been converted into a two-room shack. One was a bedroom with a double bed and another three-quarter bed jammed into its foot. The other passed for a living room with a table and chairs and a toilet. There was a shower outside. It was a dump. We called the place the "Den of Iniquity."

In our minds Long Beach was still classy then. It had nice tree-lined streets with pretty single-family houses. Lots of people lived there allyear round. It was a big step up from Rockaway where we had summered for years when I was a kid, right up to end of my college days. In Rockaway, our crowd stretched out for half a block in the sand and at night we hung out near the jukebox in front of the penny arcade on the boardwalk at 55th Street and danced the Lindy. We knew everybody.

Then we started fanning out, starting jobs, following the money, which is why we stepped up to Long Beach, a few miles up the beach from Rockaway. Jackie was already in his father's retail coat business in Harlem and I was the editor of a small weekly on Long Island. Hesh was with us, too, that year. He had just started in his father's garment manufacturing business and had his own car.

A few weeks before that summer began, North Korea had invaded South Korea and Truman had declared a police action and the U.S. was sending troops to Korea. We had all missed doubleU-doubleU-2 by a hair, and the idea of war was far from our minds. The vets had come back and were getting established. Some of the people in our crowd were getting married. We were all twenty-one and, at that moment in time, none of us had permanent girlfriends.

But girls were very much on our mind. In fact, that was the principal reason why we had rented Mrs. Miller's converted garage. We had a place to take them. Remember in those days we all, girls and boys, still lived with our folks. Few of us had cars then. This was before anybody in our crowd made it.

We'd barrel in to the "Den of Iniquity" after work on Friday night, jump into sport clothes and hit the boardwalk in front of the Nassau Hotel. A huge crowd of boys and girls about our age would gather there and eye each other until by osmosis groups would intersect and, if we were lucky, we might pair off. In those days this might lead to what they called heavy necking, which meant you might get your hands inside a pair of panties and, if you were really blessed, you might do some dry humping and get yourself a hand job. Things were opening up, though, and girls were supposed to be getting a lot bolder. You wouldn't have known by the experiences of the three of us.

In the context of today's world this might sound awful and insensitive, as if women were merely considered sex objects. They were to us, of course, but, deep down, both genders were looking for the same things. You got it. Love! The kind that Frank Sinatra sang about. The kind of love that made your heart ache with longing and the fear of losing it drove you mad with jealousy. Parting, losing one's love, gave the worst pain imaginable. Finding a girl to love and love you was the most important thing you could do. That was a fact although few would admit it.

Of course, we hid this craving for true love behind lots of noisy macho and exaggerated reports of our sexual peccadilloes. In those days, too, virginity was a prized possession. The girls were taught to save it until marriage. The boys were supposed to come to the marriage bed with experience, a double bind if there ever was one.

But don't forget, the technology of birth control was pretty basic. You wore a condom or pulled out in time. Girls were worried sick about getting pregnant. Abortion was illegal and those who did it were sleazy and unsanitary. Sex was a dangerous game, we knew, but well worth the struggle and the risk. Lucky you can't see the tongue in my cheek.

The three of us were barely okay in the pick-up department. I was pretty good-looking then and had my share of stares, but my tongue would hit the roof of my mouth and stay there when I tried to make an aggressive approach. Jackie was no better and Hesh was short. He had to make do with a kind of clown approach.

Some nights we just stood there in front of the Nassau hotel, cracking jokes, fooling around and hoping that some girls would make the first move. We were just about the worst there was on first moves. How we envied guys like Ziggy who was part of our Rockaway crowd and could make out like crazy even in Long Beach where the girls were slightly more stuck-up than the Rockaway females.

Ziggy wasn't even clean-cut. He had a cap of curly hair hanging low over his forehead, a big nose, swarthy skin and dark eyes. His father was a butcher. But he had a line on him like a magnet and dark eyes that could fix a double whammy on any girl who came into his field of vision.

"Hey, doll," he would say, immediately getting intimate by putting both hands on their shoulders and looking deeply into their eyes. "I've never yet met a girl like you, who is both good-looking and mysterious." Inside of five minutes he would have them eating out of his hand.

"You just compliment them, is that what you do?" Jackie would ask.

"It's all a question of sincerity," he would say. "They believe in me."

"God, you must have plenty to spare."

"More than enough."

"I'd be happy with your seconds," Jackie would say. We all would've.

"Sometimes I get so damned bored with it I haven't even got the will to unzip my fly." Ziggy liked to flaunt his abundance.

It was Ziggy who came up with Big Judy.

It rained a lot that summer. When it rained you couldn't go to the beach or the boardwalk and everybody disappeared, especially the girls. Our way of killing time on a rainy Sunday afternoon was to play poker. It usually grew into a big game, about seven guys. We played for what was then considered high stakes, a quarter and a half.

One Sunday Ziggy shows up with Big Judy. God knows where he found her. She wasn't bad looking for a big girl, not too much in the belfry. She had big tits and an ass to match. We tried to question her, but she shrugged a lot in answer to our questions. What we got out of her was that she lived with her grandmother in a house in Long Beach for the summer and that she was now working as a salesgirl in a store somewhere.

Ziggy was sweet to her, holding her around the shoulders and occasionally giving her a peck on the cheek. We hadn't started the game yet and were just sitting around the table getting rid of the restlessness. Also, it wasn't often that we had a girl present.

"She something?" Ziggy asked.

We all agreed just to be polite. She might not have been my choice, but she was, after all, a girl and that was something. Ziggy winked at us and squeezed one of her tits.

"Biggest tits in Long Beach," Ziggy said with a phony air of pride. Then he kissed her on the cheek. All Big Judy did was smile, but she never took Ziggy's hand off her tit.

We covered up our surprise with winks.

"Bet you'd all like to see what they look like?" Ziggy said. Again he kissed Big Judy. It was a kind of kiss of reassurance. The fact was that I was a bit embarrassed to be watching. Maybe the rest of us felt that, too, but not one turned his eyes away.

"These are my friends, doll. My best friends," Ziggy said with his usual sincerity. "One for all and all for one. Right, guys?"

We must have grunted assent, for he was unbuttoning Big Judy's blouse and she was saying nothing in protest, not even trying to stop him.

"This is going to be one big treat for my friends, isn't it, Judy? Ain't she the most beautiful thing you ever saw?"

"The best," Heshy said. Like the rest of us, he was bug-eyed, watching Ziggy open the girl's blouse and show us her tits encased in a big pink brassiere.

"Just look at this one," Ziggy said, maneuvering her left breast outside the cup. No question about its size with a big luscious nipple in a pinkish circle. It didn't hang either but stood straight out, big and fat, the kind we dreamed about.

There in front of us, Ziggy sucked the nipple of her left breast until it stood out like a big red finger. We were all struck dumb, of course. No question but that we had all grown hard-ons. If Big Judy was embarrassed, she showed no signs. She hadn't even blushed. Nor did I get the impression that she did this often. She just seemed too ordinary to be a whore.

"Show them both, doll," Ziggy said. He winked at us and sure enough Big Judy, who had been sitting down in a chair next to Ziggy, stood up, unhooked her brassiere, and stuck them out. Two beauties. No question about it. She could have been no more than nineteen and the tits were still firm and white and without networks of veins running just beneath the surface.

"God damn," Jackie said.

"The best," Hesh said, mesmerized with the sight.

"They're the real thing, aren't they, Judy?" Judy nodded slightly, although she seemed neutral about the matter. It was Ziggy who showed the pride.

"Go on guys, feel 'em," Ziggy said. "Judy's a great sport and you're all my friends." He stood up and kissed her full on the mouth, teasing one of her nipples with his fingers. "And any friend of mine is automatically a friend of Judy's."

I know one thing. I loved looking at those big tits. When she came my way, I reached out and fondled them, but I hadn't the guts, as Heshy had shown, to take one of them in my mouth.

Everyone got their feel and when Big Judy had made her rounds, Ziggy kissed her once again and addressed the group.

"Look, you guys deal me out the first few hands," he said. "Judy and I are going to go over to the other room and discuss some very major subjects." Again he winked as he led the bare-breasted woman to the bedroom.

Hesh dealt the cards for seven-card stud, but I can tell you that none of us really had our mind on the game. Besides, there was no door between where we were playing and the bedroom, although the double bed wasn't totally visible. In order to see what was going on you had to get up and walk toward the middle of the room.

Hesh dealt and during that first hand, I can assure you that we all got up at least once to get a gander at what was happening in the bedroom. It was very distracting. We managed to get through three hands when Ziggy came out of the bedroom alone.

He sat down on one of the chairs and, in all seriousness, announced:

"Now here's the way we're going to do this," he began. "You go in to see Judy after you deal. Stay as long as you want but not so you miss your next deal."

"You're kidding?" Hesh said, speaking for all of us. We knew he wasn't kidding. We also knew that there would be no hassle. Judy knew what she had to do.

"For free?" one of the other guys asked.

"Of course, for free," Ziggy said. "Judy's no whore. She just likes to be friendly." He smiled and held down a laugh with a hand over his mouth. When he had calmed down he said: "The most important thing to remember is to always treat her with respect."

"I don't believe this," Jackie said.

"You can't deny the evidence," Ziggy said.

"I just dealt," Hesh said.

"Be my guest," Ziggy said with a half-bow from the table and a flourish of his arm, which pointed in the direction of the bedroom.

"Do I use a rubber?" Hesh asked. I could tell he was a little nervous. Who wouldn't be? I was nervous as hell.

"Your call," Ziggy said. "Depends on your control." He shrugged and chuckled.

Hesh left the table and I deliberately folded a fairly good hand so that I could fake going to the bathroom. But my real reason was to see what Hesh was up to. He was up to it, all right, a little guy climbing up that big young woman.

When he came out he looked like the cat that swallowed the canary.

"That's one nice girl," he said, taking his place at the table.

By the time the deal fell to me, the others had already taken their turns. It seemed like part of the routine of the game. After they had done Judy, the others seemed unusually relaxed and immediately got their heads into the game. As for me, I was still nervous. I wasn't sure what to expect and there was, after all, something sleazy about a gangbang, especially if you were at the tail end. I frankly admit that I had been to a whorehouse once in Scranton, Pennsylvania, but that was different. You weren't so blatantly confronted by the fact that you were just one of a gang of men that had been there before you.

My mind also was not on the game. I was down about twenty bucks, which in those days, made a difference. My salary at the paper was only sixty bucks a week.

"Your turn, Willy," Hesh said. From his tone I knew he was impatient and ready for seconds and I got up from the table and handed over the deck to Ziggy who had not dealt yet.

To tell you the truth, the idea of doing Judy in sequence like this was not to my liking. I suppose I could have declined. No one was twisting my arm. Maybe I was afraid that my not going would somehow diminish me in the eyes of my friends. But I doubted it.

There was a serious side to my relationship with Jackie and Hesh. We really weren't afraid to share our dreams for the future and often as we three lay in bed in that bedroom in the Den of Iniquity, we would often exchange confidences about what we wanted to do with our lives and how we saw the future.

All three of us were sons of immigrant families, although all of us were born in the States. We knew about keeping our eye on the ball and getting ahead and becoming a success. But I swear to you underlying all this was still that thing that I spoke about at the beginning, falling in love. It wasn't manly, I suppose, to talk about it and, frankly, we skirted around the subject. But it was the God's truth. We all wanted to find someone to love and love us and have kids and that was as much a part of being successful as making money and realizing whatever other secret dreams we had.

I'm not saying that any of this was going through my mind when I went to the bedroom to see Judy. I don't know what was going through it. She was lying there, naked as the day she was born, staring up at the ceiling, her big tits like giant sunny side up eggs on her chest, her black pearly triangle of hair all shiny against the smooth white of her naked thighs.

When I came in she looked at me and smiled. She had good teeth and brown eyes and although her hair was mussed, it picked up a kind of halo from the way the sun peeked through the window behind her head.

"Hi, Judy," I whispered shyly.

"Hi."

"I'm Larry."

She held out her hand.

"Nice to meet you, Larry."

I smiled. I was more than a bit flustered and not a little hesitant. She must have sensed this, for she winked at me and hoisted herself up on the bed and reached out with both hands to undo my belt buckle. I was ready, no doubt about it.

"You want to wear a rubber?" she asked.

That puzzled me a little bit. Was she really willing to risk pregnancy or was I supposed to pull out just beforehand? What women did to protect themselves in those days was a bit of a mystery to me. But the thing I didn't want to happen was for her to become pregnant with my child. To be honest, it wasn't because I was worried about the consequences to her. I was more worried about having my sperm make a baby with someone whom I did not love, nor did I, frankly, feel was worthy of my love.

"Rubber," I stammered. In those days the word condom actually seemed dirtier than the word rubber.

She rolled it over me gently using busy little fingers that felt pretty good. Then she reached out with both her arms and drew me closer to her for a long soul kiss. She put her tongue deep in my mouth and I did the same with my tongue.

I wasn't thinking about the guys that went before me. Judy became for me a kind of sexual symbol for all women. She was gentle and giving and, despite what had gone on, she had a smell similar to the fresh ocean. With pants down to the ankles I climbed up on the bed and got comfortable at the right angle and she helped me head for home.

"Feel good, Larry?" she asked. I was surprised she had remembered my name.

"You?" I asked.

"Ummm," she said as she began to gyrate her hips.

Then something happened that came to me as a surprise. I had put my lips on hers, one hand kneaded a nipple of one of her breasts and I was pumping slow and easy trying to make it last. I must have had it in my mind to make a good sexual impression. Something macho like that. After all, she had a good basis of comparison with my best friends.

The damned thing melted away like chocolate on a hot day. I couldn't imagine why. One minute it was up to the mark, ready for total action, the next it was gone.

"Something wrong, Larry?" she whispered in my ear.

"Maybe the damned rubber," I muttered.

"Then take it off," she said gently.

I did and she tried to get things moving again with her hand.

"I can use my mouth," she said. As I say there was nothing phony or inhibited about Big Judy. She was as nice and gentle as can be. But I could tell that nothing she could do would be of any use. Such abrupt calamities happened to me later on in life; not many times, but enough to know that nothing, but nothing on earth, can do any good at those moments. Nothing.

"Never mind," I told her. Perhaps she caught some hostility in my tone. It was then that she said:

"I hope you'll still love me."

I didn't know what to say in response. But I got my pants on and zipped up pretty fast and without looking at her went back to the game.

Nobody paid much attention when I returned. Banging Judy was becoming old hat. I did the best I could to hide my sense of failure or was it rage. I wasn't sure. I tell you I was not happy with myself and not a little worried. Perhaps this experience would scar me for life, I thought, trigger a permanent impotence. My imagination ran rampant. A young man depends upon his cock to function on demand. I wanted a wife, kids. I was very depressed and it showed in my game.

"I'll pass," Ziggy said when it came his turn again to pay Judy a visit. Hell, for Ziggy it rained pussy and this was no novelty.

But Hesh wasn't one to pass it up. Neither was Jackie, although one of the others in the game passed. Then it became my turn again.

I was very frightened. I'll admit it. Another failure could spell psychological ruin. Or so I thought. Yet, despite everything, a strange feeling had come over me as I played the game and watched those who still wanted to visit Judy. By then, the takers had evaporated. They were more intent on the game. All but me who was the big loser. I think I was down nearly forty bucks. But somehow I got it into my head that only Judy could truly save me from a life of impotency and failure.

With some trepidation I went into the bedroom. Judy was waiting just as I had seen her before. Only the light in the room had changed, the setting sun giving her skin a pinkish glow. She moved over and patted the space beside her on the bed.

Fully dressed, I sat down beside her.

"I need you to love me, Larry," Judy whispered. "I really do." I think that's what she said or words to that effect. I can't remember my reaction, only that I wanted to react like a normal red-blooded American boy.

I repressed a desire to say some pretty taunting things. Hell, she had been laid, relayed and parlayed, maybe a dozen times in the last few hours. That was just sex. Not love. She must have been some kind of a nympho to have no respect for herself and do this kind of thing. Or maybe she was some retard that Ziggy had stumbled over in his travels.

As you can see I was getting very judgmental and nasty-minded. Notice I wasn't judging myself or the others for taking advantage of this poor dumb woman, but blaming it on her.

It was then that the anger that was growing inside of me suddenly seeped out of me, like air out of a big balloon that had taken all the air it was going to take. I looked at her, my eyes meeting hers. I was sure she was seeing something true in me and I was seeing something true in her. Call it a revelation, epiphany or whatever. But I knew then that Judy was just as scared as I was. Of the future, of failing, and, above all, of not being loved and loving someone else, missing out on love. When all the bullshit goes down, that was, I knew then and I know now, the number one thing in life.

"And I need you to love me, Judy," I whispered, turning my head, kissing her, deep with longing for something that I was scared of missing as much as she was. We held each other tightly for a long time and it soon became obvious that I had nothing to fear in the potency department. I didn't wear a rubber either and I didn't pull out.

We loved each other in those brief moments, clinging, tangled together in a tight knot, feeling the kind of irrepressible joy in each other that came not only from the body but from somewhere deep inside us both. I'm not sure she felt exactly as I felt, but it sure seemed like it.

"I love you," I whispered in her ear.

"And I love you," she whispered in mine.

I didn't want it to end. I forgot about the game. I'm sure I stayed past my deal. It didn't matter. I'm not sure I ever loved anyone as deeply or felt its return so keenly.

"Hey, Larry, it'll fall off," Hesh called from the table. I remember I heard some laughter and the clink of money. It had stopped raining and was getting dark. The game, I knew, was over.

Judy and I got dressed quickly, but before I went back to the boys, I held her in my arms one more time.

"I'll never forget you," I told her.

I never did.

PEELING THE ONION

"Let's peel the onion," Myra Schwartz would suggest to her husband Harry with a wink, mostly on Fridays, after a couple of martinis had taken the edge off her frenetic, increasingly nightmarish week as principal of PS 109 on Manhattan's Upper West Side.

It was their very private, very personal, very sexy ritual of seduction. Both in their late forties, they had been married for nearly ten years. It was Myra's second marriage and Harry's first and they had no children. Their relationship was the principal priority of their lives. Their apartment on West 81st between Columbus and Broadway was their fortress and once inside, they raised the drawbridge and were quite content to spend all of their time together.

Like many apartments in New York, the living room faced the street and the bedroom faced a back alley that looked out on the rear windows of another apartment house. Such proximity was an acceptable standard of living in the stacked-up space of crowded Manhattan.

The work week for Myra and Harry, who was an accountant, was tension-filled, time-consuming and required enormous concentration and discipline, and there was little room for light-hearted recreational adventures and seduction games until Friday evening rolled around, except in tax season when Harry worked weekends to get the job done for his tax-averse clients.

For Myra, running an inner city school fighting to stay within the new educational standards set by the Board of Education required a superhuman effort to stay focused in a day filled with bureaucratic bickering and backbiting by frustrated teachers and numerous students from homes of indifferent parents. Still, Myra had retained the hard core of her original idealism to educate young people and generally devote herself to the betterment of young minds.

She had started her career teaching first grade in the mean schools of Harlem, loving the challenge, and eventually working herself up to principal. She did miss the hands-on work as a teacher but had subjugated that skill to work on the larger stage, administering and inspiring other teachers to greater effort to educate their charges. She loved her work and was well respected by her colleagues and those in charge of the system.

It was, she admitted to herself, getting harder and harder to do the job, but she soldiered on with optimism and good humor, encouraging, cajoling, persuading her staff and their wards to strive to meet the hard standards which she deemed necessary to set her students on the path to compete in the real world.

With good cheer and cautious diplomacy, she had reached a level of respect and admiration and was careful to maintain her role with, above all, dignity and compassion. It was, of course, hard work, which she often likened to existing in a pressure cooker.

But once inside their fortress, she and Harry could toss away the cares of the outside world and since they needed no one else but each other, they could revel in their private world, free spirits responsible only to themselves. Few activities gave them more pleasure than the sexual fantasy games they had devised which they called "peeling the onion."

Stripping themselves of all inhibitions, they would engage in such enterprising sexual stimulants as cross-dressing, mutual and single performance masturbation, dirty talk, strip teasing on her part with all the bumps and grind movements, pornography accompaniments, vibrating sex toys and whatever sexual abandon they could think of.

And why not, they both agreed. They had strong libidos, were healthy, devoted, faithful, trusted each other implicitly, loved the enhancement of their orgasms and such activity became a cornerstone of their private lives.

"How lucky we are to have found each other," Myra would tell Harry in those special heart-to-heart talks they would have in the afterglow of their sexual activities. This was always the time for mental unburdening as they assessed their relationship and their lives.

They both had acknowledged early on that what they yearned for in a mate was total transparency, unconditional love and, above all, honesty and being true to their inner nature. Enhancing these conditions, they had established their fortress. Once inside, they could close the gate and let the outside world fulminate and fester while they danced to their private tunes, undisturbed and undeterred.

For some reason on this particular Friday winter night, they found themselves unusually sexually energetic, even for them. Perhaps the martinis were stronger than usual or had metabolized too slowly. Or the week had been particularly difficult for both of them. They would reflect on this later.

They went into the bedroom where Myra performed a particularly active strip tease while a naked Harry watched in full arousal mode. They then engaged in a number of acrobatic poses before a standing mirror. It was, Myra would remember, especially delicious and fulfilling and Harry, ever the willing participant, agreed.

But it was later, after their usual after-play discussions, that Myra noted that the blinds that ordinarily covered the bedroom windows had not been closed. The idea had, at first, amused her. Perhaps they had provided a free sex show to the people in the apartment house on their level across the alley. She wondered if it had ever happened before, but wasn't certain. In any event, she did not fret over it.

The first signs that something was amiss came in subtle ways. Her colleagues and students looked at her differently. The change was barely perceptible at first, then strangely blatant. She would receive troubling glances from her staff. Students would look at her and jab their classmates knowingly, giggling and turning away, as if enjoying some private joke.

It was confusing and, after a while, downright irritating, as if someone had deliberately put a sign on her back to ridicule her.

But when one of the eighth grade students, a wiseacre black kid with wide droopy jeans, mumbled under his breath a remark directed at her with the word "ho" in it, she wondered whether she had heard correctly and asked the student to repeat what he had said. He didn't, although his general attitude was oddly disrespectful. Because hers was an inner city school she was fully conversant with the various slang expressions of the African-American community.

By the middle of the week, she became convinced that something had indeed changed in the atmosphere, something uncommon and mysterious and mostly manifested in the way people reacted to her. She had worked for years to build trust and respect among her colleagues and students and had carefully nurtured an environment of mutual respect and was considered by her superiors and peers as one of the truly inspirational educators and administrators in New York City.

"Something is different," she confided to Harry, "and I can't put my finger on it."

"You will," Harry reassured her. He was her chief cheerleader and was well aware of her dedication and commitment to her job.

And she did. On Friday of that week, just as she was wrapping up for the day, filling her briefcase with work she would take home, her secretary, who had been acting strangely all week, came to her in tears. She was a middle-aged woman of Hispanic antecedents with whom Myra had a wonderfully supportive relationship.

"What is it, Carmen?"

The woman was highly emotional and had numerous difficulties with an errant husband. Myra had been a sympathetic listener to many of her domestic complaints.

"Something terrible, Mrs. Schwartz," she blurted. "I show you."

Wiping her tears with the back of her hand, she shut the door between their offices and sat down at Myra's desk and fired up the computer that Myra had just shut down.

Startled, Myra watched as Carmen's fingers tapped the keyboard. Then she stood up and motioned for Myra to sit down and watch the computer screen.

Puzzled, Myra obeyed. What she saw came as a physical shock. Her breath came in gasps. Perspiration rolled down her back. She watched, mesmerized and disbelieving. There she was in her own bedroom doing a bump and grind strip tease until she was naked, then having oral sex with Harry before their mirror and finally intercourse in varied positions. There was no mistaking their identity and the video was clear, complete with zooms and close-ups.

"I don't believe this. I don't believe this," she cried. She felt on the verge of hysterics. "How could they?"

"I don't know, Mrs. Schwartz. People do bad things. I think it's all over the school. Everybody knows and many have seen it."

"Oh my God." Myra tried to rise, but she couldn't muster the energy.

"We forgot to close the blinds. Obviously, someone in the other apartment house . . . " Her anger became acute. She must call Harry, prepare to do something, sue, call the police. It was a violation of their rights, their privacy. Something must be done. She felt helpless, violated.

"I'm so sorry, Mrs. Schwartz," Carmen said. Despite her secretary's obvious concern, Myra could detect an odd change in her attitude, a false note, as if this intimate view of her boss in sexual abandon had recalibrated their relationship.

When she stood up, her legs began to wobble. Then she called Harry on her cell phone.

"I need you, Harry. Come home. We have a problem, a big one."

She told him the story in halting, tearful gasps. He held her, obviously astonished, disturbed and angry. Then he went to his computer and sure enough, by putting in the address of the school he was able to view the video. He couldn't believe his eyes.

"We've got to get that bastard who did this." he said, marching into the bedroom. He looked across the alley at the window directly across from theirs. By then it was early evening and the blinds were drawn, although light seeped out of the corners, but it was apparent to her that this was where the video was shot.

"We don't have much of a choice, I'm afraid," Myra said. She had begun to calculate the fallout from the episode, remembering the word "ho" that had come from the eighth grade student's mouth. There was no getting away from the fact that this could be the prevailing attitude of everyone who had viewed the video. To most people it would qualify as a pornographic video. Of that, she was certain.

They pulled themselves together as best they could and went downstairs and around the corner to the apartment house that backed up on theirs. It was an older rent-controlled building without a doorman and a buzzer system for entering. Calculating that the apartment was on the fifth floor, as was theirs, Harry rang each buzzer on all the fifth floor apartments to gain entry by a ruse, pretending to be a FedEx delivery man.

Someone buzzed them through and they took the elevator to the fifth floor, quickly assessing which apartment was the one that looked over theirs across the alley. They pressed the door buzzer and a woman about forty opened the door. She was attractive, well groomed, and wore jeans and a sweatshirt.

"Who is it, Molly?" a man's voice called from the apartment interior.

"We're the Schwartz's," Harry said. "We live in the apartment that faces yours across the alley."

The woman assessed them, obviously puzzled.

"I don't understand," she said.

"We need to talk," Harry said. "It's rather serious."

"May we come in?" Myra asked.

"Serious?" the woman asked, obviously confused.

"Very," Harry said.

Frowning, the woman stepped aside and let them in. As they entered, a man came in from the dining room, a tall, pleasant-looking man with graying curly hair.

"We're in the middle of dinner," the man said.

"They're from across the way," the woman said. "They tell me it's a serious matter."

"Really," the man said, holding out his hand. "We're the Alperts. That's my wife Molly and I'm Bill." Harry took his hand and exchanged glances with Myra. "Come on in." They followed him into the living room.

"Can I get you a drink?" Bill Alpert asked, pointing to the couch. "Won't you please sit down?" He was affable and easygoing. Molly Alpert struck Myra as more cautious and wary.

At that moment a teenage boy came out of the dining room and observed the two couples. Myra's eyes drifted toward the boy and their eyes met. From her long experience with teenagers, she knew immediately by the sudden change of complexion and the aversion of his glance that this was the culprit.

"Is this your son?" Myra asked.

"Why yes. This is Tommy Alpert."

Myra had studied the configuration of the apartment and there was no question in her mind that this was the right apartment and that one of the windows was directly across from their bedroom. Reaching out, she squeezed Harry's upper arm, mostly to steady herself. Without another word, she rose and moved quickly to the room, which, she was certain, faced their bedroom.

"What is going on?" Bill Alpert asked, turning to Harry.

All Myra needed was one look into what was clearly the boy's room. A video camera with a tripod stood on one side of the room. Then she came back and faced the boy.

"Tell them, little Tommy dear, what you have done?" Myra said, her tone menacing.

"Now wait a minute . . . " Bill Alpert cried.

"Tell them, you little monster," Myra said, raising her voice. "Tell them what you've done. Tell them about the disgusting thing you have done and deliberately caused us enormous harm."

"Now hold on . . . " Molly Alpert began.

"Tell them, you miserable little shit," Harry cried. He was tempted to rise and strangle the boy.

"I was just having fun is all," Tommy said, his voice a whisper. He shrugged.

"Fun? Fun?" Myra raised her voice and confronted the boy directly. "Videotaping our private life? Is that your idea of fun? Sending it out over the internet?" She turned to the boy's parents. "Can't you see what he has done? He photographed the intimate details of our sex life and sent it out for anyone to see. I am the principal of PS 109. As of now, I am an object of ridicule, branded a whore or worse, because your son photographed us doing what most married couples do in the privacy of their bedroom. We have been violated, raped. Do you realize what your son has done?"

"Christ, Tommy," Bill Alpert said. "You did that?" The father was visibly exercised and embarrassed. "How could you do such an awful thing?"

Tommy bowed his head and looked down at his hands.

"I was only having fun," he mumbled.

"Fun?" Bill Alpert said. "You had no right . . . "

"He doesn't even go to your school," Molly Alpert said. "He is a private school student." She turned to her son. "How could you do such a disgusting thing?"

"He does have friends who went to your school," Bill Alpert said. "Not of the highest caliber and obviously a very bad influence."

"I wonder who the bad influence really is," Myra muttered.

"I didn't mean no harm," the boy whined. "I'm sorry."

"You stupid idiot," Harry cried. "Didn't mean no harm." He turned to the boy's parents. "Can't you see what this little moron has done to us? I am certain that this is an actionable crime and I intend to pursue this to the fullest extent of the law."

"It was stupid, disgusting," Molly Alpert cried, looking at her son. "How could you?"

"I didn't mean . . ." the boy whispered, bowing his head.

"Didn't mean. Didn't mean," Harry cried. He pointed a finger at the boy. "I intend to see that you are punished. I'm going to pursue this. Really. This boy has got to pay for this."

"Be careful on that score, mister," Molly Alpert sneered. "We're both lawyers."

"All I can say," Bill Alpert said in a placating lawyerly manner, "is that we're sorry this happened. Really sorry." He looked at his son. "We'll deal with you later, Tommy."

"Deal with him?" Myra said, her anger accelerating. "You should have dealt with the little shit years ago. It's far too late now. He's victimized us. He needs psychiatric help."

"That's it. I won't take these insults anymore," Molly Alpert said angrily, "Tommy can't accept all the blame. You should have closed your blinds. You want privacy, then that's your responsibility. He's only fourteen. Yes, he should have known better, but if you had the decency to close your blinds none of this would have happened."

Myra and Harry looked each other, shaking their heads.

"So we are to blame," Myra said. "Like parents, like child. Can you imagine how this little scumbag has hurt us?"

"I won't have this. Get out." Molly Alpert shouted. "Get the fuck out of here." Bill Alpert looked at her and shrugged helplessly. It was obvious to Myra who ruled the roost.

"Hopeless," Harry muttered as they stood up and moved toward the door.

"You haven't heard the end of this," Harry said.

They said nothing until they left the building and started toward their own

"I don't believe this. We are now the villains in the piece."

As they moved toward their apartment, they saw a crowd of people gathered at the entrance, some with obviously professional video cameras.

"What's going on?" Harry asked one of the people in the crowd.

"We're looking for the sex kitten principal," one of the women said, obviously a reporter.

Shocked and dismayed, they moved quickly through the lobby. But as they got to the elevator, the press and television people, alerted to their identity, swarmed after them, cameras clicking and voices raised with questions. They managed to get into the elevator by themselves. As they ascended they heard people pounding up the staircase.

"How did this happen?" Harry asked. Myra shrugged. No logical answer came to her mind.

"We are in deep doo-doo, Harry," Myra said.

Luckily they managed to get inside the apartment before the ringing and knocking began. Their answering machine registered that the messages were full.

Disconnecting the phone, they did not listen to any of the messages. They felt trapped.

"Go away," they shouted to the reporters who pounded on their door. After a while, they stopped.

They spent the night contemplating their situation, angered by the terrible turn of events that had impacted on their lives. They held each other all night as they tried to assess the situation and come up with some plan to face what they knew would be a troubled time.

"I feel like I'm about to face a firing squad," Myra mumbled before the effects of a sleeping pill eased her into slumber.

"Fight or flee," she remarked to Harry as she left the apartment in the morning. "I'm certainly not going to flee. I haven't a choice." Harry hugged her for a long moment. "I wish I was the one to bear the brunt, but who cares about a sexy accountant."

"I do," she said, winking, steeling herself as she left the apartment.

She walked past a number of photographers and reporters as she entered the school, saying nothing, determined to keep her head high, remaining stoic and hopeful that she was looking unfazed.

In her office, she noted that a number of messages were piled on her desk, one of them from a top executive of the Board of Education. She returned the call immediately. She was requested to come downtown today to discuss the situation.

Before she could leave, a delegation from the Parent-Teachers Association awaited her. They had brought along a cleric.

"We wanted to speak to you directly," one of the mothers who was a spokesman for the group said. Many nodded agreement. Myra wasn't sure about their motives until one of their number spoke up.

"You've done such a wonderful job, Mrs. Schwartz. We hate to see this happening. The newspaper stories are awful."

Myra had seen the headlines, which held her up to more ridicule than scorn. "Principal Goes All-Out For Sex Ed," the headline in the Daily News proclaimed. The Post was worse. "Principal's Porno Flick Gets Wide Release."

"We just wanted to say how sorry we are, Mrs. Schwartz. There is nothing worse than invading one's privacy."

"I just worry about the effect on the children," Myra said, as if it were expected. Apparently, it gave the delegation exactly the opening that was desired.

"That is our only concern, Mrs. Schwartz," the woman who spoke for the delegation said. She exchanged glances with the others in the group, who nodded their consent. "Our view is that the impact on them is—I hesitate to use the word—unsavory." The woman paused and glanced at Myra sympathetically. "We believe, despite the wonderful truly dedicated job you've done, that you must rethink your position here."

She knew, of course, that her status as role model was compromised and her level of respect had seriously declined. She had become an object of ridicule by the media, which greatly expanded the reach of her vilification. There was a great deal she wanted to say in rebuttal. She was tempted to lash out at them for the general malaise of parental indifference that was crippling their children, their reliance on overworked educators to stem the tide of their bad parenting and stupefying ignorance and appalling dysfunction. She had, she realized, fought the good fight for these people and it was obvious they were not willing to fight the good fight for her.

Before any extended conversation could ensue she explained politely that she had been summoned downtown and she thanked the delegation for taking the time to make their views known. On the way, she heard from Harry on her cell phone.

"Me too, babe," he said with surprising good humor. "The enemy has landed on my shores. Some of the firm's clients are pissed, especially the public companies. I'm not being fired, just exiled to a Siberian clientele."

"How awful, Harry."

She explained that she was on her way downtown where she had been summoned.

"It has not been a happy day," she sighed.

"There is an upside, babe," Harry said. "Some of the boys . . . and a few of the girls . . . gave me some pretty good reviews." He laughed. "You, too."

"Every cloud has a silver lining," she smirked, but his remark did lift her spirits.

Downtown, she confronted the people in charge of the New York school system. They showed outward signs of understanding and expressed horror at her victimization, but Myra could tell that they were all on the horns of a dilemma. The incident and the resultant publicity had made her a kind of pariah. She imagined she knew what they were thinking.

One of the executives around the table was more forthright than the others.

"The incident has done you a terrible injustice, Mrs. Schwartz. To have done such a thing is beyond awful. But the fact is it has not been good for the school system. It has impacted it negatively."

"I can imagine," Myra said. "Dedicated principal turns out privately to be a slut." Her sarcasm was deliberate and they all knew it, but as she studied the faces around the table she knew that, despite all her good work, she had become a liability. They could, of course, defend her, but it would not change the facts. She had become an object of ridicule, a subject of humor, a target for those who believe her uninhibited exhibition of sexuality could be interpreted as condoning and encouraging loose sexual behavior.

They did offer sympathy and support, but she knew it was merely pro forma. The ball, she knew, was in her court. What they seemed to be saying via their body language and subtle remarks was that the only course for her was resignation. She had reached a threshold for her pension and she could tell that the only sensible move for her was a graceful exit. She hinted that she might opt for this course and noted that the people around the table seemed relieved.

She thanked everyone for their verbal support. Above all, she wanted to demonstrate the sense of her own dignity. She was clearly a victim of a terrible injustice. Yes, she might still ride it out. People would forget as new gossip and scandal would feed the maws of a public greedy for such material.

After the meeting, she called Harry and they agreed to meet at a fancy restaurant in midtown. No one recognized them. They ordered martinis.

"I'm resigning, Harry, "she told him.

"But you loved that job," he protested.

"It would never be the same," she replied.

"Without a fight?" he asked.

"Why waste time on anger, lawsuits, and vengeance? Our energy will be drained. I'd always be the porno principal. I've had a good run and I can always teach at some private school. Besides," she reached out and took his hand, "we have each other."

"That we do. You and me, babe. Forever."

No crowd of reporters was present when they got back to their apartment house.

"See. We've already had our fifteen minutes of fame," Harry said, embracing Myra as they headed toward the bedroom where they began to undress, kiss and fondle each other.

"Let's peel the onion," Myra whispered, flicking on the lamp beside their bed, throwing a golden glow around the room. Soon they were naked.

"The blinds," Harry whispered as they began to make love in earnest.

"Keep them open," Myra said, giggling. "That's their problem, not ours."

THEY ALWAYS HELD HANDS

"All in all," Beth Glazer said, after a long silence, "on a scale of one to ten, I'll give her a four for nurturing."

Steve, her elder by two years, shrugged and she wasn't sure whether he agreed or disagreed with her assessment.

"Well, what's your view?" she prodded.

"I'm not sure I have a view," he said, his voice weary. He had come from his home in Los Angeles to the funeral of their mother. Beth had come from Alaska. The funeral ceremony was held at the Riverside Funeral Home. In attendance were eleven people, which included their mother's housekeeper, a doorman from her Park Avenue apartment, her lawyer, her accountant, her hairdresser, and three representatives from some charities and non-profits to which she had contributed.

The funeral director had arranged for a rabbi who had not known her and the ceremony was quickly disposed of. Beth and Steve followed the hearse to the cemetery and a man with a scraggly beard wearing a skullcap said a prayer and that was that. No one else observed the burial. Of course, she was buried next to her husband. A tombstone already existed with her name and birth date on it beside her husband's. Only the date of her death had yet to be inscribed.

During the burial, a sob had risen from somewhere deep in Beth's chest and her eyes had moistened, but she felt no great loss or sense of mourning. Steve stood dry-eyed throughout the brief ceremony and they re-boarded the limousine for the trip back to Manhattan. The black chauffeur was silent throughout the trip. If he listened to the conversation, he showed no sign or interest and they didn't care.

"Together again at last," Steve said. "Got to admit, it's where she wants to be."

"Never met people so joined at the hip."

"We were always intruders, Beth."

She knew exactly what he meant. They had discussed it often, although not lately since they did not speak that often. Their parents had never been mean to them, always kind, concerned, understanding, interested in their upbringing, their welfare. She had never felt unwanted. And yet, something had always been missing and Steve had felt it as well.

"It was all façade. They were too locked into each other."

"Do you think, Steve?" She hesitated, trying to form exactly the right sentence to match her thoughts. "Do you think that maybe we were jealous, that they loved each other more than they loved us?"

"Could be," Steve sighed.

"They did give us everything else. I mean materially. We are rich. In fact, now that mother has died, even richer. They made it clear early on that we will inherit everything and the lawyers have indicated that that was the truth."

"Wealth isn't love," Steve said. He bit his lip as if it was necessary to hold back tears. "We were their children, for crying out loud. Admit it, Beth. You feel the same way. It was as if . . . " He shook his head and closed his eyes. "Once we were grown, it was over."

"What was over?"

"Their job was done and we were on our own."

"Isn't that the way it's supposed to be?"

"Sure it is. Then why do I feel so damned guilty? Why am I not grieving?"

He turned to look at her and they exchanged glances. "You, too, I'll bet."

"I guess you might say we're ungrateful little brats," Beth said with a forced giggle.

They lapsed into silence again. Steve closed his eyes.

Steve, who was divorced, had one child, a girl now in college. Since her mother, his ex-wife, was granted custody, his daughter had little contact with her paternal grandparents. Nor had they sought her out, although they were generous with their financial gifts. Beth had never married.

He had taken the red eye from Los Angeles and was jet-lagged and bleary-eyed. She had come in the day before from Juneau and met with the lawyers who were handling the estate. Their father had been an investment banker and had made a fortune, and both she and her brother were, as they saying goes, trust fund babies, although each had fulfilling lucrative careers, and the large sum that each would inherit would make little difference in their lifestyles.

Both siblings were in their late forties and their lives had long been out of their parents' social orbit, although they called them dutifully once or twice every month but both knew that the cord that bound them with their parents had been severed long ago.

Their father's funeral was much better attended than their mother's. He had been enormously successful financially and many people owed their wealth to his careful and imaginative money management. At his death ten years ago, the Riverside Chapel had been filled to capacity and many stepped up to the podium to provide glowing eulogies.

There was no bad blood between the generations, no family battles, and Beth and her brother had been friendly as children and then took up different pursuits that separated them both emotionally and geographically. Beth had become a geologist working for British Petroleum in Alaska and had settled in Juneau.

Steve was a partner in a West Coast advertising agency. They rarely got together, although there had been sporadic visits to New York on anniversary occasions orchestrated by their parents. Anniversaries had always been the premier celebratory occasions in their parents' lives. Both Beth and Steve knew that their parents were more devoted to each other than they could ever be to their children. That had been the overriding reality of their parents' lives.

"Now comes the hard part," Beth sighed. "Emptying the love nest."

She knew there was both irony and sarcasm in her statement. She and Steve had long ago acknowledged that the apartment on Park Avenue was indeed more of a love nest for their parents than a family home. Even as children they had discovered that their parents were bound to each other so tightly that there had been little room for strong, demonstrable ties to anyone else, including their children.

"Remember, Beth?" Steven said. "They were always holding hands."

"Always."

"Like two kids."

Their parents' section of the apartment, their bedroom and sitting room, was a kind of sanctuary, hence their description of it as a love nest. It was the central focus of their living quarters and was, more by assumption than prohibition, off-limits to their children. By the time they were teenagers, Beth and Steve had become aware that their parents were conducting a lifetime love affair, sexually and emotionally.

When their father died, they were concerned that his loss would make their mother a basket case and burden them with responsibilities that neither had any wish to undertake. Although both she and Steve had long ago concluded that they were playing second fiddle in their parents' lives, they did understand their responsibilities as offspring, acknowledging the traditional obligations and duties to their parents, and to their mother in her widowhood.

To their relief, after her husband's death, their mother still went about the daily business of her life, narrower than it had been, but she did not appear depressed or anguished, which baffled them since they had expected his death to leave her devastated, inconsolable and a burden on both of them. Their father had died suddenly of a massive coronary in the shower of their apartment. His clothes had been carefully laid out for a day at the office and hung on a hanger on the doorknob of his closet. Years later, they still hung there.

Indeed, nothing, but nothing, of his possessions had been eliminated or rearranged in the apartment since the day their father had died. His clothes still hung in his closet; his study, his desk, his drawers remained exactly as he had left them. A book was still open face down to the page he had been reading. Everything in his bathroom had remained as he had left it, even his toothbrush, his shaving equipment, his toiletries were in the exact place where he had put them on the morning he died. Whatever defined his presence at the moment he expired was preserved as a kind of shrine.

Her mother's maid dusted and cleaned with a minimum of disturbance and was instructed to put everything of her late husband's back in its proper place. On a visit a few months after their father's death Beth had asked her mother when she was going to remove their father's possessions.

"Someday," her mother had responded. She asked again on other visits and got the same answer. It had long been obvious to Beth that it would never happen and she ceased asking.

"Leave it alone," she instructed her brother. "It's her call."

"Doesn't seem normal," he had said.

"It is for her," Beth answered.

"It's weird."

"Must we?" Steve asked as the limousine approached the Park Avenue building. They had agreed to go through the apartment and check to see if there was anything that either of them wanted before turning it over to appraisers and a firm that did this kind of disposal work. They had already decided to sell any items of real value and give everything else to charity.

"We do owe them some respect. After all, they were our parents."

She could sense the element of guilt in her tone. Steve shrugged.

"Actually, I doubt I'll want anything." he said. "I just don't feel any connection."

She knew exactly what he meant since she felt the same way, but she let the comment pass.

"You might want some things for your daughter. Something to remember her grandparents by." Guilt had turned to sarcasm.

"You've got to be kidding."

The apartment occupied a whole floor and was in reasonably good condition and well maintained. Not much had been done to it over the years.

Beth roamed through the vast apartment aware of her indifference and odd lack of feeling.

"You're right, Steve. There's nothing here I want to live with." She shrugged. "Or remember." She paused and grew reflective. "I feel so damned cold-blooded."

"We were strangers here, Beth. Worse. Intruders. We didn't belong. They had each other."

"Lucky them."

She detected an unmistakable air of nastiness in her attitude. Or was it envy? That kind of luck was something that so far had eluded her.

"Yeah, lucky them," Steve said, perhaps reflecting on his own failed marriage.

He shrugged and they wandered to their parents' so-called sanctuary. Steve opened the door.

"Behold the love nest," he said, trying to lighten the mood.

"I can't remember ever setting foot in this place," Beth said.

They stood at the entrance to the suite. It was lavishly decorated, the large king-sized bed covered with a brocaded spread and pillows. On the wall was a large nude whose face resembled their mother at a younger age. It might have been her, but they couldn't be certain. Framed photographs of their parents at various stages in their life together hung on the walls and stood on every flat surface. Heavy drapes, half drawn, covered the windows.

"Note the paucity of pictures of us," Steve muttered. There was one picture of them as young children, a family portrait, the children in the center, the parents on either side.

"There are lots in the other rooms," Beth said. Nevertheless, it was a telling observation that seemed to reflect the general feeling that there was no room in this place for anyone but their parents.

They opened closets and found their father's suits neatly hung in transparent plastic bags. Shoes were stored in compartments. Ties still hung in racks. Their mother's clothes filled two large walk-in closets. Chests of drawers contained their father's shirts, socks and underwear, as well as their mother's stockings and underwear.

In one of their mother's bottom drawers they found a number of boxes containing jewels, rings, necklaces, bracelets, gold chains, undoubtedly of great value. Papers in her lawyers office had validated that they had been insured and would certainly fetch lots of money, hardly an issue for either of them. Earlier they had talked of giving the proceeds to charity.

Next to their mother's bed, her side, they assumed, was an end table, a kind of cabinet. Steven attempted to open it and found it locked.

"Why is it locked?" Beth asked as she saw him struggling to open it.

"Beats me."

Steven abandoned the struggle and they moved on, opening drawers of their mother's dressing table, which still contained much of their mother's makeup, hairbrushes and other various personal grooming items. But before they left the suite, Beth stopped at the door and surveyed the interior. Her gazed rested on the locked end table.

"Curious," Steve said, noting her interest.

"Why is it locked?" she muttered.

"One way to find out," Steve said, prying open the cabinet with scissors he found in his mother's dressing table. Inside was a metal box about the size of a cigar box. That too was locked, and they had to pry it open.

"Oh my God," Beth screamed looking at the contents with horror.

Steve closed it quickly, then opened it again slowly. The initial shock over, he studied it carefully. It was a man's hand, severed at the wrist, lacquered but shriveled. Without a doubt it was once a living hand. It was obviously a left hand and on its third finger was a wedding band. They did not question the identity of the hand.

The siblings looked at each other but said nothing, as if the sight of the severed hand explained everything. No further comment was needed.

"We know what we have to do," Beth said, punching in a number on her cell phone.

Steve nodded and they left the apartment. They waited briefly and a limousine arrived. It took them back to the cemetery where they revisited their mother's grave. Both kneeled and they dug into the soft earth with their hands, burying the box.

"It was only right," Beth said as the rode back to the city in the limousine.

"They always held hands," Steve said. "Right to the end."

THE POLKA DOT DRESS

Originally published in *Which Grain Will Grow*, 1950

I went to Manhattan to look for a job. I just got on the subway and went to Manhattan. On 42nd Street all the people were rushing about. They looked as if they knew where they were headed. I had no idea where to go. I didn't even know where to look for a job. But I said to myself, "Jack," I said (Jack isn't my real name, but I call myself Jack because it is a nice-sounding name), "Jack, you have got to get a job. Look, everybody has a job. They have some place to go. They bring home money every week to support themselves with. Don't you feel ashamed because you haven't got a job?"

I am a writer. I didn't feel ashamed, so I went to Central Park. It was spring, the rich green grass glistening with dew, and the caterpillars and false noses were dropping like raindrops from the trees. It was warm, and I walked with my hands in my pockets and my jacket swung over my shoulder. I thought it made me look real tough, and I like to look real tough, even when I'm out of a job and have only ten cents in my pocket.

I saw a pretty girl sunning herself on a bench. She was wearing a blue polka-dot dress. I wanted to sit down beside her and talk to her, but I was afraid, so instead I walked past her tough and swaggering, and I wished that I had a pretty girl in a blue polka-dot dress walking with her hand in mine.

The sun was shining brightly, and when I looked at the grass I wanted to take off my shoes and run barefoot or maybe just lie down and go to sleep with the caterpillars and false noses falling on my face.

Near the zoo I heard two fat old ladies talking. They both had nice pleasant old faces; they looked like grandmothers. They were looking at some bums sleeping on the grass.

"Can't those riff-raff read signs?" one old lady said.

"It distinctly says 'Keep Off,'" the other one said.

"I'd like to call a policeman and have them chased," the first one said.

"Me too," the other one said, looking for a policeman.

I was very glad that there were no policemen around to chase the sleeping tramps off the grass.

When I heard a lion roar just then, I knew I was very close to the zoo. I walked faster now that I had some place to go. I would be a mighty happy fellow, I thought, if I could walk with a pretty girl in a blue polka-dot dress with her hand in mine.

I went up to the lion's cage. He was sprawled out in the sun with his paws in front of him and roaring. A woman behind me said that it seems silly for a lion to roar for no reason at all. I walked to the next cage and saw the lioness scratching at the bars. Then I knew why the lion was roaring. It seems a shame, I thought, and I went back to the lion's cage and looked sympathetically into his sleepy brown eyes, and I know this is crazy, but I think he looked back sympathetically at me.

I went to the monkey house and saw a man give a cigar to a chimpanzee named Jimmy.

"Is that allowed?" I asked the man.

He didn't answer, but instead he lit the chimpanzee's cigar. The chimpanzee puffed the cigar and climbed to the top of the cage. He inhaled and blew the smoke out through his nose. A few people gathered around and looked up and laughed at him. I laughed because he looked like my father.

"He looks just like a man," a little boy said.

"He seems to be having a lot of fun," his mother said.

I no longer cared whether it was allowed or not.

After the monkeys, I watched the seals splashing around in the cool green water. One of them was sleeping on a stone slab.

"What a life!" a man behind me said. "Sit around and take a sunbath and then jump into the water and go for a swim."

"It's not who you are; it's what you are," I said.

I laughed and walked out of the zoo, still wishing that I had a pretty girl in a blue polka-dot dress walking with her hand in mine. On the Mall a little boy with a sunburnt nose spoke to me. He was holding a balloon that was in the shape of an elephant.

"Look! I got an elephant!" he said.

"That's a mighty nice elephant," I said.

"It can go up to the sky," he said, lifting his arm way up in the air.

I remembered an old nursery rhyme that my mother used to recite to me:

I asked my mother for fifty cents
To see the elephant jump the fence.
He jumped so high he reached the sky
And never came down till the Fourth of July.

The little boy laughed and ran back to his mother. I took my shoes off and sat on a rock near the lake. People were rowing. Across the lake I saw a boy and a girl. They were sitting real close, her red hair blowing over his face. I wished that I could make love to some pretty girl in a blue polka-dot dress. I wished that I could kiss her cherry red lips and rub her nose with mine and let her hair blow over my face. I wished that we could go rowing and put our toes in the water over the back of the boat. I wished that we could sit on the grass and say nonsensical things. I wished that I could recite "Jabberwocky" into her ear while she kissed my neck:

> 'Twas brillig and the slithy toves
> Did gyre and gimble in the wabe

I was sitting under a tree, and the caterpillars and false noses were falling all over me. I put on a false nose. A little girl who saw me do it said to her mother, "Isn't that silly?" I knew it was silly and I even said to myself, "Jack, you're silly," but I didn't care.

There were no clouds in the sky and the sun made glistening spangles on the ripples of the lake. I watched them until my eyes began to hurt. A man from the park department with a long thin face was doing some hoeing near where I sat.

"Do you like your job?" I said.

"I like it this time of year," he told me.

"It must be fun," I said.

"Not in the wintertime," he answered.

"I'd like to get a job like that," I said.

"A young feller like you can get a better job than this. A young feller like you can get a good job, good pay, good future."

"I'm not interested in things like that," I said. "I'm a writer."

"Why aren't you home writing?" he said. He was a very smart man.

"I'm looking for a job," I said.

"You sure are looking," he said laughing. "You sure are looking!"

"What was your ambition when you were a boy?" I asked.

"I wanted to see the darkies pick cotton in Louisiana. I wanted to see the sun come up over the black hills of Dakota. I wanted to see the

moon shine down on the Great Salt Lake. I wanted to see the men sing-
ing songs on top of railroad trains. I wanted to see men pick grapes in
California and husk corn in Iowa and thresh wheat in Indiana."

"Did you see all these things?" I asked.

"Sure did! I was a hobo for thirty years."

"I'd like to be a hobo, especially in the springtime," I said.

"That's the best time," the man said. I knew he was thinking about
the time when he was a young man.

"What do you write about?" the man asked.

"I write about girls with blue polka-dot dresses and old ladies who
chase bums off the grass and lions and monkeys and seals and little boys
with toy balloon elephants and old men who used to be hobos."

"You're a funny kid," the man said.

I walked near the sailboat pond and sat down on a bench. I thought
about the whole country and then about the whole world and then
about the universe.

"It's not so big, Jack," I said to myself.

Two young men sat down next to me. They took sandwiches out of a
brown paper bag and began to eat. The sandwiches smelled like tuna
fish. One young man had sad eyes, and I knew he was a philosopher.

"Sure is good to get out of that stuffy smelly office," he said.

"Sure is," the other one said.

"Some day I'm going out for lunch and then I'm going to take my
tuna fish sandwich and throw it into this pond and never go back to that
smelly office. Then I'm going to marry a rich girl and buy an estate and
sit on my estate and get sun-tanned all day long. Then at night I'm going
to do nothing but make love to my wife and thank God for her having all
that money."

"The grass always looks greener on the other side," the other one said.

I looked out over the pond where a little sailboat was gracefully sway-
ing on the crest of the wind. An old man with a long stick was following
it along the shore.

"Some beaut!" a little boy said. He had a pleasant high-pitched voice. I wished I were a little boy or an old man having fun near a sail-boat pond. But I was a young man and what would make me happy would be to make love on the grass to a pretty girl in a polka-dot dress. I was sorry that I was afraid to speak to the girl in the blue polka-dot dress sunning herself on a bench.

It began to get late. The sun dipped quietly behind the large trees and the children began to disappear from the park. I had started out to get a job. I did not know what kind of a job. I know now. I went home and wrote about Central Park, and when I went to bed I had a dream. And in my dream I was making love to a pretty girl in a blue polka-dot dress.

THE OTHER PEOPLE

Originally published in *1950 American Vanguard*, 1950

You felt your wife pinching and prodding you to wake up, and when you opened your eyes you could see her face, scaly and flabby, with the lips all colorless from using lipstick, and her cheeks dabbed with remnants of rouge that were nearly worn off on the side of her face that she slept on. The clock on the bureau was ten minutes fast, so you knew that you had a few minutes to lie around and stretch the sleep from your weary bones, but you had to be careful not to doze off again, although you certainly did feel like doing it. It was better to talk, so you talked in a hoarse sleep-wracked voice to your wife, while you watched her crawl out of her pink silk nightgown with the rip near the right hip; you saw all the curves and the folds, the ripples and the waves of her spreading form that you knew so well. Every few moments you would look at the clock where the minutes seemed to tick by slower than usual, and you wished that they would go faster, even though you really wanted to stay in bed. Soon you just couldn't stay in bed any longer or else you would be late for work, so you threw the red-checked quilt off you and crept on to the floor which was pretty cold for October. When the cold water hit your face you winced, but it revived your senses and made you feel pretty good. A quick shower, a shave, a sweet toothbrush, and a hair comb, and you were as presentable as you could be with chronic red eyes and a broken nose.

There was a half of a grapefruit waiting for you on the kitchen table and the sound of the percolator and the smell of coffee made it feel like Sunday morning, although it was but Wednesday.

Her hair thatched loosely together, your wife bustled about the stove. You saw that she wasn't deriving any pleasure from making that coffee; her flabby face reflected feelings of disturbance, of discomfort, of pain. And after you left the house she would go back to bed and wish that she could sleep alone all the time, but now she didn't really care for she felt icy inside and had a headache and was worried about her change of life. She wouldn't even wait until you finished your breakfast before she went back to bed.

The coffee, made too fast, was weak and tasteless, so you just ate a piece of toast after your grapefruit and washed it down with water. You looked at the clock and saw that it was getting late; now it seemed as if the minutes were ticking faster than usual. Bending over the soiled bed, you kissed your wife on her dry scaly cheek. She wouldn't move and you would smell, while in the realm of her vapors, all the stinks and odors that were your very own, but were hers now because she had received them from you in the blood flow of creation. All the rotten stinks and smells and slops were hers, and they were yours too, but she lived in them; she had nothing else, while you mingled with the vapors of the outside, and lived in a thousand other stinks and smells and odors which you absorbed and brought back to her and she kept them and nurtured them and they permeated her, and she couldn't escape from them.

In the street you joined the parade of people walking to the station with the sunbeams dancing through the nooks of fences and walls and ashcans. Nobody noticed the sun, it was just there, bright and warm and friendly. The people marched, out of step, but with one goal in sight and that was the subway station where a dark metal thing would open its jaws and swallow people and people, and would vomit them out again at other stops along the line. You walked with the rest of them just as you did every other weekday morning in the year, except when you got your two weeks' vacation with pay and then you went away from city and subways et al. and got yourself a sunburn which lasted for at least two weeks more, then it left you and everything was the same as ever.

A big hell-like hold, open, and with stairs leading down greeted the morning paraders who poured and poured into its never-filling space. You felt in your pocket for change and found four pennies and a dollar bill. An old graying Negro stood in the change booth and slid you the change for your dollar. Through the creaking turnstiles then past the reeking dirty toilet rooms and down the darkened steps spotted with spittle; past a newsstand where you bought the morning paper. The parade continued, and you were one of the marchers, jostling, jogging, reeling in time with the tempo of humanity; forever moving in the circles of beating pulses. People huddled together near where the doors would open and talked or read or looked at the tracks and at the people who were far more interesting than anything else. For these were the corpuscles of the city blood beating through its veins.

You heard rumblings from the darkness and knew it was the dark black thing approaching to receive the people that stood waiting on the dirty platform. Everybody heard the sound and huddled close together. You found yourself pressed against a pole with vulgar ditties and foul language written all over it with pencil and black crayons and all sorts of people jammed you up against it. The black thing rattled into the station and its heart stopped beating as it opened its jaws and people flowed into it. Pushing and pressing and heaving they wrapped themselves around one another until there was no room for even the foul air to intrude. Some people never got on, but stood on the platforms, their eyes gaping at the compressed mass of flesh and bones trying to fit into the mouth of the dark black thing.

Your hands were stuck in a human vise and you found that it was impossible to read your paper. An old man with withered yellow flesh and rotting insides that produced a foul nauseating breath stood looking at you with sick weary eyes that said many things that had been said many times before by other sick and weary eyes. A young woman whose skin was still tight and fresh and who bore the unseen marks of having just come from the closeness of her lover's arms and could still taste the moisture of his breath on her lips stood packed against a young, embarrassed lad with horn-rimmed spectacles. He was embarrassed because he could feel the roundness of her tired breasts beneath her dress and was afraid that she would create a scene that would humiliate him. A man whose hair was spotted with gray tried looking about him disinterestedly, but his great sad eyes betrayed the troubles that wore him down and thwarted his life.

As the dark black thing jogged along, the mass moved with the rhythms of its gyrations. The fans 'were going, but the foul air kept circulating back and forth, weaving its way amongst the people. A man who had spent the evening before pouring alcohol into his guts now made the car stink with the rumblings of his stomach. Everybody breathed in the filthy odor but no one said a word, although you could see the signs of discomfort in all the faces. Next to you stood a young woman who reminded you of your wife because she had flabby cheeks. She was breathing heavily and her breath was none too sweet because she was three months pregnant and had pains in her stomach but continued to go to work because she had to make enough money to pay for the hospital bills. With each swerve of the train, she got paler and paler and every few moments she would well up and purse her lips as if she were going to regurgitate. Through the side of your eye you could see that she was going through some sort of pain but after a while you didn't look and only hoped that she wouldn't throw up or if she did she would turn her head the other way.

The smell of a thick musty perfume would suddenly fill your nostrils and then disappear on the wings of the drafts and breezes that flew through the air. After a while it wasn't the odors that really annoyed you but rather the tightness in your cramped limbs that made them ache and smart, like a prisoner in shackles yearning to be free. Occasionally you would steal a glance at the suffering woman rammed against the small of your back. You were hoping that you weren't hurting her and even strained against the crowd that pushed you toward her.

You knew that all the people locked in that dark black thing, racing through the veins and arteries of the city, were thinking the same things that you were thinking or had thought or would be thinking—that the pain and the discomfort must be endured and that it would soon be over and then the sun would kiss your bodies again and you would forget the pain. Yet it was always the same thing. It wasn't you, but the other people that made the annoyance, it was the other people that caused the hardships and the pain, the crowded places, it was the other people that caused the wars and made the laws, and spread disease and destroyed, and pilfered and smelled, and spat, and took the rent, and raised the prices and hurt little children and old folk. It was the other people that suppressed you, and stifled you, and bore down upon you until you were chained and imprisoned, and you found yourself crushed together with the groups of the other people until you became the very thing that had destroyed you—the other people.

So you stood cramped and paralyzed and wedged in amongst the other people and kept watching the pregnant woman trying to hold her breakfast in her stomach and you began to think that she was fighting a losing battle because the half-made life in her guts was pushing and kicking into her flesh and you wondered whether she remembered the pleasure with which she had begotten the pain. The dark black thing was plodding along at a slower arid slower rate because other dark black things with other people jammed into it were slowed up in front. You wished that you could get at least one hand free so that you could read your paper even if you couldn't read but only one page and had to read that over and over again.

Then the dark black thing stopped moving altogether and you could only hear the monotony of the fans and the scattered coughing of the other people and even an occasional voice whispered that it was terrible and that the same thing happened every morning and why don't the city take care of its subways, and someone would chime in that she was absolutely right and something should be done about it. But nothing could be done because it was the other people who were at fault and you were the other people and you did nothing. But how could you do anything when you were busy watching the sick pregnant woman and hoping that she would get off soon even though you knew that nobody got off until you at least passed under the river and that was still about fifteen minutes away. When you stopped looking at the pale sick woman for a moment, you saw that other people were looking at her too, but nobody could actually do anything because the other people were rammed tight against them and they couldn't even move their arms.

You tried to think of different things such as your wife or the boys at the office, but that didn't help much because there was a horrible effluvia passing through the stagnant air and it made you slightly dizzy and nauseous so you looked toward the sick woman next to you and saw that the fresh new stench had not improved her condition.

Then it happened. You had just turned your head a moment when you heard the gut-cry that heralded the sound and smell of vomiting. All the pleasure and the pain and the new life and the stink of menstruation and the medicinal odor of sperm and secretions and the insides of a pig and the flow of a cow and the growths of a chicken and the sweat of a fruit—all in one foul ugly gushing mess, lumpy and pulpy and stinking, rushed out of the pregnant woman's mouth and on to her chin and her clothes and her hands, and onto the back of your coat and your pants and your shoes and your hands.

You looked at her and you could see that she was sorry and humiliated and sick and she looked at you with red swollen eyes that also seemed to have vomited some sort of fluid and you felt pity, but it was a strange sort of pity because at the same time you also wanted to kill her for making the ugly stink and soiling your clothes and you wished that she had turned her head and thrown up on someone else, the old man with the dry yellow flesh, or the young lad with the horn-rimmed glasses or the young woman who bore the unseen marks of her lover's closeness, but not on you because you didn't know what to do now and besides you were terribly shy and had a weak stomach. Everyone was looking at you, and some turned white while others held their noses and you knew that one and all wanted to leave and so did you and the young humiliated woman who felt crucified by the other people's eyes and who was sorry that she had not fainted because she couldn't bear the eyes and couldn't even bear the smell of her own vomit. You could hear her earnest entreaties of sorrow as she took out her handkerchief and started to wipe the slop that her guts had produced from the back of your jacket, but instead she made things worse and it began to run down your sleeve until it was a thick creamy substance with lumps and it made you dizzy just to feel it in your hands. The other people were literally crushing themselves in their effort to push away from yourself and the young pregnant woman who had tried cleaning up the mess with her little pocket handkerchief but instead ended up wallowing in her own vomit. Her face was covered with it because she had forgotten and tried to blow her nose into the handkerchief and realizing her error she tried wiping it off again which only made matters worse. You stood there praying that the dark black thing would move again and quickly reach another station.

You wanted to disappear or crawl into someone's pocket but it was no use because you were here and just couldn't stand around as if nothing had happened. Then you remembered the newspaper that was still in your hand, and you used that, and strangely enough you found that you had plenty of room now and if you wanted you could read your paper but you didn't want to now.

You wanted to tell the other people to close their eyes and they would have, if they weren't so curious, but it annoyed you to see them trying not to look but looking just the same. The dark black thing began to move again and you heaved a sigh of relief because the stench was becoming unbearable. You knew that the people who had not seen what had happened were straining their necks to see a miserable young woman trying to wipe herself free from the ugly stench and telltale stains and a man with chronic red eyes and a broken nose trying to do the same thing. You wanted to scream at these curious other people and ask them if they thought that their guts smelled any differently, and they probably did, but worse. The black dark thing began to slow up again and you were getting dizzier and dizzier and it would only be a matter of minutes before you yourself would throw up.

You looked at the young pregnant woman and saw that she was crying bitterly and it made you want to move mountains to help her but there was nothing you could do so you said nothing and turned your head away. All you wanted now was to get away from the stink and the people and the eyes and all these things that kept going around in circles, and you knew that if the train did not reach a station soon you would lose consciousness and fall right into the puddle of slop that was seeping into the leather of your shoes and made them slide when the dark black thing pitched and lurched.

At last the train was going full speed again and you breathed a great sigh of relief and so did all the rest of the people who were pressed up so hard against one another that they could hardly breathe. And when all these other people would leave the dark black thing they would curse each other and especially the young pregnant woman for adding to their discomfort, and so to speak, putting salt on their wounds but soon their antagonism would die down and they would feel pity for the poor pregnant woman and later they would think it quite amusing that the man next to her, the one with the chronic red eyes and broken nose, should have been cruelly victimized and they would tell the story for many days among their friends but not all of them would think it very funny.

You no longer looked around you but you closed your eyes and gritted your teeth and hoped and hoped hard. You didn't think any more of why this misfortune had happened to you, and you just accepted it and prayed that after you got out you would be rid of this miserable burden that made you feel as if you were nailed to a cross and people were sticking knives in your belly. The stink was awful and you could feel the drops of cold sweat on your brow and your throat was parched and your hands were sticky and slimy. You didn't even care about the other people any more. They were part of the structure of the dark black things like the cold metal and the dirty glass and the yellow straw seats and the dusty emergency cord, and you knew that they were wishing that they were part of the dark black things so they would no longer have to smell the abominable stench that turned their stomachs and made their heads ache.

When the doors opened you dashed on to the station and rushed away from the dark black thing; you knew that you were making a trail with your dirty shoes but you didn't care and you didn't even look for the pregnant woman and try to help her. In fact you no longer cared what happened to her. You ran up the stairs and bumped against people who sniffed at you and then turned their heads away and you wished that they would all go to hell. Next to a tattered phone booth you found the entrance to the men's room and already as you passed through the little corridor you could smell the urinals and the unflushed toilets, but this didn't make you any sicker. There was an old drunken man with a torn blue jacket sitting on the toilet and talking to himself. You were thankful that he didn't notice you when you came in. The sink was so dirty from the dried spittle that lined its walls that you were afraid to put your hands into it, but you had no choice and had to rinse the foul stuff from your hands. There was no soap and you had to manage as best you could although the very best you could do was to get the pulpy matter off but the smell remained no matter how hard you rubbed. Your jacket was all spotted so you took it off and tried to clean it. In a little while you found that it was soaked through and through with water and you couldn't possibly put it on again. The drunken man was still making all sorts of hideous sounds and you were thankful that he didn't notice you because you were in no mood to humor drunks.

Back on the station again you realized that you were in no condition to continue on your way to work; you were nervous, you stank—a dry pungent piercing odor that embarrassed you and made you hide and avoid the other people. Getting into a dark black thing that was going back in the direction of where you lived, you quickly sat down in the most obscure corner you could find, although actually they were all about the same. The car was comparatively empty and that fact seemed to relax you a bit.

To your complete surprise the dark black thing suddenly began to load up with students at the next station and a dark gangling youth with a multitude of books sat next to you, sniffed about him in the obvious way adolescents have, then he changed his seat. You tried not to notice, but it annoyed and irritated you beyond all measure. The students kept coming and corning until a young girl sat next to you but she too changed her seat; then another girl—the same thing. You felt as if all those young eyes were looking at you and many of them were. You could hear some of them say that there was a terrible stink in here or some similar remark. Many were leaving the car and you wanted to call them back, to tell them that it wasn't really your fault but that another person—other people—it was they, her, that caused the trouble. Please, it wasn't you, your heart wanted to cry out, please. It was the other people, the other people made the mess. Why should you suffer for them? Please it was the others please please—but nobody would sit next to you.